RANDOM HOUSE

HOUSE

LARGE
PRINT

AIR DANCE IGUANA

3

WE APPROACHED A CLUSTER of uniforms, hairy eyeballs from no one I knew. A stocky man who looked like a retired Marine turned to check us out. He wore slacks, an open-neck dress shirt, and a beige sport coat. He approached and reached his hand toward me.

Bohner butted in. "This is Rutledge, Detective. He's—"

"I can see the camera, Deputy. Sheriff Liska called and said to expect someone special." He half smiled and studied my face as if he wanted to recognize me. "I'm Detective Chet Millican. Dressed as you are, I take it you're undercover FDLE."

Local-level cops always held the Florida Department of Law Enforcement in awe.

"I'm a civilian," I said.

Millican looked me up and down. "Ex-cop?"

I shook my head, tried not to stare at his military-perfect silver crew cut.

AIR DANCE
IGUANA

TOM CORCORAN

R A N D O M   H O U S E
LARGE PRINT

**The Library of Congress has established a
Cataloging-in-Publication record for
this title.**

ISBN-13: 978-0-375-43423-5
ISBN-10: 0-375-43423-2

www.randomlargeprint.com

FIRST LARGE PRINT EDITION

10   9   8   7   6   5   4   3   2   1

This Large Print edition published in accord
with the standards of the N.A.V.H.

This one's for Larry Gray,
whose grand life
inspired so many others.

ACKNOWLEDGMENTS

I offer special thanks to Marty Corcoran, Carolyn Inglis, Bob Dattila, Jerry and Elsie Metcalf, Charles Wood, Carolyn Ferguson, Sandie Herron, Marshall Smith, Teresa Murphy Clark, Lee Gurga, Sofia Karma Cello, Pat Boyer, Sonny Brewer, and Dinah George. Also to Janice Legow, who urged a youth to write and gave him a typewriter. Here's what happened.

Grief works its own perversions and betrayals: the shape of what we have lost is as subject to corruption as the mortal body.

—Barry Unsworth,
Sacred Hunger

"Revenge may be wicked, but it's natural."

—Becky Sharp in **Vanity Fair**
by William Makepeace Thackery

AIR DANCE IGUANA

1

A COCKATOO'S SCREECH PIERCED the dead man's silence.

I scanned the home across the canal, its second-story porch, then checked the morning sky. A high-coasting turkey vulture had spooked the caged bird. Moments later a yachtsman eighty yards to windward began dock-testing his unmuffled outboards. An oily blue cloud drifted down to shroud the suspended corpse. I knew that the body deserved more respect, that Ramrod Key should go quiet until the medical examiner lowered it from the boat-lift davit. On a deeper level, I hoped that people would treat my death with brief dignity if they learned that I had died, even if I'd been strung to a winch before dawn and hung like fresh-caught fish in a waterside market.

The cockatoo screeched again.

I switched lenses and went back to photographing the victim. In contrast to the late-June warmth, he looked trapped in midwinter with his blue, frostbitten hands.

Bobbi Lewis raised her voice to beat the outboards. "What the hell happened to his left shoe?"

"He wore out the toe fighting for altitude," I said. "The killer dangled him just high enough to offer hope."

"But no chance to survive." She sipped from a lidded Styrofoam cup. "Are you done here? Someone on the forensic squad said you might be dawdling."

"You should fire me," I said.

"Talk to Sheriff Liska. He might create a part-timers' retirement program. Meanwhile, I like the way you work."

"My long career of evidence jobs?"

"Don't belittle yourself. You've got a mind for this game. But I really meant two mornings ago with sunlight sneaking between the miniblinds."

Once in a while she softened her hard-cop demeanor.

"This early sun is screwing me up right now," I said. "I need to take some insurance shots with fill flash."

"You're right, Alex. This is not the place for romantic chatter."

"We have our jobs to do."

"Darling, that's wonderful and insightful. The scene techs want to do theirs today."

———

When my phone rang at 6:40 that morning, I knew that one of the overlapping jurisdictions— either Monroe County or the City of Key West— needed help. The rude wake-up was my own damned fault. Several years back, after fifteen years of freelance ad agency and magazine work, I had started accepting crime-scene gigs for extra cash. But I kept stepping into crap that I couldn't scrape off my shoes, and I had come to dread the sight of my own camera. I'd never wanted to be a cop, yet every time I saw a victim up close, I wanted justice.

That's not exactly true. My job wasn't justice. I wanted revenge in the spirit of decency, contra-dictory or not. I had invented a few versions and barely survived. Revenge almost always claims two victims.

Dawn calls were never a good sign. I let it ring through to the answering machine.

One minute after the ringing stopped, my cell phone buzzed. I was awake enough to be curious, so I reached for the nightstand. No surprise: the window identified Detective Lewis of the Mon-roe County Sheriff's Department, my lover for the past four months. Somehow, on our amorous roller-coaster ride, we had managed not to mix our personal lives and our jobs. Now she had bro-ken a rule, had dialed my unlisted cell number to hire me for work she knew I wanted to avoid. In spite of a long list of reasons to ignore it, I took the call.

It summoned me to a hanging next to a canal. I found it tough to decline, especially since Lewis's persuasive manner didn't invoke whining.

I consoled myself with ten minutes in my outdoor shower before I left the house.

Lewis moved to shade under the victim's elevated house. She wore crisp khaki slacks, clean sneaks, a star-logo-emblazoned white polo shirt, and, clipped to her belt, the Monroe County badge. At five-eight, with the shoulders of a competitive swimmer, she looked capable but not powerful. I wished I had a dollar for every man—criminal or not, and including other deputies—who had made the mistake of thinking he could bully or belittle her.

She studied the dead man, glanced over, and caught me staring. "What?" she said.

"Are you zoned-out?" I said.

She shook her head. "You know what I see?"

There would be no correct answer. "What do you see?"

"A prehistoric praying mantis that spit out a one-string marionette."

"Very creative," I said.

"Can you top that?"

I looked at the stanchion, the swing arm, and the cranelike davit's on-off switch, well out of the victim's reach. I considered the noose and restraints and, as if part of the man's punishment, the spectacle. "To me, it's a professional hit," I said. "Thought out, drawn out for cruelty, and foolproof."

"Good start," said Lewis. "Go farther."

On what scale of analysis? I took a stab at animal simile. "I see an iguana with a hemp necklace."

"Where's your action verb?"

"An iguana dancing on air for his breakfast."

"That's what you see?" she said. "An air dance iguana?"

"It beats an upchucked marionette."

"Now you've twisted my creativity."

The neighbor up the canal revved and shut down his twin outboards. A last thick cloud of fumes drifted toward us.

"Have you put a name to this guy?" I said.

"Plumb Bob."

"What did you smoke this morning?"

Lewis lowered her voice. "His name was Jack Mason. People called him Kansas Jack. With your new escape from downtown, Alex, you'd have been his neighbor. You could have bonded with him, shared a few beers."

"That's the third time you've called it an escape, Bobbi. You make it sound like I'm running away from you, and I'm not. I'll be one island up, a mile from here. What does that do, put our homes eighteen minutes apart instead of fifteen?"

She shrugged. The phone on her belt buzzed. She unclipped it, suppressed a grin, and strode away.

The cockatoo screeched again.

We ought not reveal this weapon to the Third World.

Morning sunlight sparkled on the canal's surface. Cool yellows enveloped Kansas Jack Mason's drooping body. His eyes bulged—hence my iguana impulse. He wore shorts and black socks. His shoes were utility specials, the black oxfords I had sworn off on leaving the military. His lean face and muscular arms suggested a man who might have shoveled coal in his youth, or snow, or manure. His belly bulk supported Bobbi's assumption that he was a drinker. He'd probably done little labor of late beyond bending his elbow.

The breeze finally offered me a favor, turned the corpse so that my camera caught reflections in the duct tape over his mouth. I tapped the shutter button six times, at different angles, then zoomed and focused on the rope around his neck. In my childhood I'd seen a diagram of the correct way to structure the knot. A person today would be investigated, hounded out of town and state for showing a youth how to tie a noose. As if the skill might lead one to a hellish career. My knowledge hadn't inspired me to hang anyone.

Tomorrow I would start nine weeks of house-sitting on Little Torch Key. After almost thirty years in Key West, I would learn about life twenty-seven miles from the big island, among fish and birds and people who had elected to live closer to open water. Kansas Jack had existed at the bottom end of Lower Keys style. In contrast to nearby homes with their clean pea rock, proper trees, shaped shrubs, and slick watercraft, his place was a dump. He had arranged empty buckets under a homemade lean-to with a weedy thatched roof. Each five-gallon plastic bucket had its own category: plumber's trash, wood scraps, parched aloe clusters, boat-motor parts. A row of pineapples along his home's east wall had sprouted and wilted, been wasted. A veteran center-console Mako named **Swizzle Rod** rested sun-bleached and engine-free on a boat trailer with two flat tires. Its blue Bimini top had frayed to pale pennants, and its name had faded to a pink swirl on the transom. If the man's demise hadn't been so evil, his hands hadn't been bound by monofilament fishing line, I could have suspected murder-suicide. Kansas Jack had killed his environment, then took himself out. But this scene spoke only of murder, at the ugly end of a sad spectrum.

I heard a distant helicopter, then a go-fast boat out in Newfound Harbor Channel. With the exhaust fumes dissipated, the smell of sour plankton captured my nose. I framed a shot of the yard, the expanse between the davit and the house.

"Take your time, Rutledge."

I knew the voice.

"Gaze about and soak up paradise," he said. "We got all fucking week."

I had known Sheriff Fred "Chicken Neck" Liska since the early nineties. Before his recent Monroe County campaign and election, during his tenure as a city police detective, he had prided himself on his disco-era outfits. For the past year or so, I'd been surprised each time I'd seen him in khakis and the badge-embroidered polo shirt. I asked one time if he missed his old image, the Nik-Nik shirts, and he shrugged and mumbled something about "protective coloration."

I knew only two tactics to counter Liska's sarcastic banter. Remain silent or speak in homilies.

"Everyone's in a hurry," I said. "We came to the Keys to slow down our lives, but we speed up after we're here awhile."

"We got a rain issue," he said, sticking his

thumb to the northwest. "The print people want a shot at that davit. Plus, we got a situation up the road. I need you there for an hour or so."

"Should I have my booking agent review my contract?"

Liska ignored me. His mouth formed an odd smile as he peered at the corpse. I could almost hear his brain shift from its management hemisphere to its true detective side. "That tan, his forearms?" he said. "That's his lifestyle in a jiffy. He never wore a watch."

"I thought about that. The man was barely scraping by. He might have been one of the last old-time Keys dwellers not pushed out by all the incoming wealth."

"Think he got to see himself die?"

"It was dark, no moon," I said. "Or do we know that?"

"He was found at first light."

"Somebody hooked him up and turned on the davit winch," I said. "He heard pulleys, motor whine, and the twang of the cable adjusting itself on the take-up reel. He felt himself going away slowly. Probably smelled himself, too, while his murderer got in his car and drove home. From the surroundings and the stand-still drama, we might assume it wasn't a robbery."

"Don't ever assume slobs don't have money," said Liska.

"Who found him?"

"Woman down the canal, going out for smokes at daybreak. She idled by and spotted him swinging."

"She runs for cigarettes in her boat?"

"Florida snatched her license after four DUIs. She commutes to the store in her Boston Whaler. Happens a lot in the Lower Keys. She even drives it to church. What's **that** fucking noise?"

I pointed to the cockatoo. "Bird."

"If it wakes the dead, maybe our jobs will be easier."

"I just saw two more shots I want."

"I have a crime-scene crew waiting on your ass. You've got ninety seconds."

"Where's your regular photo ace? That schmuck from Marathon."

"I fired him."

Bobbi Lewis watched me snap my lens covers into place, stuff gear into my canvas shoulder bag. "Did you shoot any digital?"

"If the courts require film, why double up?" I said.

"I just thought, if you had two or three, you could e-mail them to me. Might help me write my scene report."

I pulled my eight-megapixel Olympus from

the bottom of my bag, then walked a semicircle to capture the surroundings. "Regarding my al-leged escape," I said, "you've got an open invita-tion. Aren't you looking forward to a few days in the boondocks?"

"I have a full-time job, Alex. I used this year's vacation time when we were naked in Grand Cayman."

"Weekends, maybe?"

"Weekends, yes," she said without smiling. "Thank you."

"There's another photo I want when you cut this one down," I said. "The sticky side of that duct tape on his mouth."

"We've tried that before," she said. "No one can read fingerprints on top of duct-tape threads. It'll get tossed out as inconclusive, so why bother?"

"Can't hurt to take a couple shots. Let's at least preserve the evidence."

"I'll try to arrange something." She pointed. "The sheriff is waiting in his car."

"One last thing?" I said.

"Probably not."

"You called me out of bed before seven. You owe me one."

"Maybe so," she said. "Tell me what."

"Forget you're in a hurry long enough for a smile."

"With this kind of shit going down, I save smiles for the weekends, too."

"You're tough."

She raised her hand, pretended to scratch her forehead, and slid me a quick half-grin.

2

KANSAS JACK'S CHARACTER VAN was hand-painted a poster tone of royal blue. Faded bumper stickers covered its rear end. SAVE TIBET, STOP GLOBAL WHINING, SAVE OLD STILTSVILLE, and FUCK FEMA. BLOW THE BRIDGE. All of them wishful thinking. Jack had written **Swizzle Rod** with a red Magic Marker on his gray vinyl spare-tire cover.

Beyond the yellow tape, Sheriff Liska's personal car was wedged into a patch of palm trimmings, puddles, and toppled garbage cans. Just past the Lexus, my old nemesis, Deputy Billy "No Jokes" Bohner, leaned against his green-and-white's front fender. A Kevlar vest under his starched white shirt bulked his torso. He mopped his doughy face with a paper towel, turned an eye to me, then looked away.

Liska lowered his passenger-side window. Cool air escaped the leather-scented interior. He said, "You doing okay?"

I leaned down to speak. "What's with your lady detective?"

"Is she letting her mind run free?"

"That gets it."

"It's her first step in solving tough ones. So far it works." The electric window started upward. "Hop in."

I opened the door, noticed the light-colored carpet, and checked my shoes for mud. The cold, dry air hit me like I'd opened a freezer.

Liska said, "How do you feel about what you saw?"

"It wasn't random. Someone hung him for show."

"You just restated two facts," he said. "I asked how you felt."

"I heard you, and it forces me to ask what's going on. Is touchy-feely the new fad in crime solving? She had me visualizing sci-fi back there."

"She told me your cute 'air dance' remark," he said. "Answer my question."

"Start with numb," I said. "I didn't know him. He didn't have style, but he had a right to not be dead. Someone hung him, and not one neighbor is out here bleeding sympathy or demanding justice."

"Perfect," he said. "You're getting better at this. Another year, you might be a good cop. Like I said, I need you up the road."

"Thanks for the upbeat words, Sheriff. Is it another murder?"

"Does it make a difference? Murder, car wreck, B and E—a picture's a picture."

"I've seen too many bodies the past few years and one too many today. Why would I want to sign up for more?"

"You're getting used to it, in spite of yourself. You can stay on the clock."

"Given my choice, I'd rather sell used cars in Tampa."

"You could do well," he said. "It's a growing town."

I didn't answer him. I watched a letter carrier drive box to box.

"Why the attitude?" he said. "You too good for the work?"

"Let's just say that the work is not my destiny. I take photos, ninety percent of the time not of dead people. Except for these crime gigs, it's been a rewarding occupation. Fundamentally, I'm into sunshine and smiles. Do you feel a need to transform my life?"

"I want to help you reach your potential."

"But it's your version, not mine," I said. "I have thirty hours to prep my house for a two-month rental, and I'm low on film. I wish to decline."

"We got people waiting for you up there. Do I

need to pull you off the clock, send you there against your wishes, and chalk it up to civic duty? Take it from a veteran civil servant. You'll find it harder to cash that unsigned check."

"My only civic duties are jury service, paying taxes, and not committing crimes."

He turned to face me. "You could've stayed home in bed. Why'd you even come to this one?"

"My inner need for fantasy."

"Follow that thought. If your girlfriend asked you to go to Marathon, you'd do it?"

"Dud question, Sheriff. She's got a conscience. She knows she burned up today's favors by dragging me to this one."

Liska stared out the windshield. He looked tired, whipped, not at all like the eccentric but legendary case-closing cop of a few years ago.

I said, "Why me instead of Lewis, or one of your other detectives? Surely they know how to use a camera."

"She's busy with this, and they aren't **my** detectives. You would be, and I respect your input."

"It's getting deep in here."

"You're right," he said. "The truth is, I want you to represent me."

"You want to deputize me?"

"Call it what you want. You'll be a consultant."

"On photographer's pay?" I said.

"We can negotiate an adjustment. How did you get up here?"

"My motorcycle."

"The forensic officers aren't leaving soon. It'll be safe. I want your opinion and a few pictures. I arranged for a chauffeur." He pointed. Deputy Bohner, still hanging close to his vehicle, was chatting on a cell phone.

"I ride with your duty bully and take his crap? His venom is his reason to live. For the fourth or fifth time, I don't want to deal with it."

"I can't imagine you'd let that doofus intimidate you. When I was elected to this job, he was my opponent's campaign manager. I beat him, so you can, too. Give me your film, and I know the argument. You own the negatives and the rights. Like you could ever want keeper photos of low-life death."

I wanted my silence to convey refusal. I offered no response.

"Remember the last time we saw each other, Rutledge? I came by your house to deliver a fat check and a word of thanks. You were happier about the money than my words of appreciation."

"Sounds logical to me."

"You were in your backyard, taking a shower. Was that your version of sense and logic?"

"We're still on solid ground, Sheriff," I said. "I guess I wanted to be clean."

"It was pouring rain in a thunderstorm. Lightning flashed twice while I sat waiting on your porch. One bolt struck out on Fleming Street."

"Do you live your life thinking the next flash will blow you out of your shoes, the next oncoming car could be a head-on?"

"No," he said. "It takes too much time to worry about what-ifs. It's time better spent on what's next. Or earning a few bucks to pay for what's next."

"Why should I buy the future? It's going to show up anyway."

"Oh, you **are** an optimist," he said.

"Comes from photographing more smiles than corpses."

"Have I done you any favors or cut you slack in the past?"

"I suppose so," I said, "but I have to believe I've got a credit balance."

"You never know, Rutledge. It can't hurt to bank another blue chip. And you'll get paid for doing it."

"Do I invoice you straight rate for this road trip?" I said.

"Whatever you see, don't fuck around discussing it with other detectives. Report to me directly and hit me for a full eight hours."

"I could stand ten."

Liska grinned widely and slapped his palm on the steering wheel. "You see? Natural-born cop."

His grin looked fake and his eyes looked sad and wary.

Deputy Bohner opened his cruiser's right-side door and gestured as if offering a Louis XIV chair. The royal treatment, a couple of weeks before Bastille Day. I set my satchel on the grimy floor mat, then reached to pull the shoulder strap.

"Belt up," he said.

"What am I doing, raking leaves?"

"We have our rules."

"Nice carpet."

He sucked snot up his nose. "Rubber's what they give us."

"Must grind your quality of life. You boys haven't joined the union?"

Bohner hurried to his side of the car, keeping his eye on me, not trusting a civilian near his siren switch and radar rig. He cranked the motor, heavy-handed the shift lever, and fixed his eyes on the dash-mounted computer. Oblivious to our surroundings, he whipped a three-point turn, just missing a mailbox shaped like a grouper. Through the eight blocks from Kansas Jack's house to U.S. 1, Bohner tapped his keyboard. His eyes never left the monitor. He tore himself away to check traffic before turning toward Big Pine Key, then mashed his pedal as if taxpayers were buying the gas.

"How far do we go?" I said. "Liska didn't tell me."

He pointed to the northeast as if to show me our exact destination. "Four miles past the Hump." He won ten local-lingo points. It had been years since I'd heard the old nickname for the Seven Mile Bridge.

"Could I get a more specific clue?"

"All I got's an address in Marathon," he said. "The boss told you it's another killing, didn't he?"

"In a roundabout way. Are we late on-scene?"

"I don't know about you," he said. "I'm on the overtime clock."

He'd been on duty during the predawn hours? "I thought rookies drew the all-night shifts."

"Usually, yes," he said, "but late hours don't bother me. Once all the drunks get home, my workload drops big-time. Every so often I get a shot of spice."

"Like a murder?"

"Or two."

"Dead people don't get to you?" I said.

"They kill the boredom. I hate risking my life for seat-belt citations."

With no traffic ahead, he goosed his Crown Vic up to sixty-five. We sped across Little Torch Key, and I caught an over-the-shoulder glimpse of the house on Keelhaul Lane where I would spend my next eight weeks. A few weeks ago

Johnny Griffin, an old college friend, had asked to rent my Key West cottage for July and August. A man's home is his castle, and I didn't want the hassle. I tried to squelch his idea by quoting two grand a week, but he didn't back off his request. I warned him that I still wanted to think about it. Then Al Manning, a watercolorist who had fled Key West for a stilt home on Little Torch, asked me to help him find a house sitter. Someone to water plants and pay utility bills for the summer while he prowled the museums of Europe. His mention of a motorboat and an outdoor shower convinced me to volunteer.

I called Johnny Griffin and we cut a cash deal. By Labor Day I would hold sixteen grand in crisp hundreds. The money would help pay off my house by year's end. With my money worries defused, I could have my own summer vacation, spend weeks paddling Manning's kayak through mangrove channels, taking his outboard to Marvin Key, counting clouds above Picnic Island.

On the flip side, being stuck in a cruiser with No Jokes offered nothing but crossfire.

Liska had plugged me straight into it. He knew that Bohner and I had a history of pissing matches. Our spats weren't so much bad blood as disregard for each other's view of mankind. The deputy, because of his badge, always assumed an upper hand. He hated what he perceived as my useless calm. My advantage was not giving a shit. I could have told him that most inner peace was outer illusion, but I didn't want to lose ground.

Except for an oncoming speeder whom Bohner blue-lighted, then elected not to stop in the Key Deer zone, our ride was uneventful. He rolled a steady seventy over Bahia Honda. Then, with oncoming traffic, he fell behind slowpokes on Missouri Key. We paid the price for his being the fuzz. No one in front of us would dare blitz the limit. He regained lost time by kicking up to eighty and passing twelve cars on the Seven Mile Bridge. I sensed that the clear road ahead ticked down his anxiety a notch or two. He let his computer drift into sleep mode.

Rolling across Knights Key into Marathon, Bohner threw me a curve. He shook a slim yellow box. "Gum?"

I suspected only a power washer could get the marching soldiers out of my mouth. "I haven't had Chiclets since I don't know when."

"One or two?" he said.

"Two, if that's okay."

No Jokes Bohner civil and generous? Something read hinky.

A quarter-mile farther we slowed quickly, skidded on gravel to go right on 10th Street South. A forest of signs greeted us: DEAD END, PRIVATE, KEEP OUT, DO NOT ENTER. The stained posts at the entrance to Florida Straits Estates were decorated with four-foot leaping dolphins in pale aqua. Someone had painted hot-pink lipstick on them. A shirtless big boy stood out front, a forty-ish ex-linebacker type, square-jawed with shaved sides and a mullet cut gone ponytail. A tattooed panther crawled his shoulder. I didn't guess he was the hired greeter, like they have in Wal-Mart. He could have been waiting for a bus or dooms-day. He didn't look like he cared which came first.

We drove thirty yards of two-track concrete before Bohner's tires crunched on scallop shells and dirty marl. The manufactured homes on Trailer Heaven Lane were presentable with paint schemes more stylish than their shapes. Sea Cloud Terrace was a step down—old trailers and several parked cars sporting primer paint and mini-spares.

Bohner waved at another deputy, slipped past a roadblock at Pearly Gate Court, and parked a few yards from the action. Liska had asked for my opinion and a few pictures. I took one camera, shoved my bag into a shadow on the car floor, and made sure Bohner clicked the locks. Approaching the scene, he took his time, swiveled as he walked, as if his legs were hinged to his shoulders. He was my ticket in. I slowed my pace so I wouldn't arrive first.

This end of the trailer park looked like a motor court in the style of Florida, 1952. Any form of maintenance had last been done before 1992. It now was a museum of disuse and poverty; the "estates" were Nomad car trailers and weathered Winnebagos parked a lifetime ago. Fenced yards held remnants of long-dead palms. Two Hobie Cats sat on a vacant lot, their faded hulls crusted with mildew. Plastic bags hung from thin shrubs like out-of-season holiday streamers. The stench of a rancid Dumpster fought down the odor of death. Most residents had replaced their broken glass with cardboard flats. The most common window treatment was the black garbage bag. Two sour-faced women in stretched tops and cheap sneakers sat on slat steps in front of their open doorways. I suspected that oxygen reached their lungs only through cigarette filters.

I came around a corner and caught sight of the murder victim. Like Kansas Jack, he was hung from a davit.

Bohner spit out his gum. "Christ," he said. "They didn't tell me he was a swinger, too. Couple more of these, we could make wind chimes."

His patronizing smirk went cold. "Tallahassee consultant?"

"No," I said, "I'm a freelance photographer. Anything but weddings and babies."

Our discussion began to draw attention from nearby uniforms and forensic personnel. He shook his head and inhaled enough air to double his size. "Take your cameras off my crime scene. Deputy, take him back where he came from."

"Call the boss," said Bohner.

Millican sneered and exhaled to show his exasperation. "I still got a hard time calling him boss," he said. "It was plain Chicken Neck back in the city. If I wanted it bad enough, I might take credit for making up that nickname. Why isn't our surefire detective right here right now? You don't see hangings all that often, unless they're suicides in a locked room. In the old days this would interest the hell out of him."

Bohner said nothing.

Millican quieted his tone. "I'm starting to think Fred Liska's reputation exceeded him."

"That makes him not your boss?" I said.

Millican jerked as if I had slugged him. He stared up an empty flagpole for a moment, then shook his head. "I've had a crew on hold for eighty damn minutes. I was waiting for a snotty civilian to fall by and nose around? This is too much bullshit."

Bohner shrugged, a helpless gesture. "All due respect, sir, but put it in your report. The man told me to bring him here, and I'm betting he told you to grant access."

"Stay put," said the detective. He walked away and slapped his cell phone to his ear hard enough to knock himself sideways.

I changed my mind about not wanting to be there. I wanted to force my presence on the belligerent dickhead, wallow in his crime scene. For the moment I wondered about Bohner. He had fired back two good answers and given me words of assurance. That and his offer of gum put him out of character four times inside of ten minutes.

"Don't mind Millican," said Bohner. "Man likes to think he's King Shit."

"How come I've never met him before?" I said.

"Liska hired him about seven weeks ago. A long time ago, probably before you were born, he used to be a Key West cop. The last thirty years he's been a detective somewhere up in New England. Florida draws these old guys, so I guess it figures he came back to the Keys. Hell, he's got his retirement bennies plus a county salary. I heard Liska didn't really want to hire him, but we were shy a qualified man in Marathon."

Detective Millican walked toward us. He spoke with a scene tech en route, kicked some gravel, stared at me with a quizzical look, then motioned Bohner aside. The men conferred for a minute, then Millican ordered the uniforms to stand back.

"You're clear to stay," said Bohner. "Don't get into their turf, but check it out. Get a feel for the crime."

"That's my job description? Get a feel?"

"I got it thirdhand. Have yourself a look-see, a little picnic. Maybe Liska wants insights. Good luck with that."

"Is a look-see like a listen-hear?"

He didn't miss a beat. "I'll ask Millican. It might be like a fuck off."

"What time was he found?"

"Just after sunup." Bohner aimed his finger at a trailer with warped side walls. "The wine expert who shares his mildew palace came outside to barf off the stoop. He said he thought it was a davit repairman working early and he went back to bed. A woman in his dream told him it was a dead man noosed high. He came back out to look and went flippo, started screaming to the neighbors."

"Dead man have a name?" I said.

"Milton Navarre."

"A phony one."

Bohner looked bored. "What makes you think that?"

"It's an exit off Interstate 10, near Pensacola."

"An exit?"

"Milton and Navarre Beach are towns up there."

"Whatever. I worked in the jail, I had a prisoner named Bobby Detroit. I put him in a cell with a hophead named Gainesville. Everybody got a kick out of the Map Twins. This guy here, I see him like the stiff you photoed back on Ramrod. Another slug who doesn't have to worry about West Nile virus."

"You missed the sensitivity-training update?"

"Being this way helps me keep my bearings." He looked at me like I had lost my mind. "I thought you had a sense of humor."

"I sold it to you guys."

"That may be true, but watch yourself. None of it trickled down to Millican."

I wasn't sure what the sheriff wanted, but Millican was right. Liska could've come to Marathon to get his own facts instead of sending me. Chicken Neck had made his rep as a city detective, then jumped away, won the election, and became sheriff. I had no police knowledge beyond what we all see on TV shows and the few tidbits I'd picked up working local crimes in recent years. I certainly had no methods for working up plausible theories. What weight could Liska give my opinion, anyway?

My task came down to a short agenda. I wondered how the men were connected; I had no doubt they were. Near-identical murders the same morning don't occur by chance. With that fact given, I wanted to know whether two killers or one had hung the men. Also, had Kansas Jack and Milton Navarre known each other? Had they known their killers, simply answered their doors without suspicion? Or had they been wakened, pistol barrels to their noses, and marched outside to their executions?

The wind had picked up. Navarre swung like a dead-weight pendulum.

I took forty photos in three minutes—of the davit, the dirt under Navarre, his neighbors, his palace, the Dumpster, his distance from the dredged canal, and close-ups of his face and the noose. He wore the plaid pants common to street people and nothing else. He probably had gone five-eight before his air dance, close to six-even with his neck stretched. Kansas Jack had been low-rent, but Navarre, at best, was one step up from a weedsleeper. He had a carbo belly, but unlike Kansas Jack, he wore no duct tape. He may have been handsome once, but his new ruggedness spoke of tobacco, whisky, sunshine, and coffee. Dried blood coated his teeth and lips. Copper splotches covered his chest.

With so many cops and spectators, my shots

of the general area would be useless unless the killer had returned to gape and gloat. I fitted a wide-angle lens, shot the crowd without even peering through my viewfinder, then quit and looked for Bohner. I wanted a beer more than a ride. I felt assured that my return trip to Ramrod would come first.

Detective Millican approached. "How would an expert like you describe the corpse?"

"No shirt, no shoes, no problems."

"That's the dead man's point of view. Now he's my problem."

"Guess that's the deal. I get to go home."

"Tell me again why you came," he said.

"If you find out, let me know. Are all these nearby trailers occupied?"

"If any was empty," said Millican, "some liquid-brain would find his way in."

"Who owns the davits? Do they go with one of the trailers, or does the landlord maintain them?"

"I don't fucking know."

"How is the electric hooked up?"

Millican shrugged.

"Can anyone operate them, or is there a lock on the switch box?"

"I don't know," he said. "Call ahead before you come next time."

"I feel unwanted. It's a shame because this is how I like to spend my Thursdays."

"We'll call you when we need to test another steel cable."

Bohner left a circle of deputies, joined me at his car. "Navarre was a plumber, part-time if ever," he said. "No one enjoyed his company. His income was lean and mean, but he had cash for cheap bourbon."

"The goofball that found him," I said. "He's not a suspect?"

"He's got a passive defense. He was in a bar on the highway at three A.M., too drunk to walk. The saloon owner drove him here, rolled him into the trailer's front door. That lovely fact, and his knuckles aren't beat up from tapping the vic's teeth."

I pointed to a trash can full of empty bottles. "Is the murder weapon in there, or was it chucked in the canal?"

"The murder weapon was a noose."

"Then why no duct tape? Why didn't the victim call out for help? Even if he was passed-out drunk, getting hung would've wakened him. He died before he was yanked up the davit."

"Fuck." Bohner pivoted on one foot, left me standing there, and strode the best he could back to Millican.

A minute later I watched the result of my logic. A black deputy with a grim face and rubber gloves pushed the dead man's roommate into his cruiser's backseat. I heard him promise the dude a shower and a shave. Two deputies began to string yellow crime-scene tape around the trash can. Detective Millican's body language broadcast a massive grudge.

It wouldn't spoil the rest of my day.

On the way back to Ramrod, I asked Bohner why Liska had fired the Marathon-based photographer.

"The boy heaved every time he saw blood," said Bohner.

"How was his photo work?"

"Fuck if I know. You need to be blessed with genius to point and shoot? He was a jerk-off. I just hope you're not his replacement."

"I fit the same category?" I said.

"You're the boss's buddy. True or not, you'd be seen as a rat."

"What's to tattle?" I said. "Does everyone have a side scam? Or is it just laziness?"

"Don't get the wrong idea, Rutledge. Things are clean these days, you compare it to the eighties. Worse than that, the seventies."

"That doesn't mean the Keys haven't gone downhill."

"You're into another subject," he said. "Like crime changes, the county changes."

I shut up, listened to the tires on concrete, and didn't attempt to decipher his analogy.

We came off the Seven Mile Bridge and slowed to pass a trooper who had stopped a Mustang convertible. The three men in the rental car looked half asleep, but we knew they were two-thirds blitzed. If they were lucky, the Florida Highway Patrol wouldn't call in the drug-sniffing dog. One way or another, their holiday cash would be collected at the hotel with no reservations.

"You napping or thinking?" said Bohner.

"You must be thinking, too, or you wouldn't have asked."

"That call you made on there being a murder weapon. It's the first time I've seen why Liska respects you."

"I don't know about respect," I said. "He hires me, I work cheap, and I take good pictures. I shot four rolls on Ramrod. They'll prove Kansas Jack was hung by his neck and not his ankles. I came up here with you and shot another couple rolls that will prove the same thing for Navarre. Hung by his neck."

"You'll collect your hourly rate," he said. "What's to complain?"

"When's the last time you saw a davit hanging?"

"These past eighteen years I've seen and heard it all, but never a davit. I mean in the Keys we got more davits than pelicans, but not hooked to people. Now we get two in one day."

"That's my point," I said. "It's too weird to be a coincidence. It's a single crime with two crime scenes."

"I don't think anybody would doubt that, Rutledge."

"Did you look closely at the victim on Ramrod?"

Bohner shook his head. "I was told to stay out on the street."

"I'm a civilian?"

"Excellent point."

"Then why am I the only person who's had a close look at both of them? Why not two or three detectives investigating, comparing notes, all the shit they do? Where's Sheriff Liska? Why isn't he here in the car with us?"

Bohner forced a bored look on his face. "Ask me ten more I can't answer. I do my job, and I do what they tell me."

"Well, I didn't beg for this, and I can't stop thinking it's going to bite me in the ass real soon."

"Got me already," he said.

I was going to let his statement hang, but he'd opened a door. "How so?"

"The last few years I get my kids four weeks every summer. The rest of the time they live with their bitch of a mother up in Raleigh. Last summer I was a dictator worse than the bitch. My twelve-year-old, going on eighteen, told me she never wanted to come back. The boy kept complaining about always being wrong, no matter what he did right. At first I thought tough shit, but it started to eat at me. I bit the bullet, went to the shrink the boss keeps on retainer."

Hearing an introspective No Jokes Bohner talk about himself was as odd as having to view two davit hangings in a single day.

"The shrink have an opinion?" I said.

"He told me I was addicted to power but didn't have any, so I overused my resources. In a word, I was pushy."

Bingo, I thought. If I had to pick from the dictionary, **pushy** would be it. "That was it?" I said.

"He suggested I lose the push, and he sent me to meditation class."

I couldn't picture it. "For what?"

"To lower my blood pressure."

"Did it work?"

"You bet. I can still be myself, but I won't seize up and die from it."

"Did they sign up Millican for the same program?"

Bohner sniffed and shook his head. "I expect his deepest thoughts come during TV wrestling. If they had dog fights, he'd watch them, too."

"Sounds like perfect inner workings for a detective," I said.

"The reason I brought up fighting dogs, I once heard him compared. He sinks his teeth into something, he doesn't let go. Back there he got his feeding eye on you."

4

I AIMED MY OLD Triumph motorcycle at the dropping sun, rode across the Saddlebunch, where concrete utility poles like prison bars hacked my south view. Along this stretch the preferred move was to look north to where shallow channels snaked out of the Gulf of Mexico into basins carpeted with sea grass, vegetation thrived, pockets of mangroves expanded as they had for centuries. Stark, stained boats had anchored in bay shallows not a hundred yards from U.S. 1, their boxy shapes pure function, their work gear simple and worn. A line of menacing clouds filled the gulf horizon and fed a gray squall that washed the Mud Keys. Even the stench of dead plankton at the tide line drew me to calm.

On Stock Island I looked for and didn't find Liska's car at his office. I U-turned and rode into Key West against the flow of mainland-bound single-day tourists and workday commuters rushing home to the Lower Keys. After inspecting two corpses and having my rational chat with Billy Bohner, I was too wiped to deal with the gas grill or a restaurant meal. I had emptied my kitchen stock so I could vacate the cottage and make room for Johnny Griffin. My best option was a chilly six-pack and slippery chicken from Dion's.

Before going home, I stopped on Olivia to give the Marathon film to Duffy Lee Hall, my darkroom tech and friend for years. I found him in cut-off Levi's and work boots piling coconuts on his yard trash, stacking them like cannonballs.

"Why did Liska, of all people, bring me your film?" said Duffy Lee. "I figured you were in jail."

I explained my day, the road miles and similar victims.

"Awful way to go," he said. "I ran a proof sheet. I assume that geezer on Ramrod had to listen to the davit's electric motor in the dark."

"Wait till you see the shots on this new roll. Different rules, same result."

"Liska was not wearing, by the way, a vintage polyester shirt."

"He's abandoned his seventies look," I said. "Now that he's more in the public eye, he's working a new dimension."

"He wants me to scan the best prints and e-mail him JPEGs."

"Our nostalgia king is wiring himself into the future."

"I don't know," said Duffy Lee. "He looked rough, like he was wired to a bad habit. Maybe all these years on the job have caught up with him."

I shut off my motor and coasted past my porch into the backyard.

During the winter I had paid a carpenter to build a shed for my vintage Triumph. He made it sturdy, big enough to also hold my bicycle and a gas can. He strapped it to a concrete base and painted it two-tone gray. Its shingle-roof runoff goes to my mango tree. My neighbor in the lane, my dear friend Carmen Sosa, joked that if I ever fell short of cash, I could disguise it with trellises, hook it to cable, and lease it as a trundle-bed bungalow.

My small home on Dredgers Lane offers a credible version of paradise. I'm walking distance from saloons, fine food, not-so-fine food, a convenience store, a hardware, and a bike-repair shop. It felt great to be back, and I sensed my first twinge of guilt for having peddled my right to live there for the next eight weeks. Then I put the guilt in perspective: years ago I joked that all I needed was a boat outside my door and a canal with backcountry access. Al Manning's stilt house on Little Torch would deliver those two perks in less than twenty-four hours. I looked

forward to a change of scenery, however temporary. I also looked forward to cutting back on my
work schedule, at least locally.

Inside the house I put the chicken and all
but one beer into the refrigerator, turned on the
stereo—Christine McVie's solo CD from the
mid-eighties, a personal favorite—opened windows, and spun my fans. I had twenty minutes to
shower before sundown mosquitoes and no-see-
ums would turn me into a blood feast.

Praying for an out-of-state job offer, I called
my message-retrieval number.

First up was Teresa Barga, the city's media liaison. We had been lovers for a year, until the grass
turned greener and her falsehoods grew legs. I
still felt burned by her betrayal, and word had
come back that Teresa now referred to me as her
"recent unpleasantness." How do you fight that
crap without turning into a sleaze? It's a gentleman's task not to talk after a breakup; how do
you avoid being branded the bad guy?

In chipper voice Teresa let me know that the
city had hired a full-time police photographer.
The young man possessed skills, but he was not
a prince. "The operative word," said Teresa, "is
butthole. Apparently he's aware of your reputation. He asked for your phone number, which I
told him I lost. I just wanted to warn you, let you
know. That's it from the city."

Sometimes even I failed to keep the city and

county in their separate slots. Key West was in Monroe County. The county encompassed the Florida Keys and a small chunk of the Everglades. The county seat was Key West. So, while each entity had its own government, politics, and law-enforcement units, the overlap of jurisdictions confused even judges and lawyers. When people referred to "the city" or "the county," they usually meant the official entirety rather than a specific location. Once in a while they brought geography into it.

The next call came from my close friend Sam Wheeler, canceling our lunch date for next Wednesday. Two days ago he had borrowed a fellow fishing guide's van and helped me move my stuff—including my '66 Shelby—to Al Manning's place in one trip. The most important box carried my "read-these-soon" books, new novels by Gautreaux, Rankin, Furst, and Rozan. "Hope you got squared away in Little Torch," said Sam. "I kept the van for ten days and now it's next stop Weeks Bay, Alabama. I needed some time in my cabin, and Marnie started her book, so she won't miss me."

Sam's housemate, Marnie Dunwoody, worked for the **Key West Citizen.** Last year she felt inspired to write a series about island changes from the Depression bust to the current boom days. Six weeks ago a New York editor with a home in Key West called to praise her series. He suggested that Marnie find an agent so he could buy an expanded version of the series as a book. Marnie faced daunting research. Aside from old newspapers, several weak novels, and the fine pictorial books by the Langleys, little had been written about the period.

Her voice came up next. "I assume you were up the Keys. My boss at the **Citizen** asked me to write for page 1. Please call. I'll be here at the house. I also need to borrow your copy of **A Key West Companion,** the Christopher Cox book."

Next came Sheriff Liska: "I need your written report faxed or e-mailed to me by eight-thirty A.M. Don't get your jock in a wad. You can whip out two hundred words no problem, something I can show the county prosecutor. Compare the scenes, tell me what those dead men said to you. And ask your darkroom tech to get me some Marathon-scene photos ASAP."

Liska was followed by a familiar voice from a Naples ad agency. "Hi, Alex, Connie here. We have an open shoot, four days at our inflated rates, plus rental car and one twenty-five per diem. It's a pinewood furniture catalog for a shop in Blairsville, Georgia. You fly to Atlanta Thursday noon and drive two hours into the mountains. We see a fine weather window for the duration. We like you for this, but we have to know by Monday."

An out-of-state job offer. If I had known my

prayer might work, I would've gone for an extended fashion shoot in Tahiti.

The last voice was the city's new photographer. He identified himself as Bixby, and recited his phone number. "I've heard great things about you, and I'd love to buy you a few of whatever you drink and pick your brain. At your convenience, of course. Maybe you can give me tips on dealing with locals and getting behind the scenes. If you ever want to let me know, for instance, that somebody famous is in town, I can make it worth your while. My name is Bixby. Just the one name, like Sting."

I deleted all six, popped another, stripped my shirt and shorts, and went to shower. I felt skeeters brush against me, but none of them bit. I must have been the wrong temperature.

After two pieces of chicken, I returned Marnie's call. She was finishing her **Citizen** piece and wanted info on the two snuffs.

"I don't need much," she said. "The sheriff's press liaison faxed me a short page of details. The Marathon detectives have a man in custody with no charges filed."

"You going with coincidence?"

"On no proof, Alex?" she said. "My editors would eat me alive."

"Two in one day and both on davits?" I said. "That's coincidence over the top."

"Maybe you saw something else that links the murders. One of your evidence tidbits that the police missed."

"You may want to stress poverty, which rules out theft."

"Poverty links a whole lot of Keys residents," she said. "Anyway, time has taught me that unless cops are abusing them, poor people make shitty headlines."

"How about researching the last time the county had a nonsuicide hanging?"

"I hate that kind of low-rent story. It's like covering a bank holdup with no suspects, so you're forced to write a fat sidebar on the history of bank holdups."

"I don't know what else to tell you, Marnie. I was as close to the dead men as anyone. Beyond timing, poverty, and davits, I didn't see a thing that linked them. The forensic experts could have a different story. A couple of matching footprints or witness sightings of similar cars."

"So maybe I should camp out on the medical examiner's front porch?"

"Heard from Sam?" I said.

"Not yet, but he sometimes forgets how to use machines like telephones. If you hear from him, remind him that I'm alive."

"Before you go," I said, "I just thought of a detail you might pursue. The Marathon victim had head wounds. He might have died before he was lifted off the concrete."

"No similar injuries on the other dude?"

"None that I could see."

"Has Liska ever put restrictions on you regarding talking to the press?"

"No," I said. "But if you say in print that I was the only one to view both scenes, I might become the killer's next target. I might get to do my own air dance."

"Your what?" she said. "Oh, I get it."

"You understand my reluctance?"

"Alex, we all have our jobs to do."

5

I DISLIKE OBJECTS THAT promise to improve my life but end up confusing it, and buying a "plan" is even worse. But my new living arrangement dictated a cell phone. I could remove billing issues by unplugging my house phones for eight weeks and let incomings forward to my mobile. And Johnny Griffin could use his cell to make or take calls while he occupied the cottage. No overlap, no problems. The soundness of the arrangement was crumbling fast. For the second straight night the new buzzing bastard interrupted my dream sleep. Four people had the number, and Sam Wheeler hated cell phones. He swore he would call only to inform me of his own death.

Dumb-ass me answered it. The next time I crossed Cow Key Bridge, I would chuck it seaward. I should have known that the police can get any info they want. To compound the crap,

Officer Carlton Tisdell was the last Key West cop I wanted doing me favors.

"Rutledge, you got a brother?"

My clock said 3:08. "Last count I had two."

"Is one the mongrel here on the curb?"

"Does he have a name?"

"Timothy Rutledge."

"Ah, shit."

"I heard that," he said.

"Is he dead?"

"He's doing his best but he's not there yet. Come collect him before he dies of being repulsive."

"Where are you holding him?"

"I'm giving him a break, saving you taxpayers the price of a metal bunk. Call it a credit to my bank of good favors. We're watching traffic out front of the Bull and Whistle."

"Thanks, Tisdell. I didn't know he was in town."

"Save your chatter for people who treasure your image."

I called a taxi and asked it not to honk in the lane. I changed my T-shirt and pulled on shorts, deck shoes, and a ball cap. A bartender friend once called a fifty-dollar bill a postmidnight miracle worker, so I dug into my secret stash. The night's perfect miracle would have my brother evaporate without being harmed.

A pervasive hum of climate control filled Old Town. The air smelled of dense frangipani and what passes for dew in the tropics. A tree-frog chorus croaked a rain warning. An east breeze ruffled palms, and frond shadows danced beneath streetlights. The cab stopped on Fleming as I walked from the lane. I knew the driver, a freelance writer who wrote a weekly column for **The Miami Herald.** I hated to include him in my wee-hour drama.

"Where to?"

I said, "Caroline and Duval," which told him I was on a mission, kamikaze or rescue. I thought it best that he think kamikaze. Taxi drivers hate to pick up drunks because they so often barf in the car.

He was no fool. He knew me and pegged it a rescue. "Charming," he said.

"I guess we'll find out." I tried to run a preview through my mind.

Our parents had imposed an alcoholic and myopic outlook on life. Our job was to shut up and be "good." We couldn't afford vacations, new sports gear, Indians' tickets, Vernor's ginger ale, or theme-painted lunch boxes. Even Raymond, the oldest of us, wore hand-me-downs from cousins. We were told that finer things were for finer people.

Raymond never left Ohio. He did two years at Kent State, married his pregnant girlfriend, and moved to Toledo, her hometown. He worked his way through the union ranks in a steel-fabrication plant, took six-week vacations each year, and made more money than all of us. He stayed married, and would retire with full health benefits inside of eight years.

I fled Cleveland Heights in the late sixties, to a state college, then the Navy. In the seventies I landed in Key West, an island few in Ohio had seen and fewer understood.

Tim, on the other hand, rode a downhill sled. After high school he tried to escape, but each time he U-turned. When he was twenty-one he married a young heiress to an Akron tire-and-rubber fortune. The morning after their wedding, the newlyweds missed their flight to Hawaii. Her family found them honeymooning in a Canton hotel room with an underaged black hooker, a case of Cuervo 1800, four grams of cocaine, a box of poppers, and a mini-canister of nitrous oxide. Even with his political clout and wads of cash, it took the bride's father months to squash the paperwork and send the groom packing. Tim's cash reward for going away was chugged and snorted inside of two months. His life from then on was repeat, recharge, and repent.

I hadn't seen Tim in seven years, and those few days had been rough. Our father had collapsed and died during a Christmas reunion. My brothers and I had taken down lights and decorations and gone into funeral mode—long faces and enough cocktails to keep Mom subdued. It went down as we had been trained. Booze cures all, even though it killed the old man. We were never sure if our mother was grieving or just relieved and going through the motions. The standard mourning script was, "Mom looks dry. I can get it," and one of us would pour a Canadian Club and Coke. My four-day trip went to ten. I hit my body's limit for cold weather and came down with bronchitis. After my recovery, back on Dredgers Lane, I swore to forever stay south of Miami between November and March.

Tim had been the stalwart brother that time. I was full of cold pills, sweating, trying to sleep under a pile of blankets. Raymond had fled, claiming he needed time with his family. Tim stuck it out, dealt with the out-of-towners who'd come to the funeral, attended to our mother, stayed sober, showed—of all things—kindness and a personality I hadn't seen since grade school.

Eight years before that, I had kicked Tim out of my house. He had pissed off every Key West friend I had, started a fight in Louie's Backyard, been tossed out of the Full Moon Saloon, eighty-sixed from the Green Parrot—no mean feat—and rolled to my doorstep twice by city cops. I demanded that he not return to Key West, ever. I'd felt like a failure because I'd never found a way into my brother's skull, a way to save him from himself.

In recent years I had wondered whether the stalwart Tim was permanent or temporary. If I saw him again, would it be the rational Tim from the days following our father's death or the manic Tim who'd forced me to slam my door? Now I had my answer. He was back on the island, drunk, probably fresh out of cash, with a cop attached. I know the argument: you can't control things that are out of your control. But at least, for a short time, I'd seen a glimmer of hope for Tim's future, something to hang on to, to make me feel like less of a failure.

I couldn't bring him back to my house. Johnny Griffin would begin his occupancy in less than five hours. I had promised to vacate by eight A.M. so Johnny could check out of the Casa Marina and drop off his luggage before starting a day's fishing in the Northwest Channel. The last thing I wanted to do, on the first day of a lucrative rental, was to confront my tenant with a drooling fool who looked like my twin. Also, I didn't want to relocate Timothy twice inside of six hours. Best to rent him a room where he could sleep it off, and maybe have a bus ticket delivered to his room before checkout time.

I took one small consolation. The money I would spend could amount to a screaming bargain.

From a block up Caroline Street I spotted Tim flat-assed on the sidewalk, his back against the bar's outside wall. Officer Tisdell stood close by, bullshitting two young women who didn't look any more sober than my brother, or old enough to drink. Fitting the hour, Duval was packed with stragglers and stumblers. Thumpa-thumpa cars cruised, filled with sneering boys, a few rock-hard young girls. Music blared from open saloon windows. I asked the driver to stop and wait on the far corner.

He spoke his second one-word paragraph: "Wonderful." If the cabbie had told me my ride was over, I would've countered with at least a twenty. He stuck with me, however, and I stepped to the curb. Tisdell broke away from the young women, glanced at me, shifted his stare to my brother, and said nothing.

Tim heard the cab idling and raised his head. His eyes filled with sullen fear. "Man, you know I didn't want this," he said. "You know I wanted this time to be different."

I said, "Why fuck with tradition? Hop in. You don't have a ditty bag or anything?"

"Shh." Tim looked out the corner of his eye at Officer Tisdell. "I told him I hitchhiked down." He misjudged his curb-to-cab step, but I caught him as he fell. He smelled more of body odor than alcohol. In the backseat he said, "Cop doesn't need to know about my car."

"You remember where you left it?"

"On that street near Louie's Back Yard."

"Why over there?"

"The parking spots aren't marked 'Residents Only.'"

"You're getting smarter in your old age," I said.

"At least I'll never be as old as you."

A clever line that I had heard him say before. I heard it as his prediction that he would die first. My sadness expanded.

He said, "What's new?" but didn't look eager for an answer.

"New, old, what are you talking about?" I said. "Nothing changes. You roll in, and I spring for a room."

"Yeah, well." He jammed one hand, then the other, into his front pockets. He mumbled something that I chose to ignore.

I knew an all-night clerk at the Blue Marlin who would accept fifty to find a hundred-dollar room. The room might have been used from ten until midnight, then vacated, but why be choosy. I asked the driver to go left on Whitehead.

"Don't need no motel, Alex." He was still wiggling his hand in his pocket. "I met a guy in the bar, big fucker named Tanker. He said he needed a roomie to kill the boredom, and he said, 'Split the rent, more money for beer.' It made good damn sense, so I said okay. I had his address right here."

"Fish it out."

"I swear I had it. I think the fuzz pulled it out when he searched me for dope."

"He didn't find dope?"

"My drug of choice has always been beer."

The bullshit continues.

"The cop kept the address?" I said.

"It fell in the gutter back there."

"Are we sure of this, Timmy?"

"Pretty damn sure. The guy in the bar's name was Tanker Branigan."

Without a speck of hope, I asked the cabbie to go back to the Bull and Whistle. We cut east on Fleming, hung a left on Duval, and got caught behind a pedicab at the light on Caroline.

Tim sat up, peered through the windshield, and pointed at the far corner curbing. "Fat damn, there it is. Don't you see it?"

When we were much closer, I saw a yellow speck on the pavement.

I didn't doubt that his liver was shot, but his eyes were perfect.

The address on Johnson threw me. The street runs east from the Casa Marina, where digits and decimal points define mansion prices (1.2 would be a starter home; 2.5 might be average). I had never traveled beyond White on Johnson, but in the 1800 block prestige was hard to find. Concrete block ruled. We stopped at a two-bedroom side-by-side duplex dump—a "du-du" in real estate parlance. I reminded myself that, in today's Key West, a clean du-du was .8 and rising.

A bleary-eyed young woman with shoulder-length brown hair opened the door. She was about five-three and wore boxer trunks and nothing else.

A slurred man's voice from inside called, "Who the fuck is it?"

"Two guys I don't know. I got it handled." She squinted at me like she needed glasses. "Don't tell me I got the cutest little titties you've seen the last three hours. I'm too tired for horseshit." She aimed her finger at Tim. "What's that?"

"He met a man named Tanker, and he had this address in his—"

"I gave that address to one boy, not two," yelled the unseen man. "Boy named Tim."

"I won't be hanging out," I said, loud enough to be heard inside. "I was helping him find his way."

"Let him in, Francie," said the man. "Find him a pillow. Make him take off his shoes before he sleeps on that sofa. We'll hit his wallet for rent bucks before he wakes up. Tell him, if he's a bed-wetter, I'll kick his ass."

The young woman brushed her hair behind her ears, then stood back so Tim could stumble in. "You look like his little brother," she said to me. "Your girlfriend wouldn't let him stay?"

"Kind of like that." I fought an urge to look at her breasts. "Thanks for your hospitality."

"Do it," she said. "Look down."

I did, for an instant, then looked up.

"Save 'em to your hard drive? The next time they're out you won't have to be so uptight."

"I'm sure they'll look fine long into the future."

"You could've said that in two words." She shut the door.

She had to be somebody's daughter.

"You get an eyeful?" I said to the taxi driver.

"In a week's time, I see it all," he said. "Some you laugh your ass off, but most of them you don't want to know. Not that I wouldn't give Francie a passing grade. I've had her in my cab six or seven times the last few weeks. Brought her here twice."

I set my alarm to give me three hours and a shower before my tenant showed up. The buzz came at 6:55, and I woke clutching a softball-sized wad of pillow. I blamed tension and the two murder scenes, then Francie flashed through my mind. I couldn't recall my dream, but I cursed the clock. Drawn-out thunder rumbled to the west. I twisted the slim wand, opened the blinds. Orange light painted high branches of the blue-shaded trees. A garbage truck backed out of the lane at Daytona-qualifying speed. Perfect time to stagger out on a half-night's sleep.

I jammed on a Black Fly ball cap and headed to 5 Brothers for coffee. The warm wind carried dampness from neighboring foliage, the jacaranda, sea hibiscus, and sausage trees between Fleming and Southard. From someone's TV, I heard Katie Couric, then Bob Seger's three-word Chevy-truck gold mine. His old hit, "Like a Rock," had earned him more in two seconds of network time than the previous day had put in my pocket. Not that he didn't deserve it. I walked past an elegant magenta bougainvillea that shrouded a trash can full of yesterday's shrimp, then registered the irony and the poetry. Seger had written his song about love, and now it pitched trucks. I had bought my cameras to document beauty, and all I'd shot lately was death.

Shopping at 5 Brothers reminds me of my first days in Key West. Signs out front read: HOT BOLLOS, CAFE ESPRESSO, CAFE CON LECHE, CUBAN SANDWICHES, CONCH FRITTERS, PAPA RELLENA, CROQUETTES, EMPANADAS, GROUPER SANDWICH, and JUGO RELLENA. Three men on an outside bench spoke Spanish, quickly and all at once. One held a **Key West Citizen** with the headline TWO DEATHS LINKED?

A raindrop hit my arm as I opened the door. More drops darkened the sidewalk. I knew the drill. My walk home would be humid but not drenching. Summertime blue-sky showers rarely lasted more than ten minutes.

The store's bins were filled with potatoes, plaintains, and onions. Three narrow aisles split four steel-framed racks, which displayed **rojo criollo** and Edmundo soft drinks, picnic supplies, Cuban condiments, and canned food. The top shelves held expensive-looking skillets and pots, though I'd never seen anyone buy them.

I worked my way to the rear deli section, into the usual scramble at the old-fashioned cash register, the bilingual orders for coffee, pastries, and breakfast sandwiches. A flash of eye contact with the person behind the counter was an invitation to place an order. A delay, even for an instant, was the equivalent of being sent to the back of the line. I asked for café con leche and a guava cake. By the time I had paid and shuffled to the front door, the rain had let up.

I crossed through rush-hour traffic on Southard, bicycles and cars, early birds going to work. Halfway to Fleming a male voice behind me said, "Mr. Rutledge?"

If someone in Florida calls you Mister, they've already screwed you or they want to get in line. This voice was just twirpy enough not to be a cop. I turned to find a movie version of the hot-shit metropolitan newshound, Jimmy Olsen eagerness all over his face. Two Nikons, a standard and a digital, hung from his neck. His khaki vest had fifty zippers for forty pockets.

"I'm Bixby, from the K dub PD."

Oh boy. The new full-timer would dig his own ruin. He had made up a nickname for the Key West Police Department. I wished I could be a fly on the wall when the sergeants heard it. The day's first flight of tourists roared eight hundred feet above us. I said, "Blow it out your ass," but the jet ate my words.

"I'd love to get a few minutes with you, if you don't mind. I left my home number with your service. I know your schedule must be tight, so if you ever need help, I'll carry lights, hold cameras, anything to watch a real pro work, to get my career in motion."

"What's this, at this hour? Are you stalking me?"

"No, no," he said. "I went to the graveyard for dawn shots. No one told me they keep the gates locked until seven. I was in the grocery. A man saw my camera equipment, he pointed you out." Finally he studied my face. "I'm disturbing you. If this is a bad time—"

"Okay," I said. "Let's call it a bad time. Why don't you call my secretary and make an appointment."

"Yes, sir." He slid a reporter's notepad from a vest pocket.

"His name is Liska." I gave him the sheriff's direct office number.

"You're the best," he said.

My cheap practical joke reminded me that Liska was looking for a fax. His words had been "Tell me what those dead men said to you."

An old Raleigh ten-speed with ape-hanger handlebars was parked at my screen door. Duffy Lee Hall sat on my porch.

"I would've brought you a coffee," I said.

"Had mine an hour ago. One more would rocket me to the Tortugas."

"What's up, home delivery?"

He slapped a large manila envelope. "I got your packets, and I printed some extras." He spread four eight-by-tens across my table. "Were you like me and a million other ninth-graders? Did you learn to tie a noose? How to loop coils around the rope, and feed the rope back through them?"

"Sure. Fascinated the hell out of me."

"Maybe it was a rite of passage, a ritual for all boys. Like throwing jackknives into the dirt, to see how close we could come to the other guy's foot. Or doing forty downhill on Schwinns, defying death every way we could think of, positive we never would die."

"All of the above," I said. "My specialty was to fake being wounded by an enemy sniper. I would spin and fall off the garage roof, shooting the sniper on my way down."

"Check these shots. The group Liska gave me, the coils go one way; the roll you gave me, the coils go the other way. I don't know about you, but it was hard enough to learn the knot, much less bending it backward."

I studied the pictures. "Two bad guys, you think?"

"More likely two than an ambidextrous hang-man." He stood to go. "That should be enough to keep you out of this one, Alex."

"Duffy Lee, I have no desire to get into this mess."

"But I'm just saying, you don't want to be sandwich meat, chasing one murderer and out-running another at the same time."

6

CARMEN SOSA HAD AGREED to cover the domestic side of my house rental. Once a week she would wash sheets and towels at her place—three houses down the lane—and make sure that garbage cans reached the curb on proper days. Everything else, including kitchen tidiness and soap in the outdoor shower, went to my tenant. Carmen would charge me a "major wine" for each visit. I was to vary the vineyards and surprise her. "No bottle before its time," she said. "And no trash under twenty bucks."

I wanted to bury myself in the bed to recapture lost sleep, but I stripped and remade it and rolled a Burgess Cabernet into the laundry bag. Walking the lane to deliver Carmen's first task to her back door, I smelled baked bread and frangipani. Carmen's sago palm had gone berserk, grown two feet since I last noticed it. The sensory ambush launched new misgivings about my desertion of Dredgers Lane, but I fought back with images of solitude on Little Torch, my coming days in the kayak. It also helped to picture myself fanning 160 pictures of Benjamin Franklin looking much like Jack Benny.

Back at the house, I wanted to write Liska's fax in longhand, get it done before Johnny Griffin showed up. I began with the scene address, my time of arrival, and the presence of Bohner and Millican. My first narrative sentence read, "No footprints available at Marathon scene due to F.O.P. meeting on site." Then I heard the screen door open, and Liska's voice.

"Wake up, Jerky Boy," he said. "You sleep sitting up, you'll pitch off your chair and hit your head." He wore a shirt and trousers similar to those of the day before, perhaps the same ones.

I looked outside. Bobbi Lewis had parked her unmarked county cruiser next to Liska's Lexus in front of the house. She stepped onto the porch behind him, smiled at me, skipped hello, and closed the door. Not that I'd expected a kiss in front of her boss. From five feet away I could smell her shampoo. Liska eased himself onto the chaise longue and pursed his lips for an extended exhale.

"You don't believe in fax machines?" I said. "I was just working on my summary."

"This is beyond faxing your report," said Liska. "A couple things came up."

"About these hangings?"

"And what else?"

I glanced at Bobbi. She peered into my eyes, perhaps noting a bloodshot effect. "Let's get it done and behind us," I said. "I've got some things happening in the next hour or so."

Liska raised his open hand to give Lewis the floor.

"It fell to me to snoop Kansas Jack's belongings," she said. "We wanted to notify next of kin, and we needed clues to who dragged him outside in the middle of the night."

Liska said, "After giving him time to dress and put on his shoes,"

"Kansas Jack may have met his killer elsewhere," said Lewis. "He may have been followed home, or else he brought the murderer home. I spent yesterday afternoon and evening inside his house."

"More pleasant than outside?" I said.

She sneered. "He didn't have central air."

"Find anything you could use?"

"Depends how you look at it. His life was a short story. Kansas Jack Mason didn't exist prior to forty months ago."

"So he rented instead of owned?"

"He owned the house," she said, "but just barely. He arrived in the Keys and paid cash. The broker on Big Pine remembered him. She suspected back then that he'd spent his last penny to close the deal."

"Where was he before he came to the Keys?"

"He didn't exist," she said. "No record of his paying telephone or utility bills in the United States, no Social number, no credit history, no relatives. It'll take us a day or two to hear back on his fingerprints."

"His income since then?"

"The neighbors say he did odd jobs that he found word of mouth."

"Did he mix and mingle, or stay in his cave?"

"He was a happy-hour drinker, as opposed to a late-nighter, but he didn't hang in one bar all the time. They knew him at the Tiki Bar, of course, the No Name Pub, and the bar at Mangrove Mama's. No one at Boondocks knew his name, and none of those other places had seen him this week."

"I don't suppose his neighbors heard or saw anything odd," I said.

She shook her head.

"So you'll send his prints to Kansas?"

Finally she looked away from me. "The nickname's a problem. I always thought they came from other people, but these days, in the Keys, a lot of nicknames are self-imposed. People want to puff up their self-image, be Bonefish Bruce, or Pedro the Pirate, or Bad Bob. State handles are bargain models. You get them when people can't recall shit about you except where you lived in a prior life. Women take only the state names, like

Carolina or Texas. Men get the state plus their first name. Hence, Kansas Jack."

"What the problem?" I said. "You think he made up the part about his home state?"

"Kansas doesn't fit his style. No argument, he was a lowlife. But you look around his yard, inside his house, he was tuned to the Keys like he'd been here for fifty years. He was a walking survival manual."

Liska snorted. "Except he didn't survive."

"You remember who sold you this house, Alex?" said Bobbi.

"Sure. A retired man, Horace Fields, nicknamed Weedy, originally from Michigan. We made our deal on a handshake."

"What do you remember about him?"

"I haven't thought about him for years. Can I make you coffee?"

"Already had it," she said. "Back to Weedy, okay?"

"He was a pilot in the 1930s, a real pioneer, and he trained pilots for the Army during World War II. He settled here after the war and flew charter hops to Havana in the forties and fifties. After Castro, he worked for Curry's Chandlery until it burned. He admitted that he sold me the cottage for fifteen grand more than he ever thought he'd get for it."

"He have family?" she said.

"He sold because his wife died," I said. "He

had two kids, or at least that's all I knew about. A boy in college on a baseball scholarship and a girl a couple years out of high school. Weedy wanted to go back to Michigan to live out his years."

"Gotcha," said Lewis.

"With all this other crap going down, why do you want to know about Weedy Fields?"

"I found two things in Kansas Jack's house that might give us clues to his past." Bobbi unzipped her belly pack, removed a small photo, and handed it to me. "Why would Kansas Jack Mason have a picture of a young woman standing in front of your house?"

Right away, the sparse vegetation around my cottage told me the print was made before I arrived in Key West. The girl was in her early teens and wore a tough expression and a light-colored dress that came to midthigh. I recognized her immediately, even with her hair shorter than I'd ever seen it. I felt alarm and disappointment knowing that her photo was among a murdered man's possessions. "It's Horace Fields's daughter," I said. "They called her Pokey."

"Weedy and Pokey?" said Liska.

"It's a town full of nicknames," I said. "You of all people—"

"Let's get back to the picture," said Bobbi. "You get to know her when you were buying the house?"

I shook my head. "We met after Fields and I signed the papers at closing."

"The daughter came to the closing?" said Liska.

"No, she didn't live at home. The neighbors told me she moved out when she was still in high school. She'd taken up with a boy in the Navy, and Horace pushed her out of his life, never spoke of her."

"Then how did you meet her?" said Lewis.

"We closed our deal and left the lawyer's office, and Weedy took me to the Boat Bar for a beer. He told me that he'd shipped some things to Michigan, sold his furniture, and left five boxes in the utility room, stuff that his late wife wanted to give their daughter. He gave me the girl's phone number and tried to give me fifty bucks to store the boxes for a month or so. If she didn't show any interest, I could put the stuff with the trash. I told him I didn't want the fifty, so he bought a round of drinks for the old boys in the bar."

"Did you call her?" said Lewis.

"Sure," I said. "She came by a week or so later to see if it was worth her bother. She looked happy to have it, but she was in a small car, an old Camaro, and couldn't carry much of it home. She came back a day or two later in a borrowed pickup truck and took it all in one trip."

"Her nickname was Pokey?" said Lewis. "You recall her given name?"

I shook my head. "You could check old records at the high school."

"And how old was she when you met her?"

"I think nineteen, almost twenty," I said, "so this picture's well before my time."

"You never saw her again?"

"She came by again, maybe six weeks after she got the boxes."

"My, my," said Bobbi. "Please tell us about it."

I glanced at Liska. He dodged my eyes, gazed at the porch screening.

"She showed at the door," I said. "She wanted to come in and walk around. Wanted to remember better times or something like that. She told me about her mother, went out in the backyard and cried, then got in that old Camaro and drove away."

"I see," said Bobbi. "And that was all that happened?"

"Sorry to bore you, but that was it," I said. "You found two things that caught your eye?"

Lewis looked at Chicken Neck, as did I. He nodded, gave her an okay.

She reached again into her belly pack, extracted a silver Zippo lighter, and handed it to me. One side of the lighter was engraved in two columns. At the upper left was "1-12-73." Just under the date was the word **Nevada,** under that

"R.I.," which I took to be Rhode Island, then a space, then "M.J.W." Three more sets of initials were stacked in a similar column to the right: "E.J.B.," "J.P.McW.," and "H.P.E."

"How do you see it?" said Lewis.

I said, "Four men from Rhode Island went to Vegas or Reno a long time ago."

"Assume it's four dudes in Vegas," said Liska. "What's with Rhode Island?"

"Maybe all four of them grew up there," I said. "They met by chance at a blackjack table and decided to commemorate the occasion."

Liska shook his head. "Too nice a souvenir, especially if they bought one apiece." He dropped it face up on the porcelain table. "A home state can't be that goddamn important."

"I was on a ship in the military," I said. "Three hundred men aboard, but I knew which ones were from Ohio. You stood the midwatch, you bullshitted to kill time, and home states were important. Don't ask me why. Maybe a base point for pointless conversation."

"Okay, the military," he said. "Vegas isn't exactly a liberty port."

"So they were Air Force. Maybe they worked at that secret air base in the desert out there, Area 351, or whatever it's called. Maybe they were test pilots or UFO controllers."

Lewis shook her head. "Your brain is running away from you."

"You were in the service," said Liska. "You ever take a vacation with two other guys?"

"No," I said. "Except for a half-day train ride in Europe. Maybe it was the other way around. Four men from Nevada were assigned to a Navy ship out of Newport, Rhode Island."

Liska turned to Lewis. "Detective, was the medical examiner going to perform back-to-back autopsies?"

Lewis checked her watch. "Forty minutes from now. I should go."

"Can I make a suggestion?" I said.

Bobbi turned her head and stared at me. "You look awful, Alex. I suggest you go back to bed."

It was not a good time to tell either of them about Tim. I stared back.

"Okay," she said, "make a suggestion."

"Ask Larry Riley to consider two perpetrators while he works. I know it's not the examiner's job, but . . ."

She looked for Liska's reaction, as did I. Liska didn't move.

"I'll ask him," she said.

Liska watched her walk to the county vehicle. I saw his eyes drift below her belt line, then to her face when she turned to get into her car.

Backing out of the lane, Lewis had to swerve her cruiser to allow another vehicle to pass. Johnny Griffin—my new tenant—in his rented van. He was head-to-toe khaki with wraparound sunglasses on a string and zinc oxide on his nose. Ready to fish all day. He looked up the lane, watched Lewis's unmarked Crown Vic turn onto Fleming. When he opened the porch door, I introduced him to Sheriff Liska.

"Are we all friends," said Johnny, "or do we have an issue here?"

Liska looked bored. "We need to discuss your misdemeanor lease of this residence. Four local ordinances will be trampled the instant you carry your suitcase into the house."

Griffin blanched. "I'm out of here."

I fought back quickly. "Hold on," I said. "The sheriff used to be my deal killer, but I fired him yesterday. His job is out in the county. Right here, he's just another slug on the porch."

Griffin still looked confused. "So I stay or don't stay?"

"I'll help you carry in your gear," I said.

I stepped outside to follow Griffin to his van. Just loud enough for me to hear, Liska said, "I'm a fucking slug." He remained in a funk while Johnny and I unloaded duffels, two briefcases, bags of groceries, and boxes of business files. Liska's sulk didn't reassure Griffin, and I feared I might have to make a monetary concession to ease Johnny's mind about Liska's petty prank. But I kept my mouth closed. Before Johnny left I swapped him a set of keys for a narrow bank envelope full of hundreds.

"Thanks for welcoming my friend to the tropics," I said.

Liska was back to staring through the screen, studying my yard. "Did he hook his sense of humor on light tackle?"

"I think he borrowed it from Detective Lewis."

"She's my best detective," said Liska. "Intense and eccentric, but good."

"She was trying to accuse me of having an affair a long time ago."

Liska turned, tried to read my eyes. "That she was, so let me talk straight, two things, package deal."

His deals tended to go lopsided in his direction. "My curiosity awaits."

"I see officers come and go," he said. "I'm a crusty cop and set in my ways, but I'm not so stupid I could slap aside a man who . . . what the fuck word do I want, contributes? Stands up? You saved my ass three times in recent years. Cases got solved, you were the unsung hero, and I got the official recognition. Whatever you've got, most never will. So, thanks a bunch, and that ends my 'attaboy' session. Part 2, and I might get into your space here, but I know you pretty well, so I apologize in advance. Lewis was burned pretty badly about three years ago. He was a hot-dog lawyer from Dallas with one of those seven-figure houses on Truman Annex. She took the initiative, fell in love, and had a mad fling. Fifteen weeks into it, not only was he killed in a private-jet crash, but his wife showed up in Key West to close out his affairs. The dude never mentioned a wife. Since then she's dated two or three gents, but her cold feet ruined the deals. If she invents jealousies and starts arguments, it doesn't mean you're not doing the right things. It's her issue, and you have to stay steady."

I felt mild relief and surprise. In his abrasive way, Liska had boosted my spirits. "Thanks for the background," I said. "Are you feeling okay?"

"It's my back," said Liska. "I tried to carry a heavy box while I was on my cell phone."

"You were shoulder-holding with your chin, right?"

"I turned my spine into a question mark."

"And your next ten days, too."

"Today I see the chiropractor and go for massage therapy. Tomorrow, the acupuncturist and the reflexologist. The day after that, the healer. If worse comes to worse, I can go to a real doctor."

"You ought to hit the evidence locker for a muscle relaxer. Save you a lot of driving around. Or is that what you already did?"

"What's that supposed to mean?"

"I have noted your disdainful approach to crime busting."

"I may not be perfect, but there's not a soul in this county that can do better at what I'm supposed to be doing."

"Except you. Listen to the word **supposed.**"

"Maybe I've been experiencing a failure of passion."

"Little trouble in the bedroom?"

"My dick does fine, when I can get it employment. This is on-the-job."

"You don't give a shit?"

He jerked his head aside and wouldn't look at me.

"Twenty-four hours ago you wanted me to be the great cop of the future," I said. "Two minutes ago you said I had the right stuff. This long-faced follow-up tells me that police work is not a dream occupation. Is this depression your loneliness at the top or facing the daily grind?"

His eyelids drooped as he stared at the floor. "Maybe both, maybe something else. But you've got the wrong impression of your side of the table."

"What do I become, your secret stand-in?"

"Something like that," he said. "My eyes and ears. I might even be able to put you on the payroll, something administrative."

"Which of us campaigns for reelection?"

"I'm not thinking past next week. If I'm not careful, I'll screw up today or tomorrow. If I confessed all this to an employee, I'd crunch my propeller."

"I can't stand behind your office chair whispering cues," I said.

"I think you're scared of real work."

"Not true, Sheriff. If I ever, in my life, take a true job, I want my phone to ring at least half the time with good news. If I took this job, every fucking call would be another dead person in the county."

"You're exaggerating, and you're underestimating your talent. I know how you are. You go on a mission, you never let up."

I laughed. "That's how Bohner described Millican yesterday. He sinks in his teeth and never lets go."

"Millican's a subject I don't have the energy to discuss. But I will say this. From this moment onward, if you happen to follow your nose, I don't want to learn any new developments in the **Citizen.** I will be your first ear, and that's an order, not a recommendation. If I were a mental and physical basket case, I'd still have the muscle to put you in a world of hurt."

Liska threatening? This was too far around the corner. "If I learn anything," I said, "it'll be because it fell in my lap."

Liska bit his lip, shook his head, and looked down at the page of paper he'd been holding the whole time. "I'm sorry now that I sent you up there with Billy Bohner. This written report you didn't finish? You didn't get the simple shit right. It wasn't Tenth Street South."

"My evidence is empirical. I read the sign. That's where we turned."

He pushed himself out of the lounge chair. "Your eyes are failing you."

"I'm a photographer. My life's in the details. Bohner made a fast approach to Tenth, jammed his brakes, and cut a Mario Andretti turn like he knew where he was going."

"I do details, too, and I was in the dispatching room when the call came in as Thirteenth Street. The officer on the horn is the superstitious type. He wouldn't say the number. He wrote it down and said, 'Corpse, Unlucky Road.' "

"I stand by my version."

"Why argue?" Liska pulled out his cell phone, punched a number. After a short wait and a ten-second conversation, he snapped the phone shut. "The call came in wrong, so I told him Thirteenth Street. How did Bohner know where to go?"

"Maybe it showed on his computer."

"Good, but not true," he said. "With two deaths so much alike, I didn't want a media feeding frenzy. I ordered Web and radio silence on the location. It was word of mouth or landline phone only."

"What time was the call?"

"Six-fifteen."

"You were in your office that early?"

"I was at the Freeman Substation on Cudjoe. I had a breakfast meeting with the Border Patrol, which meant I brought coffee and doughnuts. That's where we got the call. Why did you tell Lewis to think about two killers?"

"Did you get your prints from Hall this morning?"

"Yep," he said. "I passed them to her. Something you saw?"

"The noose knots are identical, except they're reversed as if one was tied by someone right-handed and the other by a lefty. But they both learned at the same school."

"Do we know how to find you?"

"Al Manning's place on Little Torch. Call here, it'll jump to my cell. I'll fax an invoice with my temporary address. Lewis has the other number."

"That's too much info, Rutledge. We'll chase you down if we need to follow up on this chat. Other than that, I'll take you at your word. If your phone doesn't ring, it's us."

He swung open the screen door, stepped out, and let it slam shut behind him. I couldn't tell if he was faking or hobbling with pain. Just before he got to his car, he reached for his cell phone. He looked back at the porch as he spoke, locked eyes with me, and appeared to make a mental decision. I saw him say no to his caller, and could tell by the way he moved his head that he was issuing orders.

I had understood his wanting to be secretive over the years, to hold his cards close during his city time and his short tenure as sheriff. But this was the first time I'd seen him so far out of character, the first time I had seen him act suspiciously. His voice had given him away more than his actions and words. I hadn't heard the sluggish tone of an injured or depressed man. I had heard quivers of anxiety.

At least his job offer was off the table, relegated to history. And I was commencing, as the Navy called it, my "holiday routine."

I stuffed my shaving kit and cell phone into my camera satchel, watered a ficus, and stopped for a minute before I locked up to picture young Pokey Fields, not three years out of high school, standing in my main room. I looked around the house—gathering memories just as she had— and thanked my lucky stars that I'd hedged the truth with Bobbi Lewis in describing my relationship with the girl.

My next week would be neither routine nor holiday.

7

I RODE THE TRIUMPH away from Key West into damp air under broken midlevel stratus. Whenever I rode in humid weather, my shirt doubled in weight and salt caked my skin. It felt like a fine way to begin a vacation. A swollen cumulus line above the reef resembled far mountains and reminded me that I'd forgotten to call the ad agency in Naples.

Nearing Boca Chica, I watched a succession of jets drop for touch-and-gos, then launch eastward to altitude. Their percussion split the sky, their grace inspired a traveler's freedom. The highway that skirted the naval air station became my course to calmer waters, its odd dips and rises mimicking the lazy chop of open ocean. All I needed was a steering vane and a guiding dolphin at my bow. I didn't need a roadblock. Or complications.

The northbound traffic off Big Coppitt picked up speed as it passed Boca Chica Road. Riding

the incline past the entrance to Shark Key, I
looked south to sailboats anchored in Similar
Sound. A sole angler poled a pale blue skiff west
of Pelican Key. I turned my head forward just in
time to see a brake light, and throttled down before I pancaked myself on the ass end of a Honda
Odyssey. Traffic slowed to a walking pace. A
minute later, from the Channel #4 Bridge rise, I
saw vehicles crawling to Bay Point and red and
blue flashing lights declaring an emergency up
the road.

Probably the phone call Liska received as he
left my house.

I had no wish to wait for a wreck mop-up.
I began to turn back for a crab-cake lunch at
BobaLu's but decided that any move away from
an afternoon's quiet on Little Torch was the opposite of progress. I opted for patience and tried
not to fry my clutch. Twenty minutes later I
reached the flashing lights. A squad of deputies
had blocked Bay Point's entrance roads. Deputy
Bohner motioned me toward him, no doubt assuming that I had been called to the scene. He
was in civvies, grabbing a few overtime hours.

I stopped between two cruisers and loosened
my helmet strap.

"Ever get suspended?" he said.

I thought about high school, my brother Tim's
constant after-school detention. I had pulled the
same juvenile crap, but I was never caught. Then

I matched Bohner's words to his odd sense of humor. "Do we have another davit job?"

"You could specialize, Rutledge," he said. "Your own gallows portfolio. No matter what, we got our wind chimes."

Glaring truth from Billy Bohner, of all people. With "gallows portfolio" he had defined in two words my collective work in law enforcement.

"How's Liska dealing with it?" I said.

"From a remote location," said Bohner. "No sign of him yet."

"How far down is it?"

He directed me onto West Circle Drive.

I passed the tennis courts and ran the stop sign. As I slowed to turn right and cross the bridge to the trailer subdivision down Beach Road, a deputy waved me farther down Bay Drive, toward the more exclusive neighborhood. "What I heard, they don't need you down there," he said. "It's on the left."

If a link existed, the killer had changed his pattern, found a victim with a fatter wallet. The large, elevated home sat on raised ground on a double lot. Beyond its white five-foot fence, healthy palms, and new shrubs sat a dark green BMW convertible and a black Ford Expedition. Two edgy but quiet Yellow Labs paced around stakes in the side yard. A Carolina Skiff with a Yamaha engine rested on a trailer under the house. The oversized mailbox was awash in surreal, hand-painted tropical fish. I parked across the street, shut off the motorcycle but remained seated. Gawkers hovered two houses away.

Bobbi Lewis had set up a mobile office on the hood of her Crown Victoria. She was surrounded by uniforms. She looked up, perplexed, and said, "You've surprised me, Alex. Liska said he wasn't sending you. He asked me not to call you."

"Are you the only one here who knows that?"

"I assume so."

"Why would the sheriff make that decision?" I said. "I'd have been the only person to view all three crime scenes."

She bought time, looked around, scratched her neck. My words forced her to confront a fact that already bothered her. "You can hang," she said, "but please stay over there." She pointed to the next house to the north, a ground-level bungalow built before insurance companies, via the feds, mandated elevated living spaces. "Leave your camera bag in my trunk so nobody will mess with it."

"Including me?" I said.

"Orders are orders." She reached through her car-door window and pressed the remote trunk-release button.

I set the kickstand and put the bag in her car. She told the uniforms I didn't require an escort.

The first thing I learned was why they didn't need me.

Bixby, the new city photographer, paced the concrete apron behind the high house. In cargo shorts, zippered vest, and hiking boots, he was a 170-pound peacock in high strut. He screwed a lens onto his camera body, changed his mind, chose a shorter lens. He half-crouched, fired off eight or ten clicks on his autowinder. His moves and mock decisions may have looked professional, but his positioning sucked. He was wasting film. Wasting a crime scene.

The victim looked well fed; his neck had stretched perhaps twice as much as Kansas Jack's or Milton Navarre's, and his eyes bulged as if he had tried to stare down death as it approached. He wore bathing trunks and what looked like a pajama top, though, with Keys styles, it could have been a formal supper shirt. I took him to be in his late forties. No duct tape, smashed teeth, or ripped buttons. The rope was the same color as that used on Ramrod and in Marathon, but it wasn't knotted to a true noose. If there had been two fewer loops, the victim could have fallen from his death collar, fractured his ankles, and crawled away alive. I wondered if his weight had caused the rope to twist him around and around until he quit saying to himself that he hadn't guessed that twirling would be part of it.

Beyond the fact that a dead man hung from a boat davit and flies had come to play, nothing here resembled the two prior deaths. Nothing but the sadness of another early exit.

Bixby disguised his indecision as concentration. He paced off distance, then cowered when a forensic tech barked at him for encroaching on the circle of evidence. He bracketed exposures, twisted dials to change shutter speed and aperture. Duped by his camera's meter, he shot into the bright horizon without fill, then toward the street with a flash. His pictures would flop.

I didn't think it mattered.

"What do you see, Alex?" said Lewis. "Another air dance iguana?"

I hadn't heard her approach. "More like a strangled manatee."

"I just chatted with Liska. He was surprised to hear that you'd showed up."

"I am here by mistake and coincidence," I said. "Isn't that how some people die?"

"Not the ones I investigate. Planning and malice lead to all of them, even the suicides."

"Was the victim married?" I said.

"His name was Lucky Haskins, his first name given, not a nickname. The wife is Tinky, short for Tinkerbell. Shaped like her old man. A family friend got her out of here, took her to a home on Sugarloaf Boulevard."

I pointed to the woman in dark slacks, a buttoned blue top, and aviator sunglasses who stood under the house writing in a spiral notebook. "Is she related to the victim?"

"She's the new detective with the city police," said Bobbi. "Her name's Beth Watkins. She came from California two weeks ago and by coincidence rented the house next to me on Aquamarine."

"She works for the city and she's out here on Bay Point?" I said.

"She wanted to observe county crime-scene procedures in case she needed to coordinate in the future."

The Watkins woman glanced up and saw us looking. Her hair was short, straw-blond. She looked thirty, give or take, comfortable with herself, with a pleasant calm about her. Lewis waved her over.

Beth Watkins recognized my name when Lewis introduced us. She reached to shake hands. "Your name came up at the city this week," she said. "You're the photographer who saved a detective's life."

"And you were hired to fill that detective's slot?" I said.

"Yes and no," she said. "A man recovering from a gunshot wound, no police department would tell him to pack it in. I believe, officially, he's on indefinite medical leave and I'm covering his workload. Whatever he does in the future, my

job sticks. Meanwhile, I'd better get back to taking notes."

"Nice meeting you," I said.

She flickered a smile. "I saw you arrive on that
Bonneville. It's an 800, right?"

"It's a 650," I said.

"What, like a '70 model?"

"Exactly. It's a T-120R."

"Sharp." Watkins turned and walked toward
the under-house shade.

Bobbi started back to the street. I had seen all
I wanted to see, so I followed. "What's Liska's
opinion of this spree?" I said.

"He thinks we'll lose the whole cluster to the
state cops."

The Florida Department of Law Enforcement
had a reputation for claim-jumping high-profile
cases. They also had a rep for clearing tough
ones. "Maybe they're headline-needy this year," I
said. "Speaking of which, this morning's headline
could be the reason for this."

"I agree," she said. "Plain and simple suicide."

"The rope is similar to the other two, but if he
killed himself with that knot, he lived up to his
name. My guess is a family dispute with a copycat factor. Whatever it is, you ought to get ready
for an insurance nightmare. The FDLE might do
you a favor."

"I'd rather keep the investigations," she said. "I

think the first two are linked, but this one's self-induced."

I couldn't imagine someone taking himself out the slowest way possible. "I'll bet you a naked boat ride."

"Are you betting that it's linked to the other two?"

"No, just that it's a murder," I said.

Bobbi reached inside her car and popped the trunk release. "You don't want to know?"

"Why you won't take my bet?"

She shook her head. "Why that schmuck is working for me."

"Orders are orders, right?"

"I guess so."

I started the Triumph and felt the wet tap of summer, a raindrop on my wrist. I didn't want to ride through weather with my camera gear, but it was better than hanging out where I was a lump on a log. I rolled to the Overseas Highway. The useless traffic jam was worse than before. Bohner and the deputy at East Circle continued to block all access to Bay Point. Confused residents were U-turning, pulling to the shoulder, jamming the Baby's Coffee parking lot. A group of college-aged kids tossed a Frisbee on the north shoulder.

I checked the sky. Blue sky and blue water on the bay side. The squall was just south of me, moving westward.

Bixby would conclude his photo debut in a downpour. Welcome to the tropics.

Al Manning's across-the-street neighbor got to me before I could get inside. He was hanging a wet suit under his stilt home when I turned onto Keelhaul Lane. I parked my Triumph and began to loosen bungee cords. His ambush was perfect. I had no escape.

He strolled over, full of cheer, stuck out his hand. "Wendell Glavin," he said. "Native Floridian."

I told him my name, then said, "Calusa, Tequesta, or Seminole?"

His smile faded. "None of them tribes, but that was funny. I was born in Green Cove Springs. You watching the place for Al?"

"For the next two months," I said.

Wendell was in his mid-fifties, pear-shaped, with a graying beard, the chatter of an old salt. He was a perfect blend of retired blue-collar worker and Hemingway look-alike. "I hate to say this, Rutledge," he said, "because we don't lock up much around here. We had us a murder over to Ramrod yesterday."

"I read about it, Wendell."

"Devilish way to go. You best keep your gun near your bed, my friend. You ever been married?"

"No, sir, I dodged it a few times."

"You're better off. I'm a two-time loser, but the second one stuck around till just last year. She got to be a monster to live with, but she paid for the divorce. The neighbors is all right. Couple old hippies like me at the south end. 'Bout the worst you can say of any folks up and down this street is they got carpenter ants or termites, and that's like saying they got noses. The woman at the end on your side, she's never out of her muumuu and bedroom slippers."

"Al didn't tell me that detail," I said.

"He probably burned your ears talking bait and tackle. All these years, he paints and fishes, then fishes and paints. Me, I'm into diving. I just plain live for Looe Key."

"You knew him before he moved up from Key West?"

"No, but I sure am happy to have him for a neighbor. Al's the kind of friend you don't often find. He's helped me every time I needed it."

I had brought nine boxes and two duffel bags to Manning's. I needed to unpack, find my essentials, place them within easy grasp. Al had left typed notes for me in every room. The first was in his kitchen.

Don't kayak during mini-lobster season. Too easy to get your butt T-boned by touristas. If you ride the bicycle after dark, leave a last will and testament on the kitchen table. If you hear a mosquito spray truck, roll up car windows and close up the house. If cooking, pull your fish off grill, finish it in the microwave. Paper goes in trash can. Food trash goes into the freezer until Monday and Thursday pick-up. Your recycle stuff goes out Wednesdays.

I opened a beer and carried my duffels to the bedroom.

Turn on this white noise HEPA air filter before you sleep. With a north wind, you don't hear US 1 traffic. With an east wind, you won't hear early-morning sportsmen in high-powered sleds on South Pine Channel. A west wind, you muffle my neighbor across the street who coughs all morning. A south wind, you mask the cooing rats with wings some people call doves. Dust, who cares?

Manning wanted me to live his life.

His home was monk-simple, with sisal floor coverings and pine furniture. He explained his décor the first time I visited. Hurricane Georges, in 1998, had blown in two sliding glass doors and ruined furniture that had belonged to his grandparents. "Insurance didn't cover my broken heart," he said. "If the storm had been worse, I might not have seen the wreckage. I replaced the heirlooms with this stuff, a step above motel, a step below time-share. My curtains, cushions, and end tables from Target. My CD player, TV, DVD, microwave, speakers, and amps totaled eight hundred bucks at Best Buy. The juice and wine glasses all came from Publix. Place settings, Kmart. My one stab at style was the blue-and-white restaurant dishes. Goodwill, seventy-five cents each. The extra insurance-settlement cash goes toward my high life."

I asked him to define his high life.

"New fish and old wine."

I unscrewed the frame of an air-conditioning vent and stashed all but four hundred of the cash I'd received from Johnny Griffin. Then I wandered room to room, read Al's other notes, and stacked my books and CDs where I could read their spines and grab at will. I organized the bathroom counter, set out my pit wax, shaving soap, and hairbrush, then took **The Sibley Guide to Birds** to the porch hammock. I tried to identify a few that swooped through the yard and over the canal. Five hundred pages and no binoculars. I read about prairie warblers, then gave up.

My next try was the cell phone, its multilingual booklet. I pledged myself to a half-hour tutorial. I would get the hang of it or fall asleep trying. Within six minutes lightning over the straits stole my attention. Then rain from the east blew through the screens. I took my stuff inside and confronted my dilemma: a half hour into my vacation, my long-awaited escape from the mundane, from hurry and stress, and I was wit's-end bored.

Then the little bastard buzzed at me. For the second time in two days, Bobbi Lewis's phone number glowed on the inch-square screen.

"Can you come back to Bay Point with your cameras?"

"Safety in redundancy?" I walked to the fridge.

"The kid's a klutz. He was standing on the seawall, framing his last shot. He fell in, bag and all. He blamed moss on the seawall."

"Moss has a bitch of a time on east-facing surfaces in the tropics."

"His cameras were ruined, but his exposed film was sealed in plastic canisters. I still want a few backup shots, just to be sure. How soon can you be here?"

"Did Watkins leave with him?" I said.

"She came with me."

"So she offered the services of the city's new boy?" I said.

"Ten days ago."

"Did Liska overrule you, and make you hire me for the Kansas Jack job?"

Her silence answered my question.

"What's he going to say when you disobey his orders and hire me back right now?"

"I can deal with that."

"Is the body still there?" I said.

"The medical examiner wants it down immediately."

"It's pouring here and the squall is blowing your way. There's no way I can get there before the downpour."

"Shit," she said.

I knew the answer before I asked: "Do you have a camera in your cruiser?"

"Don't do this to me, Alex. Please at least try to beat the weather."

A huge thunderclap provided my answer.

"Shit," she said again.

"Listen to me," I said. "Are you listening?"

"I'm right here."

"Take pictures of the rope, the noose, and the davit's on-off switch. Then have someone stand next to Mr. Haskins so you can judge the height of his feet above the ground."

"The camera's automatic everything, but I'll screw it up."

"Autofocus is fine, but don't use auto exposure. Make sure it's 100-ISO print film, not slides, and set it to f-11 at 1/125 of a second while the sun's out. If clouds cover the sun, drop to f-8 at one-sixtieth."

"I'll screw it up," she said.

"I know you won't, but if you do, I'll owe you that boat trip we discussed."

"If I do, you can take your own naked ass for a ride."

8

I WAS SCRUBBING SALT film and bird crap off Al's skiff Saturday morning, dripping sweat onto my sunglasses, thinking about my failure to mention brother Tim to Bobbi or to Liska. I could blame hectic events, but the longer I waited, the more awkward I'd feel, especially with Bobbi. I'd already failed to fully disclose details of my friendship with Pokey Fields.

On her third visit, six weeks after I bought the cottage, Pokey parked that old Camaro half into my yard and asked to come in. She had worn a tight T-shirt, skimpy shorts, custom sandals, and fishing-fly earrings. She could have fit in with the town's hippies, though few Conchs had mixed with the island's free-thinking new arrivals. She told me that her mother had been a frail, uneducated woman who interacted only through shared work. She pointed out kitchen shelves that the two of them had installed, spoke of helping her mom paint the bathroom and peel up old linoleum to expose the Dade County pine flooring. In the backyard she showed me code markings her brother had cut into bark high on the mango tree. She recalled a jungle gym by the rear fence, began to weep, then came back inside, stood in the living room, and absorbed memories.

"You wouldn't have a cold beer, would you?" she asked me.

I didn't give her age a second thought. If she lived with a sailor, she was old enough to drink beer on a warm afternoon. I opened two and motioned toward the porch, but she sat on my rattan rocker. She sipped the beer, studied the walls, then stared at me. "Do you like what you're looking at?"

I'd noticed that she wore no bra, but hadn't thought she'd caught me looking. "What's not to like?" I said.

"You can have some, if you put some hurry into it. I gotta be home." She stood, put her bottle on the floor, and drew her T-shirt above her head. Her breasts had a slight droop as if she'd been heavy at puberty then lost weight during her teen years. She began to unzip her shorts. I could see that she wore no panties.

Now her age came into play. "I don't want to offend you," I said.

The zipper stopped. A pleasant tuft of pale pubic hair behind her thumb, the hint of a stretch mark from her weight loss. "I was afraid of that," she said. "My first boyfriend at least said I was cute and threw a great fuck. My new boyfriend tells me I'm shaped funny and have zits and I'm too ugly to get anyone else to ball me."

"He's full of shit," I said. "He's wrong and an asshole to say it, especially if he thinks you believe him. You're a lovely girl and you'll be a beautiful woman if you stay away from jerks who put you down to elevate themselves."

Self-conscious, still hurt by my hesitation, she raised her hands to cover her breasts. Her shorts fell to her ankles. She looked at me, almost fearful.

I smiled and looked straight at her eyes. She finally grinned, giggled, and stepped out of the shorts. She raised her beer and chugged it, came across the room. I promised myself never to forget the sway of her breasts as she leaned to kiss my forehead.

"Why me?" I said.

"You're the first person been nice to me in a year and a half." She retrieved her clothes and entered the bathroom. When she came out in her shorts and shirt, her eyes still red, she thanked me for letting her revisit her childhood.

I asked about that childhood. My early years hadn't been great, but as her tale spilled out I felt lucky for what I'd had. Her father had buried himself in work and couldn't relate to anyone but her older brother. Even then, he was overbearing and belittling. Her mother, a chain-smoker and a chain-boozer after five-fifteen "when the working day was done," had explained that she was too exhausted from raising the boy and figured Pokey was smart enough to raise herself. After that, Pokey went anywhere for friendship, among the junior high troublemakers, the island's psychedelic newcomers, the tough sailors in the Boat Bar and the Big Fleet. She was disciplined for small infractions, and called lazy for reading books. If she stayed away from home for days at a time, it was no problem because she was less trouble out of sight.

When she finished talking, I felt an enormous urge to make the world right for her. An impossible task, of course, but I wanted her to know that she could shoot high as well as low in her pursuit of friends and a satisfying existence. My first step was to open a box of books still waiting for bookcases to be installed in my new home. I pulled out a random handful, gave her at least six or seven. The ones I recall were an old paperback of **The Sun Also Rises,** an early Kesey novel, McGuane's **The Sporting Club,** and a copy of **The Last Picture Show.**

As weeks went by, she dropped by the house maybe four more times, gave me back some of the books (but not all), and waited for me to offer more. She rarely spoke of her boyfriend, but when she did she compared him to her first lover, whom she had come to idealize. Whenever I asked specifics about that first one, she deflected my questions. I got the impression that she had moved from Key West to one of the Lower Keys. For a while I wondered if my nosiness had driven her away, because the visits stopped without warning. After that year, my first in the house, I never saw her again.

Why, all these years later, would a murdered deadbeat on Ramrod have her picture? Had Kansas Jack been one of the Navy men who used her for sex, then treated her like dirt? Or had he been the one that she idealized?

I heard throaty glass-pack mufflers out on Keel-haul Lane. A low-slung Caprice station wagon with a bent Ohio front tag bounced into the yard and coughed to silence. Last winter's crusted slush outlined its dark teal fenders, and mismatched hubcaps rode the side I could see. Key West has a tradition of funky Conch cruisers, disused, painted, and sculpted. This beast rode in its own category.

Three doors swung open. Tim and his new roommates had come to call, each with a breakfast brew in a coolie. Not to risk running short, Tim also carried a twelve-pack. In Levi's and loafers, he was James Dean with a one-day sunburn. His T-shirt sleeves were rolled close to the shoulder seam, and he looked broad through his shoulders and biceps. I wondered where he'd found time to work out. His hair was slicked to a pompadour, and his belt buckle rode his right hip.

The young woman wore a ball cap, a gauze-thin tube top, pube-hugger shorts, and sunglasses. A tiny cell phone was clipped to her elastic waistband. She approached me with her hand extended. "We didn't get around to formalities the other night. I'm Francie." Her grip was firm and confident, and when she lifted her shades, her sleepy brown eyes glistened with mischief. "We put our informalities behind us, didn't we?"

"I rarely open my eyes that time of night," I said.

"Shit," she said. "They were snowballs in a bowl of ink."

Tanker Branigan reached over her shoulder to shake hands. His forearm was as big around as my calf. His hand felt like a warm towel. "You know my name and it's Irish," he said. "Now we can close that topic. How you doing today?"

I pointed to the blue sky. "How could I not be perfect?"

"Right you are," said Tanker. "Bird songs are crisp and the air is sweet. The barometer is spinning cartwheels."

Odd words from a man who looked as dense as his body. He carried the bulk of a pro wrestler, a barrel chest, and a beach-ball gut. All of it wrapped in a Sloppy Joe's T-shirt, a half-acre unbuttoned Hawaiian overshirt, and black Bermuda shorts. His face showed no emotion, no judgment, but his eyes scanned beyond me as if danger lurked in the yard palmettos. I suspected that an agile man occupied the large torso.

Tim hung back, raised his Michelob as a toast. "Hey, brother."

"Welcome to daylight," I said. "How did you know where to find me?"

"We ate breakfast at Dennis Pharmacy. I sat next to a lady who asked if I was related to you. We got to talking."

"Her name Carmen?"

He shook his head. "This charmer was Teresa, and she was as tasty as the scrambled eggs."

"I didn't know she had my new address," I said.

"She called somebody on her cell phone to get it. You didn't mention the other night you were moving."

"Would you have heard me?"

"I reckon not," he said.

Francie turned to me. "Me and Tanker are going to Big Pine, just the two of us. You got custody of your brother for the next two hours. I've never been to that giant flea market. I collect tacky tourist thimbles, and Tanker collects antique postcards."

"From the Keys?" I said.

Branigan shook his head. "Pre-Castro Cuba. Spanish architecture and Art Deco hotels, and old Havana restaurants."

"Don't get him started," said Francie. "He won't stop talking until you're an expert, too."

A minute later the station wagon departed, lopsided with Tanker at the wheel and Francie shotgun, handing him a fresh beer. Tim had plastered rock-radio stickers on his Caprice's back end. In the bottom corner of the rear window he had stuck a decal with PEACE in a circle, a line angled through it.

He looked around the yard, waggled his bottle at the skiff. "Don't let me get in the way of your labors. I love to sit on my ass and watch hard work." He pointed to his twelve-pack. "You at least drink on weekends, don't you?"

"Yes," I said. "But only with girls in the morning."

"Very good, brother. Very fast."

Tasks were a fine way to pass the time of the surprise visit. I coupled that concept with the knowledge that my brother wouldn't stop nailing his foot to the floor to accommodate me. I returned to the scrub brush and hose. Tim pulled a lounge chair from under the house and dragged it close to the skiff. He positioned it for sunbathing and stripped his shirt. The width of his shoulders was no illusion, but his chest was so white it looked pale blue. Except for his hairstyle, his face resembled what I saw each day in the mirror. His premature age lines gave me an idea of how I might appear in ten years.

"Brother," I said. "You have a beer belly."

"My waistline goes in and out with the tide. One more black mark on my heap of family dishonor."

"Hey, I was only razzing."

"Daddy had a beer belly, too, Alex. I inherited the tail end of the genetic choo-choo."

"Always the victim."

He cast his eyes aside. "Always the speech."

"Haven't we done enough Dad-loved-you-best routines?"

"We could do it a thousand times," he said. "It's not going to fix me."

"The point I was trying to—"

"It was always you making points. You and Raymond were the boys, and I was an outparcel."

"Like I said, the victim."

He led it slide and twisted another top. "Speaking of which, you see the paper this morning? Weird place you live."

"I don't get it delivered here," I said.

"Two men hung from boat davits the day before yesterday, twenty miles apart. Then another yesterday, the same way, back down the road. It doesn't synch with your Overseas Highway's lightweight reputation."

"They were beyond weird. I had to photograph them."

"Shit, Alex. For the newspaper?"

"The cops. I do part-time to help cover my cost of living."

He disapproved. "The police payroll?"

"It has side benefits, brother. What do you think kept you out of the gray-bar motel?"

"Did I thank you for that? If I didn't, I appreciate your help."

Thirty years he had been spewing morning-after apologies and thanks. As usual he couldn't talk without leaving me openings. They were easy shots but the process always fatigued me. This time I decided to stay quiet and roll with it.

Tim sipped his beer and studied the canal, gauging the territory. I couldn't guess how much of it he absorbed.

"How did you get to be a photographer?" he said. "All I remember was a box with a plastic window that looked like a fly's eye."

"The light meter?"

"Whatever. I hated when you aimed it at me. I felt like that fly eye was inspecting me from a hundred angles, putting all my secrets, a hundred versions of me, on film. Secrets I didn't know I had."

An old mystery solved. My first camera, a Kodak Instamatic, had disappeared from a crate of belongings I had left behind while I was in the Navy.

"It was just a light meter, Tim."

He waved it off. "So back to your becoming a pro."

"When I arrived in Key West, I kept seeing things that we never saw in Ohio. Funky houses, shrimp boats, Cuban groceries, tropical plants, the crazy characters who lived here. It was like a foreign country. One night I saw some slides a friend shot with a new Olympus camera, and I couldn't believe the colors and the sharpness. The next time I had a paycheck, I went and bought one. From that day on I've been the ultimate tourist, always a camera in hand."

"Self-taught?" he said.

"I kept pressing the button, buying film, and throwing away bad ones."

"Cool," he said. "Ready for that beer?"

"I think it's time." I found another chair, and we sat and stared at the canal.

"I still think about that night in the drive-in, Alex, when I let my mouth get ahead of my ass."

"You were about to have both handed to you," I said.

"And you saved the day, driving your date's car. Or her father's car, that old Buick Riviera. You pulled into the restaurant parking lot and saw me in trouble, you aimed right for that dude who wanted to rip me apart. He backed off, and you ordered me to jump in."

"I meant the backseat. You landed on Susan's lap."

"Whatever," said Tim. "I knew what was good for me. But then that guy jumped in his buddy's GTO, and the chase was on."

I stupidly thought that my silence would prompt him to drop it.

He didn't let up. "I probably didn't tell you back then, but you scared the shit out of me. You outdrove that son of a bitch and you lost them doing figure eights in the city park. Susan loved it. You might've heard her breathing, but I was on her lap and I could feel her heart beating. I think it turned her on. Her perspiration smelled like an orgasm."

"You knew the difference between that and fear?"

"Well . . . I always had a thing for her, too."

I had no response to that.

"You did me a backup favor," he said.

No escaping now. "What was that?"

"You dropped me off on the street behind our house so I could sneak through the Goldsteins' yard and go in the back door and not get caught drunk by Daddy."

"Sounds right," I said.

Tim pretended to read the label on the beer

bottle. "Did you also forget that you went back to the drive-in that night? You taunted that GTO dude yourself and got him to chase you again. Maybe you wanted to show him you were good instead of lucky."

"You know it didn't go down like that, brother."

"You're not still sticking with your old story, are you? Maybe today, all these years later, you can tell me the truth."

"Which truth would that be?" I said.

"You got him to chase you through the same route, but faster. You took a right and a quick left and crossed the river bridge and that GTO fish-tailed and disappeared from your mirror. It ran off the road at something like seventy, but you didn't go back to look. You took your date home and put the Riviera in her father's garage and made sure your stories matched—except you two couldn't have known that the passenger died in the wreck and the driver would go to prison for DUI manslaughter. Then the hero probably hit a home run—or at least got to third base with her so ready—before you walked home. That about right?"

"No." I felt sweat sticking my shirt to the chair's plastic webbing.

"What was it, Alex—they were waiting on Susan's street when you drove her home?"

I nodded. "I turned into her driveway, they

jumped out with baseball bats and started coming for us."

"Now I hear that echo from the past."

"I was about to take your beating, Tim, not to mention they'd hurt Susan and ruin her father's car. Those boys called the tune and I bolted. My point of view is that I outran them twice."

"Okay," said Tim. "Your side of the tale hasn't slipped over the years. How was it they knew . . . oh yes, the driver knew her brother Jeff because he used to swipe his dad's car and hang out with the big boys at the drive-in. He even sold the GTO driver some pot."

"I knew about his hanging out," I said. "I never knew about peddling weed."

"We were never on the same grapevine, Alex. Did Susan ever have an opinion about that guy who died? Or the guy going to jail for seven years?"

"I guess she agreed with my side of things."

"How'd you keep her quiet?" he said.

"I didn't do anything. After that night we stopped seeing each other. I think that was August, and a month later we were off to different colleges."

"Didn't you expect some legal repercussion?"

"I don't know if I expected anything," I said. "I sure feared it. I suppose the police knew the chasers were hoods. I heard they found the bats inside the wrecked car. Brass knuckles, too."

"So it was good riddance?"

"Maybe so. They could've found witnesses to your fight and traced the Riviera, but they never did and nobody came forward. I waited for that other shoe to drop for months after that. Hell, I waited all through my freshman and sophomore years."

"But you skated, just like always?"

"It's deep in the past."

"You took part in two illegal car chases," he said. "Speeding, reckless driving, stop-sign violations. How's your conscience on that?"

"Like I said, they made their move and I reacted. My conscience never came into play."

"Gotcha."

It was time to clam up. Once again Tim had shaped history to his favor, to put down someone else. In his smug slam of my conscience, he couldn't grasp that my actions that night, right or wrong, stemmed from his grief at the drive-in. If I hadn't had to rescue him, the two chases wouldn't have happened.

But Tim kept hammering. "The guy who wanted to punch out my lights has been deep in the ground ever since."

"His buddy bought the blame. Can we change the subject?"

"But, Alex, you knew they'd smashed that GTO."

"I knew they'd left the road," I said.

"You didn't go back to see if anyone was hurt."

"I could've learned the hard way that they were fine and ready for action."

"Didn't that give you a weird sense of power?" said Tim.

"Not wanting to be injured?"

"Leaving them there to maybe die. You could've made a difference."

"What's your fascination with all these details, Tim?"

"Hell if I know. Why is it something you want to sweep under the rug?"

"I had one thought in my mind," I said. "I wanted my girlfriend, her father's car, and my ass as far away from those fools as I could get. Now it's history."

He was quiet for a minute before he said, "Ever wonder what ever happened to Susan?"

"Mom told me a few years ago that she was divorced twice and finally landed a rich boyfriend. They live on an island near Spain."

He finally went quiet. I went back to work on the skiff, spritzing cleaner, scuffing my knuckles as I jammed the scrub brush into corners, finding pockets of mildew that Al had ignored all year.

"After that summer," said Tim, "with Raymond and you gone, I got to be the orphan."

"You mean 'only child,' right? I can't imagine you stuck around the house much."

"Why bother?" he said. "The old man didn't get it. Even when I was in junior high, he didn't understand I wasn't that bad. I was a fuckup, I won't argue, but I wanted to be good. He didn't believe I was smart, maybe smarter than he was. So I did what any red-blooded American boy in my shoes would do. I tried to prove to his nasty ass that I was dumb and evil, and I did it to piss him off and disappoint and embarrass him. Except it pissed me off, for some fucking reason, that you could ignore him. You didn't let his bullshit get in your way. You went off to be good and smart on your own. I had to stay back and fight my little fight."

"So here we are today," I said.

"Yep, in your Keys."

"Having arrived by different routes of travel."

"More different than you can imagine," said Tim.

"What will you do here?"

"Are you asking do I still want to be a decent human being," said Tim, "or did I waste all those wishes living a shitbird's existence?"

"As pilots say, that's the runway behind you."

He nodded. "And life is a long series of drag races and siestas. I know you've got this ledger in your mind where you owe guilt debt to the world or Mom or your friends on the island. But your debt just grows as you get older, gets heavier and never goes away. All I want is a balance sheet that zeroes out to a guilt-free ride. Anything wrong with that?"

Out of Tim's mouth, that assessment amounted to towering optimism. Maybe my kid brother was starting to grow up.

"A zero balance sheet." I laughed. "The old man died owing me money."

"He died owing me more than that."

"Like there's a written guarantee?" I said. "I won't argue that he started the wound. Maybe you need to get over it before you dig yourself a deeper hole."

Tim drained the beer. "I suppose we all exist for a reason, pieces in the cosmic puzzle. I'm through digging my own holes, Alex. On top of that, I'm convinced it's easier to be a decent human being instead of the alternative. I like easy."

"And it's nice not to always be looking over your shoulder," I said.

"You bet. But, as great men have said before me, fuck it all. How fast will that boat go?"

"That hull, that motor, I expect forty-five, maybe fifty with the wind on your butt."

"You need some kind of license to take people for rides?" he said. "Maybe that'd be the job for me."

"They call it a six-pack license. You take a

course, take a test, get the Coast Guard's approval. I've heard a few captains bitch that their income's dependent on the weather."

Tim shook his head. "I smell insurance and permits and sales tax, too. They don't make a damned thing easy these days. It's all stacked against little guys like me."

The Caprice rolled in with a honk and a shutdown blat from its hollow mufflers. Tim didn't move from where we sat. "Five-point-seven liters, 260 horsepower, and twenty-three miles per gallon. I paid two large and I should've paid less."

"Still sounds like a bargain."

"I never make good deals," he said. "I might get lucky every few years, but one way or the other, even the good ones nail me in the ass. That station wagon'll break down one day and leave me stranded when I need it least, you can count on it."

He pitched his empty behind him. It rose in a perfect arc but missed the trash barrel by a foot and landed in the grass. He stood, looked away, and made no effort to pick up the bottle.

"All that anger inside you," I said.

"I think some of it's drained out."

"It's a good thing you're not violent."

He grinned but it turned into a sneer. He picked up the bottle and flung it downward. It shattered in the trash. Brown glass flew and sprinkled his forearm. He brushed it off, unconcerned about imbedding shards in his skin, then stared into the trash can as if searching for truth. "I'm not violent? Who ever told you that, brother?"

9

TANKER BRANIGAN PRESENTED ME with two of the four dozen antique Cuban postcards he had bought at the Big Pine flea market. One was a hundred-year-old lithograph card with a picture of Key West's Havana American Cigar Factory. The other had no photograph but read, "The Cosmopolitan Bakery, Obispo Street 101, Splendid Restaurant and Bar, We Employ English Speaking Waiters."

"Some boy in hitch-up overalls thought he bent me over for these," said Tanker. "I was the better actor, and I knew what they were worth. Join me in my mercenary happiness."

"You could frame them," I said. "Sell them as art."

"He'd need a thousand damned frames," said Francie. "His walls would look better, but his party budget would go straight to hell."

Before she drove—insisted on driving—her two bad boys back to town, Francie pulled me aside, but not too far. "If you forced me to ride that boat, Alex Rutledge, I might loosen you up a bit."

"I could stand a few hours of ocean time," I said. "No offense, but I was hoping to be alone."

Francie scratched her breastbone. She understood the power of jiggle. "It's quicker and better on the buddy system."

I checked Tanker's reaction to her banter. His little cough-laugh told me he'd heard it all before.

Before they pulled away Tim offered me a beer from his dwindling twelve-pack. In a brotherly gesture of solidarity, I accepted it. As his Caprice started down the street, he stuck out his arm and flashed me Winston Churchill's **V** sign. I wondered what kind of victory he had in mind. Victory over self-pity?

Or had it been a peace sign?

I put up the cleanser and brush, coiled the hose, and chucked all the empty bottles into Manning's recycle bin. Then I stood under the house to sip Tim's beer and stare again at the canal. Our exchange had been similar to rehashes of the past, but Tim had shown a shift in thinking. He finally recognized the evil and foul luck that had grown from his bullheaded nature. He hadn't indicted our father as much as admitted to his own demons, his desire to reshape his own destiny.

Perhaps the years had caught hold of him, and

he really wanted to change. All this was one or two levels up from the days when not giving a shit was his mastered art. He'd closed it out with a vehement "Fuck it all," but I suspected that was a remnant of his old stage routine. Perhaps my inclination to back off, to ease judgment and forgiveness, wasn't the sucker bet it had been most of my life. Maybe it was time to let Tim start with a clean slate, no demerits, no probation. It sure would make my life more pleasant to call him a brother instead of a liability.

I heard a motorcycle zip Pirates Road and thanked myself for not being one of those testosterone-charged boys who thought that high-revving café racers possessed magical powers to fend off injury and death. Like GTOs were supposed to do a generation ago. A half-minute passed before the ketchup-red Ducati SS-800, growling like a miniature Ferrari, rolled down Keelhaul into Al Manning's yard and stopped behind my Triumph. The rider wore tight Levi's, Adidas sneaks, and a long-sleeved light blue shirt with a front zipper. I figured someone had the wrong address until the new Key West detective, Beth Watkins, peeled off her matching red helmet.

She pointed at the Triumph. "Alex Rutledge, you up for a ride?"

I envisioned her blasting the West Coast freeways on her European road rocket. "Your hot machine would outrun my old beast," I said. "It'd be like a Porsche Targa playing with an Austin Healey, but I give great Lower Keys tours."

"Let's go."

"I appreciate your coming by to say hello, but I've had a weird morning. I'm not up for much riding."

She checked out the beer in my hand and notched down her excitement level. "I met your ex–lady friend, Teresa. She spoke highly of you."

"I haven't seen her in a couple of months," I said.

"I gathered as much. She said she was dating your brother these days."

"Quick work on both their parts," I said. "He's been in town all of fifty hours."

"She also told me some more details about that day you and Detective Lewis secured the 'officer down' situation with gunfire involved. Again, I commend you for that."

"Thanks," I said. "But I guess my days with the city are done, what with your new full-time photographer."

"We'll see," said Watkins. "He's just finished his photo training. I was among those who approved his résumé."

"He's bound to be better than the last fulltimer. Was the training forensic?"

"It covered everything, including on-the-job success. He documented and helped solve two murder cases while he was in graduate school."

"Where was that?"

"University of Missouri," she said. "You don't seem too upset about all this."

"I wasn't looking for more crime work, Beth, especially after Thursday with the county," I said. "I'm sorry for being rude. Can I offer you anything? Water, or a Coke, or beer?"

"No alcohol on this machine, thanks, and I've got a water bottle. Did you work one of those murders?"

"I shot photos at both scenes," I said.

"Lewis told me they're being treated as separate crimes. Does that make sense?"

I shook my head. "It makes even less that I'm the only person in the county who saw both scenes firsthand. All three scenes, if you count Haskins."

"Florida gets some strange ones," she said.

"Where did you live in California?"

She placed her helmet on the Ducati's seat. "Marin County, last, but I grew up in Santa Cruz. I went to college in San Jose."

"How did you make it to the southernmost end of the road?"

"Six weeks ago I found a job ad on a law-enforcement Web site. It felt like a good time for me to leave California. I applied by e-mail. They hired me after two phone calls."

"Your opinion, now that you're here?"

"Tahiti's the true Promised Land. But I signed

up in good faith, and I can give this island a couple of years."

"You've been to Tahiti?"

She nodded but did not elaborate.

"You'll find the city unique."

"We're talking the same lingo, right?" she said. "When you say 'the city,' you mean the local bureaucracy?"

I nodded. "The attitudes and crazy crap. Our elected officials aren't all wizards. Some are good, maybe better than we deserve. But the others, I wouldn't count on their common sense."

"What's their motivation, overall?"

"Their view of the island economy is that any time you make something more complicated, someone makes more money. It almost doesn't matter who benefits. They think that, in the end, even if the island's in knots, we all get richer. A wise economist might argue the concept, but his voice would be a whisper in a wind tunnel."

She smiled, mouth only, then blanked her expression. "Did you hear about Matilda?"

"The blow-up doll?"

Her eyes narrowed. "You played with her, too?"

"I read about her last month in the **Citizen.**" To slow traffic, the police had parked a squad car on Flagler and put a uniformed vinyl doll in the driver's seat.

"I didn't realize she was so well known."

"What do you mean, play with her?" I said. "You sound peeved at her existence."

"Some of my colleagues don't know they're boorish and sexist. A few chauvinist jokers bought her a peekaboo bra and thong panties. Like a bunch of horny teenagers, they had a dress-up party two days ago in the first-floor weight-lifting room. I walked in to see one officer stuffing Kleenex wads in the bra to make her look more stacked."

"How would I have heard about that?"

"That's not the news," she said. "The duty desk forgot to bring her into the station last night. There was no sign of forced entry, so someone forgot to lock the cruiser. Matilda was stolen between sundown and sunup."

I almost asked Watkins what time she had made the heist. "Maybe they need to replace her with a male mannequin."

She dropped her eyelids a fraction and chilled her gaze. "How would that fix sexism?"

"You're right. It wouldn't." Instinct told me to shift the subject. I walked around her Ducati, admired its hardware and fairings. "Did you have this shipped with your furniture?"

"I gave my furniture to my ex-roommate. I drove here three weeks ago with four suitcases and a box of DVDs in my car. A friend rode the Ducati cross-country last week."

"A trip of large temptation," I said. "He get many speeding tickets?"

"She got three. It took her forty hours, counting six to sleep. She also has windburn and blisters on her hands and butt. She slept twenty straight hours when she arrived here."

"Is she on the island to stay?"

"She works with her husband in San Mateo, and he wanted her back right away."

"One thing you might need to know," I said. "Last month a multi-agency safety check near Garrison Bight pulled every third passing vehicle into a parking lot. The officers claimed they wanted to make sure everyone had brake lights, taillight lamps, and horns. They brought the Bill of Rights into heavy question, but they busted a few DUIs and gave seat-belt tickets."

A puzzled look wrinkled her face. "How does that affect me?"

"They also ticketed three people who worked in Key West but still held their out-of-state registrations."

She turned to look at her license tag.

"Just a tip," I said.

"Thanks." She lifted her helmet and tugged it on. "Let's ride soon."

An odd visit. I could've taken it as a put-down, a come-on, a challenge, or an attempt at insider alliance. I decided to stick with face value, a future date for a tandem tour.

She took it slowly on Keelhaul Lane and quicker on Pirates Road. Her upshifts were timed for torque peak rather than sound effects.

Someone had taught her well.

Later that afternoon I heard tires crunch Manning's pea-rock driveway. I walked to the far end of the second-deck screened porch in time to glimpse a fender, the tinted side glass of a plain white Crown Vic. Was this Bobbi Lewis's weekend visit with smiles, boat rides included? Odd that she hadn't called ahead. I was halfway down the stairs when a second vehicle rolled into the yard. The Ford had green-and-white county markings, KEY LARGO on its front fender, and it carried two men. The driver stopped with his side of the car facing me. It was not Billy Bohner.

A throat-graveled bark: "Rutledge?"

Sheriff's Detective Chet Millican stood with his rear end pressed against my car, his thumbs hooked in his belt. "Got a sec?" he said. "Couple questions for you."

I looked at the cruiser. Both occupants sat watching, not moving. "You drove all this way with two questions and you had to bring backup?"

"The man on the far side of the vehicle's a witness," said Millican. "Also happens to be my son-in-law."

"What's he going to witness, harassment?"

"Not yet. What we need, though, he's already seen."

Millican's head was a rectangle, wider than tall.

"Is this about Navarre's murder?" I said.

"Now that you mention it, how did my crime scene look in broad daylight, Rutledge?"

"Like a slum."

Millican nodded. "Where were you Thursday morning before sunrise? Humor me with a time-line."

I couldn't imagine humor making its way to his brain. "I was asleep until wakened by a call from Detective Lewis."

"Which phone?" he said. "Your home or your cell?"

I could see where this was leading. "Surely you don't believe I hung a man. How did you work your way around to that?"

"Are you refusing to cooperate? We can do this in Marathon."

"A town I admire," I said. "Your questions won't get answered until my lawyer drives up from Key West."

He hesitated, checked out my motorcycle as if memorizing its parts, then pointed his finger at the cruiser. "Turn around. Hands on your head."

The uniformed deputy was out within a half-second, crouched, with a pistol aimed.

I turned around, touched the hair above my ears. "What's my infraction, expired tag?"

"Living in a world of shit," he said. "A mouth that's full of it, too. Pull down one hand at a time to your waist."

Millican strung a plastic cuff to my wrists, yanked it tight, then turned me around and backed me up to the house pillar. He smelled of cheap cologne and failing deodorant. The day's humidity had set in and the wind had died. My first fear of being handcuffed was not being able to swat mosquitoes.

"Sure looks like our boy to me." The Key Largo deputy looked thirteen years old but had the arms of a home-run hitter.

Millican crooked his finger to summon the second man from the green-and-white. A moment later the son-in-law, a Brad Pitt look-alike with a high-pitched voice said, "That's the crook right there." He strode back to the cruiser and reclaimed his seat.

Millican put his face six inches from mine. "You showed up all smart-ass in Marathon on Thursday, I knew I knew you. I saw you on videotape earlier that morning, sliding your bogus credit card up in Rock Harbor. We must've watched that gas-station security video five times. I saw you at the murder scene, and blame it on context, your face didn't register right off. But I slept late this morning and caught your ass in a dream. How does it feel to be busted in another man's dream?"

No better, I thought, than for another man's crime. "I'd drive a hundred-fifty-mile round trip to scam gasoline?" I said. "You might want to go back and check that video."

"My eyes got me this job, bubba, and a thirty-year career before it. You accusing me of bad eyes? You don't accuse me of shit."

"You want me to take him in my vehicle?" said the Key Largo deputy.

"I'll do it," said Millican. "While you're driving Mitchell back to Rock Harbor, I can sit this goofball at the substation, maybe clear some other hot cards." He gave me a tough look. He had spent years at his mirror, perfecting the Clint Eastwood jaw set and cold eye.

"That your billfold in the front pocket?" he said.

I nodded.

He asked the uniformed deputy to pull and inventory my wallet so they could verify each other's version of events. "We might get lucky and find the card that financed his cruise up and down the Keys."

The deputy fanned the wallet contents. "Library card, driver's license, a MasterCard, a Visa, and a membership in B.O.'s Fishin' and Yacht Club. Both credit cards are current and show his name." He handed over the wallet.

Millican said, "Go up and close his door, would you?"

"Lock it?" said the deputy.

"Just pull it shut. This is Little Torch. No one commits crimes around here."

I heard the deputy reach the top of the wood stairs. Millican said, "I keep thinking about your wiseass mouth making me look dumb in front of my people. This is for your crack about my memory." He kneed me in the balls.

I heard myself grunt, felt him grab my shirt and jerk upward. I felt like I might throw up. Fighting to stay on my feet, I ran a mental movie of what would happen next. Two dozen dead-end roads could provide the setting. I would try to escape, attempt to kick an officer in the groin, maybe make a play for his weapon. No matter what else, he would claim that I spat in his face, tried to infect him with an exotic roster of diseases. After he drummed my skull and worked a while longer on my privates, he would chuck me into his backseat and drive me to Fishermen's Hospital for a "checkup."

What was the worst he could do? Broken bones? Disfiguring my hands? No way he'd risk it. He would squander his career, put himself up for a civil rights beef.

The deputy stomped to ground level and looked at my face. "He resist arrest or has he got the flu?"

"He took sick thinking about his future cell mates."

"Those HIV-positive Jamaicans? They wear necklaces strung with whiteboys' teeth." The deputy grinned, threw a thumbs-up, and walked toward his car.

"Hold a sec, so you can back me up," said Millican. "I want to clean out my rear seat before I load him. Make sure he doesn't run and jump in the canal. He might kick-swim himself to Cuba, be Castro's next houseboy."

"I give swim lessons," said the uniform. "If he passes the handcuff test, he gets to sew a star on his bathing suit. But not a **gold** star."

"You barf in my car," said Millican, "I'm going to let you escape over the Bahia Honda Bridge rail, you hear me?"

I didn't answer.

He bellowed a drill sergeant's "I can't hear you!"

"Shit, Millican, you slug me again, anything could happen." I crouched to get into his cruiser's backseat, and he pushed my head down to clear the door frame. He began to close the door but yanked it open again. "Holy shit, there's a skeeter." His open palm caught the side of my head. I felt neck tendons snap, pain bloom in my ear. "I think I got it," he said.

"You saved him from West Nile, Detective,"

said the deputy. "I can tell by this boy's looks, he's going to write you a thank-you note."

Millican grunted. "With a pencil stub and jail-issue paper, if I have anything to do with it."

The whole car smelled just like Millican.

I caught sight of Wendell Glavin standing under his stilt home across the street, peering at my parade. I could bet he couldn't wait to tell the neighborhood hippies and the muumuu lady. I was gossip fodder after less than one day in Al's house. Forty-eight hours after being chauffeured to Marathon by Bohner, I was making the same trip in a rear seat in shackles.

So much for dodging a sucker bet. A serious timeline would suggest that I was about to own a fraud charge that belonged to my brother. If I tried to explain the error to Millican, he'd see no sense in boosting my ego by hearing my argument. He'd invite me to tell it to my lawyer at the substation after they took me through the booking process, swapped out my clothes, hosed me down, and cloistered me with a few feces-tossing derelicts. From Millican's viewpoint, my ass now belonged to the county.

Tim had fucked up before getting to town. For the moment I was taking the fall.

The two cars rolled northward on U.S. 1. I

had no idea how long it would take Liska or Lewis to hear of my arrest, to ride to my rescue. I had blown off Lewis's urgent request to take pictures at Bay Point. She would be in no hurry to help me. Her closing phrase on the phone had not been an expression of goodwill. I knew her habits, her dislikes and obsessions. I believed that the sum of her traits made her a fine detective. Difficult to live with, but a fine sleuth. Above all, she was stubborn.

"Millican," I said, glad to have my voice. "We could stop for a burger at No Name Pub. Talk this thing out."

"You got dental in your health plan?"

"All this time you're devoting to my alleged fraud, I guess you solved the Milton Navarre murder."

"You called it," he said. "You floated the hot card at one forty-five. Navarre died fifty miles away between three and five. Another dude, twenty-some miles farther, died after four A.M. Connect the dots."

"That's fabulous, Detective," I said. "You should call the media, start prepping your résumé for the networks. I can see you sitting there with a high-profile attorney second-guessing the rich and powerful."

"Shut the fuck up."

"I'm praising you, Millican. The state loves hot dogs who solve multiple crimes in one afternoon. I can fake a mopey perp walk, to help your case, but the airtime might be better if you chain my ankles. My shuffle would broadcast my guilt."

"Keep talking, shit-for-brains. You're about to get so lost in the judicial process, it'll take every penny you've got to buy lawyers just to see daylight some year down the road."

"And me so squeaky clean," I said.

"That might save your life. If you had so much as a zoning misdemeanor on your record, we'd have you toes-up on a chemicals table inside of eighteen months." He turned to face me, his cheeks crimson with anger. "Did you learn to tie a noose in high school, you murdering douchebag?"

"Junior high," I said.

"I love it when I get sleazy, bigmouthed bumwads like you red-handed."

"Shit, watch out!"

He didn't react in time, didn't make it back to our lane.

I saw horror in oncoming eyes, heard ripping metal and an explosion, felt a spray of glass before I skimmed toward the reef on a red-and-orange sailboard.

"Yo, buddy, you be makin' it. We got an ambulance on the way."

It was a deputy, but I couldn't focus on his face. I was on my back, in the rear seat of the cruiser. I heard voices and squelch sounds from small radios, smelled vomit and burned rubber and engine coolant. My wrists felt broken, but the handcuffs were gone.

"Why an ambulance?" I said.

"You've been in an accident. The detective, your friend, is here."

"Alex?" Bobbi Lewis leaned down. My focus returned. She looked at me like I was a hurt child. "Alex?"

"Fuck you," I said. "You told him where to find me."

"He said he wanted pictures from the Marathon scene."

"What about . . ." My focus went away.

"No life-threatening injuries in the other car," she said. "Everybody lived through it."

"You've got a bad boy in the department."

"How's your head?"

"Hurts on the inside," I said.

"Bad?"

"Only when I scream."

10

ONCE I SHOOK THE shards out of my hair and realized that I wasn't maimed or disfigured, I promised to sign a clean bill of health and an open-ended pledge to the FOP. I offered to wash and wax fifty off-duty cruisers, anything to keep myself out of that goddamned ambulance. Having just survived a wreck in which I was handcuffed and locked into a backseat with no door handles, I couldn't imagine any injury worth the fright of being injured, immobile, powerless, and strapped into a speeding ambulance on the Seven Mile Bridge.

The badges prevailed, though I was in no shape to resist. Bobbi rode with me in the meat wagon, and drugs failed to put me to sleep. A rainstorm on the bridge did the trick. I woke up, alert but immobile, in Fishermen's Hospital in Marathon.

During the second round of pokes and prods, when I felt lucid enough to listen, Bobbi told me that a receipt in my wallet, a meal at Cafe Med on Grinnell, removed me as a credit-card fraud suspect. "No way would you pay a bill with legitimate plastic in Key West at ten twenty-five P.M. on Wednesday, drive to Key Largo, fill your tank on a bogus Visa, and be back in bed when I called you at six-forty."

"It's physically possible," I said.

"I can't imagine your losing sleep to commit a crime."

"How am I doing here?" I said.

"You've had whiplash and muscle strain. The nurse said your testicles were swollen. Is that because you missed me?"

"Only partly. Did she check for knuckle welts around my belly button?

Bobbi shook her head. "So Millican made a pig of himself."

"He made the dean's list in charm school. How about the other people?"

"He and two adults from the other car were patched and released from the emergency room. The twelve-year-old girl has a broken arm and a concussion, so they'll keep her overnight."

"Millican negligent?"

"Oh, sure, but on duty, questionable as it was. When the other car sues, the taxpayers will foot the fee."

"How did you get to me so quickly?"

"A cop-abuse call from your neighbor, Mr.

Glavin. He gave the dispatcher a description of Millican and the tag number of the Key Largo deputy. The dispatcher called me. I tried to get through to Millican, to get your status, but his phone and radio were off. To me, that was weirder than your being arrested. I left for Marathon right away."

"Thank you."

"Then I got another call. The Key Largo deputy was an eighth mile behind you on Big Pine when Millican crossed the centerline. The deputy called the dispatcher and saved you from choking on your own vomit."

"I barfed?"

"You blew lunch and you bled. I washed your shirt and shorts in that sink over there. They'll have plenty of time to dry before you leave. Do you want me to stop talking?"

"No."

"What do you want to talk about?"

"I don't care," I said. "How about three murders?"

"Is our bet still on?" said Lewis.

"Sure," I said. "Lucky Haskins died after the morning paper came out. Lucky has kids who want his lifestyle, or ex-wives he hung out to dry. Or his current wife has a beef with her future. It was classic copycat."

"Each to his own presumptions. We see it as a standard suicide."

"Standard?" I said. "You mean regular, run-of-the-mill?"

"Garden-variety, yes. In the suicide league it was plain vanilla."

"How did your pictures turn out at the scene?"

"I hate to admit it," she said. "Your instructions on the phone—you could earn side money teaching at the college."

Her phone buzzed. A half-minute later I was listening to Liska.

"I just finished a meeting with Chester Millican," he said.

"Do you have bruises to show for it?"

"Only my reputation as a judge of character. Thank God it was a sideswipe instead of a head-on. Did Lewis tell you how this all began?"

"Millican said it was a fake credit card," I said. "I have to wonder why he's screwing around with an Upper Keys security video in the predawn hours."

"He took a personal interest. His daughter and her husband own the convenience store in Rock Harbor. He didn't match the video with your face during the situation in Marathon, but he made what he called a delayed connection. That started it all."

"Did he explain why he jeopardized his job by rousting me?"

"That's a question for shrinks and lawyers," said Liska.

"He'll probably go public with a blubbering confession, and get a book contract and a movie deal."

"He said you called him a dickweed. How professional is that?"

"I don't know the term, Sheriff, so I can't use it. What's a dickweed?"

"I was going to ask you."

"Sounds like an agricultural problem, like kudzu. Maybe it's a genital fungus."

"You're a laugh a minute," said Liska. "Did you mouth off to him in Marathon?"

"I suggested to Bohner that Millican had overlooked possible evidence. Bohner passed Millican my comment, so maybe something got skewed in translation. Where does the detective stand after this stunt?"

"He's on paid leave pending an investigation of the wreck and an alleged infringement of your civil rights."

"Who alleged?"

"The duty doctor in emergency."

"Did you ask Bohner how he happened to turn on Tenth Street instead of Thirteenth?"

"Bohner and Millican are pals," said Liska. "They get together once in a while for a toddy at some bottom-feeders' bar in Marathon. Anyway, they talked by cell before you got in Bohner's car, and Millican told him to turn on Tenth."

They hadn't come off as pals on our arrival at the Milton Navarre crime scene.

"Are you okay with that answer?" I said.

"Why shouldn't I be?"

"When I arrived in Marathon, Millican thought I might be undercover FDLE. If those two had talked, Bohner might have mentioned my nonofficial status."

"What the hell do I know about one blessed conversation?" said Liska. "All I know is Millican isn't bad when he sticks to business. He made a strong point a couple minutes ago. He linked the timing, the fake card in Key Largo, the death in Marathon, and the death on Ramrod Key."

"He wanted to plug me in to that scenario."

"We'll plug somebody in to it because it makes a world of sense. Aside from a public urination in Layton—into the gas tank of a '54 Packard Patrician—those were the only three crimes in the county that night."

"Are we slick with my hospital bill?"

He hung up.

Bobbi looked puzzled. "Scenario? What was that about?"

I said, "Theories."

She looked away. "It's all we've got."

I disagreed, closed my eyes, and thought about a young woman standing on Dredgers Lane, a silver Zippo engraved with several sets of initials, and the Kansas Jack and Milton Navarre noose knots, similar but different from the one that yanked Haskins. Now a new problem, and Millican had invented a timeline. My thoughts went to Tim. He had failed my newfound trust in a way that was not out of character. Flogging bad plastic was money-motivated, small-time, typical of his old patterns, but davits and murders didn't fit. No one with half a brain would kill Kansas Jack or Milton Navarre for their cash. And, if I had my days straight, Lucky Haskins died while Tim was zoned on Tanker Branigan's couch.

The Tim I knew was not a killer.

But . . . he'd said, "Didn't that give you a weird sense of power, leaving them there to die?"

Or something to that effect.

How well did I know my brother?

I woke and realized that the action buzz around me had quit. I was alone except for a roommate behind a curtain who wheezed as he slept. The place smelled like rubbing alcohol, the air temperature was down to about fifty, the humming fluorescent lights could have illuminated a stadium. A nurse told me I was in for the night. I asked if my room was a jail, offered to sign anything.

"Your doctor of record is home in bed."

"If he's the duty warden," I said, "what does that make you?"

She shifted to a sultry voice. "I'm the Enema Queen."

"My sincere apologies."

An hour later she returned with a deputy and a clipboard. I signed eight release forms and she called for a wheelchair. The deputies refused to let me leave in a taxi. After several calls and my rants about false imprisonment and lawsuits, Liska authorized an ambulance. Because climbing the stairs to Al Manning's living area risked dizziness or hernia or some spine-related issue, Liska okayed a temporary stay at the Sugarloaf Lodge.

The nurse slipped me an envelope with a clutch of pills in it. She said, "If you piss blood, honey, give us a call."

At eleven P.M. two rookie deputies, one with vodka on his breath, wheeled my mobile bed from an ambulance to my stuffy canalside hotel room. Resentment shaped their actions. They wanted my ass past the door so their demeaning limo duties could cease. I climbed down to hobble after the wheels caught in gravel and jerked me lengthwise. They left me with two Cokes, a pitcher of tap water, and a bag of Tostitos. In an attempt to cover civic butt, Monroe County would honor my tab, including room service, excluding bar bills, until I felt able to climb the steps to Manning's living area.

A vacation within a vacation. I congratulated myself on a fine little scam. Except for the tape around my ribs—to protect my back—I was fine. Maybe the pain pills added to my euphoria. I was surprised to find that I didn't have the strength to open a soft drink, much less pour water.

I fell asleep with MSNBC buzzing through the pillow.

Sunday morning, nine A.M., I was the poster boy for Victims Unanimous. I felt aches and stiffness, like I'd been in a car wreck, but I was mobile and once again lucid. Someone had placed a plastic lounge chair in aqua and salmon, a plastic-mesh-brimmed hat, and a **Key West Citizen** next to my canal-facing door. I called the bar, ordered a coffee carafe, two large OJs, two Amstel Lights, a quad-cheese omelet with sausage and bacon, and a whole-wheat English muffin with cherry jam. The man taking the order asked if I was Dr. Thompson.

"My name is Rutledge. I checked in late, room 209."

"Right," he said. "Two Amstel Lights? Wouldn't you rather have six?"

"Two would be better."

"I'll have your order in four minutes. You need today's **New York Times**?"

"Sure," I said. "News from the outside world."

Ten minutes later, I sat under an umbrella, read "Arts & Leisure," and sipped my drinks. Four motorboats full of divers left the small marina. Eight kayakers in sun bonnets and life vests followed their group leader north to the exotic wilds of Bow Channel. The tapes around my back began to itch, so I shifted the chair twice to evade the sun. I finished half the paper, all the drinks, and half the muffin. I felt limp as sea grass, removed from reality. I began to understand why up-north tourists pay so much for their Keys escapes.

"Alex, got a minute?" Tanker Branigan stood there in gross floral jams and a hundred-gallon Chicago Blackhawks jersey. He held a twelve-pack of Michelob and a wad of bar napkins.

"Multiple minutes," I said. "Find yourself a chair."

He handed me a beer, walked to the canal bulkhead, sat on the cement. "I took a cab from Duval Street. Tim doesn't know I'm here."

"I don't even know I'm here. Why would you want to make the trip?"

"I got the address of this place from your old flame, Teresa. I guess she got it from the county."

"Is she, by chance, Tim's new flame?" I said.

"She gave him her number Friday morning.

They've stayed in touch. He heard about your accident and the credit-card accusation."

"He's remorseful and afraid to face me, right?"

"Worse," said Tanker. "I took a gun away from him at six A.M."

He let me soak that up in silence.

"Did he bring the gun with him on vacation?" I said.

"I keep a couple in the house. He found one in the Cheerios box."

"If it was me with a gun," I said, "and reversed circumstances, my fault, my brother, I might go after the bad cop. Tim wanted to target himself, yes?"

"You kicked him out of Key West once."

I nodded.

"That's why he didn't call when he hit town. He wanted to do his thing without fucking up yours. The afternoon we met—that'd be Thursday—ten minutes after we started to gab, he told me that. His opening line was he came to Key West for moontan, poontang, and rum. Then he told me about his last visit. He ended it with your invitation to leave."

"In five days he pissed off every person I knew on the island."

"Maybe it wasn't that bad," said Tanker. "People understand. Everyone has a relative over-the-top or down in the gutter."

"Well, he was both in a very short time. I worried for a couple years that he would call again, but he never did. I'd stopped worrying about two weeks ago."

"Don't forget—he didn't call, the cop did. Tim waited until he was jammed to drop your name." He inhaled, then blew air. The size of his jaw amazed me, his neck the thickness of a light pole.

"You have brothers?" I said.

"Three. Two of them were like yours."

"Past tense?"

"One split his Pontiac Firebird on a fifty-year oak, sideways on Southern Comfort. That was his junior year in high school. One took his act to Somalia with Uncle. He wanted to be a hero. He wound up just another dead grunt. I could have done a better job keeping them alive. I didn't start soon enough."

"You think about them a lot?" I said.

"Every day. I think about how they were losers and I survived. Mind you, I'm not saying a survivor is a winner. I'm saying there's shit we can do."

"Like take away their guns?"

"In a manner of speaking, yes."

"Thanks for doing that."

"No problem," said Branigan. "It wasn't unselfish. I had a roommate pull the trigger once."

I refused the image that barged toward my mind. I thought back, instead, to Cleveland Heights. "He was a selfish shit," I said, "but he treated himself worse than anyone. Growing up with Tim was like living in two separate worlds. The world that happened, that you saw and thought about, was the first third of it. The world you didn't see, that affected you the most, was the other two thirds."

"For every good act, two bads? I know it all by heart. I loaned Tim cash to drive up the Keys, to pay back that gas-station owner."

"That's the good act after the fact," I said. "Maybe too little too late."

"I told him to pay the man before he stopped for his first six-pack."

"What time of day did you meet him Thursday?"

"Two in the afternoon, two-thirty. Rick's Bar, watching a shitty baseball game, checking out drunk tourist chicks."

"You don't work?" I said.

"Don't have to. It's a short story because I worked my ass off for just a few years. It's amazing how much you can earn if you put your mind to it."

We watched a cormorant drift the canal, cruising for lunch.

"This county's been hopping the past few days," said Branigan. "Are we waiting for the next poor son of a bitch to have a short life crisis?"

"Three deaths, and the cops don't have squat,"

I said. "The one who wrecked the car tried to link Tim's bad card to the bullshit."

Tanker twisted another top. "The fact that Tim's a liar doesn't make him an evil person. I'm not sure I can rebuild him, but I'd like to help."

He caught my hesitation.

"Okay," he said. "You're thinking, the missing link just offered to help me shrink my brother's brain. I may look scary and scummy, but these days you have to look the way I look to chase honey. And I like the ladies."

"What do we do?" I said. "Make a list of rules, a working script? Or do we nail his feet to the floor?"

"We set him up to succeed."

"That won't work unless it's equal odds that he fail," I said. "He's a fuckup, but he's not stupid."

"We tilt the odds in favor of the fuckup," he said. "It'll make his success that much sweeter."

"I was right about a script?"

Tanker nodded. "I have a rule. Don't get angry, get even."

"How do we get him off the couch?"

"Give me the green light," he said.

"I appreciate your wanting my permission, but I don't govern my brother's life. He's been out of mine for more than half of my life. I've wanted it that way for a whole lot of those years. The green light is not mine to give."

"How many years have you lived in the Keys?

You can't call the shots on your own turf? You kicked him out. That's a form of control."

"I told him not to come back to my house. A block away, he's out of my control."

"But you issued orders, right?"

"Right," I said. "But my point is, if you want to help him, go for it. It's your operation. If it works out, that's great."

"It'll work out," he said.

"Also, I don't want to owe my soul to a bondsman. Please don't get him arrested."

Tanker smiled. "Not getting arrested is my top talent."

11

THAT AFTERNOON I WASHED down a pain pill with warm Coca-Cola and began to read a dog-eared copy of John D. MacDonald's **Cinnamon Skin** that someone had left in the room. The book's first line was "There are no hundred percent heroes." It was a great jump start to a novel, but conjecture more than fact. Assuming it made sense—and JDM was good at that—what about the bottom end of the scale? No hundred-percent losers, either. I closed my eyes and decided, in spite of my swellings and strains, to allow Tim a chance to turn around. I silently wished good luck on Tanker Branigan.

I came awake during a dream in which my cell phone dialed 911 whenever I sensed danger. I pissed off a yard wasp. It brought a police vehicle to Dredgers Lane. The squad car's vibes brought another, then two more until cruisers clogged the lane. My neighbor Hector Ayusa told them I was living on Little Torch, and I had lost my cell phone.

Someone was knocking at the door, not in my dream. I rolled from the bed, peeked through the jalousie slats. Marnie Dunwoody's Jeep Wrangler sat eight feet away.

"Hold on . . . I'm finding my trousers," I said.

"Why be formal?"

I popped another pill, sloshed it down with flat warm Coke, and twisted the handle.

Marnie waltzed in holding a Mountain Dew. She wore flare-gun red shorts, a backward ball cap that read SHELLFISH across her forehead, and a man's shirt with its tails knotted just above her belly button.

"Jeez," she said.

I watched her eyes go from spark to awe, as if watching a house burn down.

She checked my face, then my taped torso. "You look like shit."

"I think I drank my painkillers this morning," I said. "You look like a young, vivacious woman in the Keys."

"I came straight from karate class."

"I thought you'd quit karate."

"I let it slip last year and I got way out of shape. I'm starting to regain lost ground." She tossed me a Baby's Coffee T-shirt. "I figured you might need this. Put on your shorts and think of me as a reporter."

I lobbed the shirt back at her. "Go knock on the door and start over."

She sat on the only chair. "Why shouldn't I write your story?"

"Nothing to tell. Except I need a shower and another nap."

"A law-enforcement officer kicked your ass. You're a white Rodney King. A potential one, I should say. The feds'll jump all over this."

"My life is fine without notoriety. Trouble brings trouble, you know that." I sat on the bed, fit my legs into the shorts, and stood to pull them up. "This is a county full of cousins. Everyone is someone's brother-in-law. Isn't there a scandal you could write about? A funky lease deal on prime city property? Winos living in surplus sewer pipes? The school board going to Nassau for their budget meetings?"

"My boss is a traditionalist," she said, "and an old Conch. He remembers this Millican guy from thirty years ago. I got the impression that Millican wasn't squeaky clean at the time."

"That was then, this is today," I said. "Two lapses in judgment and he caused a traffic accident."

"I'm hearing this crap in your free hotel room."

"I won it in a contest."

"And your injuries?" said Marnie.

"I fell off my bicycle."

"I get the picture," she said. "Liska traded you a job for your silence."

"Where the hell did you get that?"

"It's going around the county offices. He wants to make you his new admin assistant."

"He offered me a job on Thursday. His description of my duties was so loose, I wasn't even sure it was real work. Whatever it was, I turned him down."

"Okay," she said, "you didn't trade your silence for a job."

"Take off your reporter's hat, and we can talk."

Marnie looked out the open door, thought for a moment. "It's off," she said. "But I'm keeping it handy."

"Heard from Sam yet?"

"No, but this is about you. How did you get yourself arrested?"

"Simple mistaken identity. Things escalated before I had a chance to explain."

Her cell phone rang. Marnie checked the incoming number and elected not to answer. "My editor, looking for a hot headline. Tell your side now. Let me put my hat back on."

I shook my head.

"So I go home with no story?"

"Things like this tarnish the reputations of good cops just as much as the ones who've screwed up. But I'll give you this. If Liska doesn't fire Millican, I'll talk a mile a minute. For now, let's fly under the radar."

"Did you get mistaken for your brother?" she said.

Oh, shit. "Where did that come from?"

"I asked Sam a couple years ago if you had brothers or sisters. He told me about Tim. Teresa mentioned him today. Smiling, I might add."

"I can't think of two people more perfectly matched," I said. "If Tim's into her thing, he'll be out of my hair. She can have all the smiles she wants."

"When did he get here?" said Marnie.

"Why don't you let it drop?"

"So the credit-card story fits his travel schedule?"

I concentrated on strips of sunlight shimmering on the motel-room wall. Then I flashed on an image of Tim holding a pistol to his forehead.

"Why get worked up over a minor scam?" she said. "By what Sam told me, it's nothing new for your brother. It's going to come out sooner or later."

"Later is better."

Marnie began to speak, hesitated, then said, "Are you afraid he did something else, too?"

"They'd probably like to think he did. The ballbuster is the timing, early Thursday morning.

Millican already speculated on a possible tie-in, the credit card to the hangings."

"We normals would call that an extreme long shot," she said.

"In Millican's stubborn head it's pure chain logic."

"Oddly enough, I can believe it. Some cops think the world around them is one big crime scene. Do you think your brother did worse than slide a bad card?"

"I have absolutely no idea, but you know the system," I said.

"He could be accused of anything that's handy."

"Sooner or later Liska or Lewis will link the surveillance video with the fact that Tim arrived in town that morning."

Marnie agreed. "That'd be step one in a long process. When did you tell Bobbi he was here?"

I went back to studying the wall.

"You're trying to keep the fly out of the web," she said, "and Bobbi's going to be hurt and pissed, two different things. You can't hide it indefinitely."

"As bad as he's been all his life," I said, "I can't believe murder's in him. I also doubt that the real killer will confess in the next few days, so the pisser—"

"I'm ahead of you," said Marnie. "If Tim's

arrested and they connect the circumstantial dots while he's in custody, he'll lose ground he'll never make up. Florida's a bad state for a mess like this."

"He'll be charged with murder, simple as hell. Conviction's a baby jump."

"What happened to proving people guilty?" she said.

"You know because you're a reporter. This century's version is 'guilty until someone finds time to show otherwise.' If it's inconvenient, God help you. The prisons are run by yes-for-profit corporations who need growth for survival."

"Which means we need to prove that he's innocent before they latch on to him."

I laughed at myself. "Unfortunately, you're right, but for you it's optional. I have no damned choice."

"What makes that funny?" said Marnie.

"I swear every time that I won't allow Tim to complicate my life. The son of a bitch got me again."

"Alex, it's Bobbi. I wanted to check on you."

"I'm feeling foggy," I said. "I'm a vegetable."

"A vegetable locked in fog?"

"Floundering in fog. A fog-floundering vegetable beats a rope-strangled manatee."

"Do you need anything?" she said.

"A glass of rum?"

"Sounds like you've already had one or two. Go back to sleep, Alex."

She hung up. By that time I was awake.

Twelve weeks before this all began, a Sarasota ad agency hired me for a photo gig on Grand Cayman Island. Bobbi Lewis—at that point a friend but not a lover—learned about it, flew down a day ahead of me, checked into a luxury room, then called Key West to suggest we split the hotel bill to save money. We shared a bed the night I arrived, but we kept our shorts on. She had a rule about making love on a first date. I played along, and she more than made up for the one-day delay. I knocked out the job in two days, sent my film to the States, and stayed a day shy of another week. Our vacation flew by, with fine meals, sightseeing, laughter, and bed. We became the tourists we'd habitually scorned in Key West. Her big surprise launched our whirlwind affair.

We came home refreshed and began to blend our lives.

During our next few weeks we discovered common interests outside the bedroom: back streets for biking, restaurants one of us knew but the other hadn't tried. Our times together were intense, but slowly, almost imperceptibly, became less frequent. I spent a whole week working in my yard, and her work schedule got tougher, made her moody, sometimes testy. Two or three times I sensed a distance between us.

What had Liska told me? **If she invents jealousies and starts arguments, it doesn't mean you're not doing the right things. It's her issue, and you've got to stay steady.**

Now, on a summer Sunday evening, a caring call. It inspired me to quit my self-indulgent recuperation, to rejoin and embrace the ambulatory world.

I could've said that in three words: I wanted rum.

I took a classic Navy shower: washrag, warm water, motel soap on the face and pits. Two swipes of a floral, value-sized off-brand deodorant from the front desk. A reed-thin toothbrush and miniature tube of paste, also from room service. I pulled on the shirt that Marnie had brought me. No use trying to brush my hair. At that moment, appearance was low on my checklist.

I walked the tarmac, crossed the dolphin-pond bridge, felt sweat itch my bandages in the heat of dusk. An orange-pink sunset was fading to pale purple and gray. A James Taylor sound-alike sang "Terra Nova" for seven people at the open-air bar. I chose not to fight mosquitoes. I continued on to the lounge adjacent to the resort's main restaurant.

A smarmy "My Way" came through the saloon's dark glass, by a crooner I couldn't name. I saw only the bartender and one customer inside. I yanked the sliding door with my back at an odd angle, and felt spine creaks and tendon snaps. Food smells tumbled through the half-open door. The crooner was aided by sugary background strings and female voices on melody rather than harmony, to mask grit in the smarm.

"Who's this jitterbug?" said a shrill woman at the far end of the bar. "He's already bought himself a souvenir T-shirt. It still has its factory wrinkles. If he's a tourist, why doesn't he have that black-socks thing going?"

The bartender, a heavy, middle-aged man, checked me out. "He's a hotel guest, ma'am. Mind your manners."

"I could tell he's not local." She sipped from a collins glass and turned to me. "Why do you people insist on filling up our restaurants?"

"My Way" faded into "September Song." Another unknown vocal stylist. Stuffed fish on the wall and the alleged music force-fed me the fact that if I could walk to a saloon, I could climb Al Manning's stairs. It was time to leave the high life.

For the moment, I still wanted a drink.

Four tall captain's chairs faced south, under a green navigation light. Eight faced east, a red nav light at their far end so regulars could find their way to safe harbor. I slid onto a south-facing stool and pointed at the rum-bottle lineup.

"Cuba Libre?" The bartender stood closer to me, wheezing through his forced smile. He glanced at my stitches, my missing hair.

"Mount Gay and soda, tall, lemon," I said. "Light on the ice."

"Obviously, this man has come to Sugarloaf to be rude," said the woman. "He won't even answer a simple question."

The bartender free-poured the rum, squirted generic soda from a sticky-looking mix gun. "Tinky, let him get his first sip, okay?"

Tinky?

She was dressed for a day of yachting. White shorts and shirt over a blue-striped T-shirt. Her light brown hair was curled and frizzed, and her tan looked high-maintenance. Designer sunglasses hung from a neon blue neck string. A small gold watch on one wrist, a collection of gold bracelets on the other.

My sip provided her cue. "Well? Do we get an answer?"

"Are you an old-timer in the Keys?" I said.

"What kind of slam is that? I am thirty-eight fucking years old, and I am a goddamn widow. Start over, and tell me. Do I look like a widow to you?"

Tinky was Tinkerbell. "You don't look like others I've known."

"So I look like a fucking 'old-timer'?"

"I don't mean you look old," I said. "An 'old-timer' in Florida means someone who's been here more than five years. You could be seventeen and be an old-timer. Did you lose your husband recently?"

She looked at her watch.

The bartender said, "Mr. Haskins was killed two days ago outside their home."

"Sorry," I said. "An accident?"

"Not hardly," said Tinkerbell. She ran a gathering ritual, picked up her drink, lighter, cigarettes, napkin, and purse. She slid off her stool and, unsteady but determined, made her way around the bar's chevron shape. She was about five-six and stocky. Not fat, but strong-looking, as if she could handle a sailboat halyard or a heavy fishing reel. She boosted herself onto the stool next to mine. "Murder by boat lift, like those other two killings this week. You're not from here, you don't know about them. Some fucker hung my lard-ass husband right outside my bedroom window. Like to piss me off. Notice my mourning clothes."

I also noticed the care she took to hide alcohol-induced slurring. I went for a pensive look and stayed silent. By her remarks and language, Tinkerbell had thick skin. I couldn't get a reading of its texture. She could have hidden Tampa beneath her blush-colored makeup. I suspected she was masking her emotions, too, with a fog of cynical bullshit.

She caught me studying her face. "I'm actually drunker tonight than I normally am. But I'm fine."

I wasn't sure how to respond.

"You agree?" she said.

The bartender raised his eyebrows, walked to the distant end of the bar.

"I agree with all of the above," I said. "You're fine, you're tipsy, and you're a widow. How long were you married?"

"Four long years. The last one, I didn't get a minute's peace for all the acid reflux and snoring. I don't mean to sound disrespectful of the dead, but you be the judge."

"Not my place to say," I said.

"Anyway, he woke me up twenty times a night. Like to drove me crazy. I could've bunked out on U.S. 1 instead of the next room and got more rest."

"Was your husband the man in the paper yesterday?"

She nodded slowly and sipped her tall drink. "They hung him right outside our bedroom."

"How far is the davit from your house?"

"Why would I know that? You think I went out there with a measuring tape?"

"Could you guess?"

"I can do anything I want."

"Give it a shot," I said.

"Thirty, maybe forty feet. You want to know how many friggin' seconds it took to walk to the boat?"

"You didn't hear them out there?"

She began to pout. Tears filled her eyes. "I wasn't in my room."

I let that ride a moment. "Were you home at the time?"

"I was in his bed, goddammit." Her tears began to flow. "I went in there to give him a little, which I did, and I fell asleep after. He, for one time in our marriage, was a gentleman. He let me sleep, and went to snore in my bed."

"And someone took him from your room?"

"Not without setting off that fucking alarm." She swayed, grasped my upper arm for support. She had crossed a bridge, said it aloud. She had slipped the last piece into the jigsaw puzzle, and given herself the answer she was drinking to avoid. Her voice softened. "He always slept after we made love, even during the day. I don't know why he went outside."

Tinkerbell fell against me sobbing. I lifted her drink from her hand, set it aside. The crying jag lasted a solid five minutes. She used up an inch-high stack of cocktail napkins to mop eyeliner and eroded makeup. A minute into her recovery, she almost launched into an encore.

I was patting her back when a man of about thirty walked into the bar and approached us. He wore a bright white T-shirt and khaki slacks, was almost chocolate-colored from too much sun. Tinkerbell looked up when he placed his hand on her shoulder, then began to gather her belongings. She slipped a fifty from her purse to cover her tab, told the bartender to put the change in his jar.

"Sorry to meet you under these circumstances," I said. "Good night, Mrs. Haskins."

Shock filled her face. "How do you know my name?"

"The bartender used it."

"He did not. When did he use it?"

"When he told me about your husband. He said, 'Mr. Haskins was killed two days ago.' "

"I don't think so . . ." Drinks and paranoia combined in Tinkerbell's mind. She tried to slide from her stool, almost fell, and was saved by the tan man. He sneered at me, and they walked out, a matched set, the same height and shape.

I tried to gauge the bartender's thoughts. "That fellow a family friend?"

"Perfect way to put it," he said. "Sad situation, for sure."

"You think he's a landscaper or a house-painter?"

"I asked him once what he did. He said he was a sportsman. Buy you one?"

"Can you make it a double roadie and sell me a bottle of wine?"

"You can put it on your room," he said.

"Open a Mondavi Cabernet, tip yourself, and mark it all down as food."

"I can make that happen, sir."

12

I WANDERED TO MY room, finished the rum roadie in two minutes flat. I wanted to sit by the canal with my wine, gaze at the night sky, watch the wind toss palms lighted by street lamps near the highway. After what I had been through, I'd be content to stare across the canal at the marina's beer signs. The mosquitoes vetoed my notion. Drinking alone in a motel room had a seedy aspect to it, but the bugs gave me no choice. Also, the clump of trees on the south side of U.S. 1 reminded me of that chase in high school, the GTO that had gone broadside into a stand of old beech and maple, my deliberate choice to keep on going. Tim's questioning of my decision had pulled old guilt to the foreground. I hadn't felt bad about not returning to assist the injured; the sound of the crash would have summoned help from nearby homes. But I had known that the GTO was a straight-line hot rod. Given a few bends in the road, I could outrun the thugs and lead them into a trap. I used my driving skill as a weapon. In my sole defense, I didn't have a ball bat or brass knucks to defend my date and myself.

Inside the motel room, with a breeze through the screens, I shifted my thoughts to Tinkerbell Haskins. Why would a widow's grief match the silliness of a college girl on a beer drunk? She had been gruff at first, but sentimental, too. How did that fit her widow's pose? A more germane question, if by slim chance he hadn't been murdered: Why might a man like Lucky take the exit road?

I did the math. A four-year marriage, a crumbling relationship. If he'd split the house, cars, and yacht down the middle, he'd shatter his life and sink his boat. Lucky would be bunking in a trailer on Big Pine, fishing off road bridges instead of his flying bridge. Many would consider that a dream come true, but Lucky might have balked. Maybe there were health problems, or he wanted to test the rope's tensile strength. Perhaps the weight of his name finally dragged him down.

Now I was being silly.

My life, far from lucky of late, was rising from the ditch. Walking to the room, I hadn't been bothered by pain. The wine was superb. I poured a second glass, told myself that I deserved it, and wondered how I would feel in the morning if I drank the whole thing.

My elevated spirits inspired me to call Bobbi Lewis's home phone.

"It's a tad late, Alex," she said. "Have you had a drug-induced insight to help me solve two murders by noon tomorrow?"

"Nope, nope," I said. "I still think you have three, the third not connected."

"That's a new touch," she said. "You sound like you found that rum you wanted. Has your mind been working overtime?"

"I just had a drink in the lounge with Tinker-bell. She offered confusing details about alarm systems and swapped bedrooms. She left with a young fellow ten years her junior and not a relative."

"Damn," she said. "But thank you. It's just that I wanted sleep."

Eleven minutes later I heard a car stop in the parking lot, a door slam, a tap at the door.

"Alex?"

I peeked through the louvers. Bobbi waved her index finger at my eye.

I let her in, coached her through a painless but extended hug, and offered to share my wine. "I got only one glass from the bartender."

"You use the glass, I'll drink from the bottle."

"This is good stuff," I said. "It deserves style."

"What am I, some street chick? I'll show you style."

I handed her the bottle. She upended it, took a small swig, no gurgle.

"Pure class," I said.

"Maybe not." In her first attempt at humor in weeks, she wiped her lips with the back of her hand, shook it off to the side. She stacked my pillows to make a backrest, then plopped on the bed. "What exactly drew you to that bar?"

I took the chair. "Plain old American thirst."

"Did you hear or see anything—beyond her escort—to make you think she played a part in her husband's death?"

"Except for a hunch, no," I said. "I think now that he's dead, her feelings have come home to roost. She loves Lucky even more since he got un—"

"Don't say it! You've been waiting two days to use that line."

"I will rephrase."

"Forget it, expert," she said. "What do you think happened?"

"A close friend or a family member."

"Killed him?" she said.

"Your tone of voice makes it sound like I'm to blame for his death."

"I'm pissed because you've been right before. I drove past her house on my way here. There was a small Mercedes two-seater in the driveway. If we double back and follow your hunch, it makes my job harder."

I reached out my glass. "You're sure that he killed himself."

She poured. "Lucky committed suicide. Tinkerbell, at first, couldn't stand the thought of it, the shame of having her husband go that way. By the time I got there on Friday, she had come to grips with it. She told me she had hidden the telescoping boat hook he used to flip the davit's power switch. It was on the concrete when she found him, and she hid it in their laundry room. By the way, I need to thank you for a suggestion. Aside from time of day, we found only one aspect of these deaths that matched all three."

"Longer throats?"

"Identical rope," said Bobbi. "You told me that they were similar, and we traced it to Ace Hardware on Summerland. They sell it off a reel, any length, cut to order. No one there could remember a single person who bought rope, even in the past five days."

"Credit-card records show anything?" I said.

"They looked back two weeks, and no one paid for rope with a card. We asked them to go back another six weeks when they had time, but I don't hold much hope."

"What about Lucky's daily routine? Was he an early riser or did he hang late in the sack?"

She paused and studied my face. "And that will tell us . . ."

"If he woke up every day at dawn and took a walk, maybe he ran into a friend, invited him back to the house for coffee. That sort of thing."

Bobbi squinted at me, daring me to have my own thoughts. "Not only was he murdered, but it was by someone he knew?"

"Worth a try," I said. "Check the probability tables. Friends and family and all that."

"What is it you want out of this?"

"It's not like I'm one of your so-called colleagues, trying to rob you of a collar."

"Change the subject," she said. "Why do you think Liska sent you to Marathon?"

"I think he feels trapped in his role of being sheriff. He has to delegate work to his employees, but he feels left out of the action loop. He wants me to be the detective version of himself, do the investigative work, keep him informed. Something inside him needs that."

"For once I feel sympathy. I hope he feels some for me, because I'm tapped for clues."

"Tell me how Kansas Jack lived each day."

She took another taste of wine. "Dirt aside, it was like the man lived in a rental condo."

"Everything new?" I said.

"It was funky but new in the last few years. He had no keepsakes, except for that photo and the Zippo lighter. Nothing looked old except for two things. Some tools and a carton of flashlights. The house looked like he had left somewhere with nothing but the clothes on his back, then did a splurge at Kmart."

"So, he was a neat freak. He chucked the used-up and replaced the old."

"But we always have junk. A cracked coffee mug full of ballpoints that haven't worked in years. Or hot pads, or an iron skillet, or dish towels from the 1970s. You've lived in the same house for how long? Maybe you don't grasp what I'm saying. I got divorced fourteen years ago, high and dry, with no possessions but a Dodge Omni and an old Scrabble game. You wash up like that, you have to find new mementos and touchstones to make you feel less temporary, the smallest bit permanent."

"So these new keepsakes," I said. "Are they to remind you of current events, or past events, or of the old keepsakes you lost?"

"I never thought about it. I guess old keepsakes. There's a shitload of the past I don't want to recall without serious editing."

"What made you think the flashlights were old?"

She looked down, let her mind go back. "The box looked beat-up, water-stained."

"How many of them?"

"It was a small box. It probably held twelve. Eight or nine were left. They were gray and had numbers on them. And one other thing I noticed. His shaving kit was an old leather job with lots of mileage."

"How about his toolbox? New, old, medium?"

"The box was new. It was Home Depot orange. Most of his tools were new, too, like the screwdrivers. But there were five or six old-looking pipe wrenches and pliers."

"How about this," I said. "Kansas Jack was in the military. Probably the Navy. Every ship had hundreds of gray flashlights, and everything in the Navy had a number printed on it. If he lived on ships half his life, he wouldn't have keepsakes we associate with homes. He was the ultimate transient. He would have a shaving kit and one set of civvies. At some point, at the end of his service, he probably swiped expensive small tools and a box of flashlights."

Bobbi smiled, sipped more wine. "Retirement pay?"

"Stands to reason."

"But he had no bank accounts. He lived his life on a cash basis."

"Maybe the retirement money's going to an ex-wife," I said. "Can you trace that info through the military?"

"Where will I get a Social Security number?"

We quit that line of thought, stayed quiet a minute.

"I don't claim this is startling news," said

Bobbi. "Larry Riley told me that when they stripped Kansas Jack's clothing, his shins were beat to hell with old injuries. He said they were the types of injuries you see in amateur hockey players and bar drunks."

"We have a shortage of hockey rinks here in the Keys."

"In my experience, when drunks get murdered, it's usually by another drunk. Speaking of which . . ." Bobbi rolled off the bed and poured more wine in my glass. The bottle went dry after filling only a third of the glass. "Sorry," she said. "I guess I took more than I thought. You want me to drive to Kickin' Back for another?"

"It wouldn't be this good. Are you okay to drive?"

"Always." She stubbed her toe on a bed leg and saved herself from the floor by falling onto the bed. "Almost always. Let me see if I can make it to the bathroom."

I heard her using my toothbrush. She came out wearing panties, carrying her shoes, bra, top, and shorts. Her other arm shielded her nipples from my view.

She went to the bed and pulled down the cover on one side. "I'm tired and too looped to drive. But, like I said an hour ago, I need sleep. Can we do this without doing **that**?"

"It's your call. This is the playground where girls make the rules."

She pretended to grimace. "We're known for changing our minds."

"Not tonight, honey. I have a backache."

"You have a sick sense of humor. Do you have an extra T-shirt?"

"No, but you can wear this one."

"Pass, thanks. Quit staring like they're going to blow away. Can you keep your hands off the merchandise?"

"You know my habits."

"You're going to hold one all night long?"

"At least until I fall asleep."

After I had crawled in and doused the light, we lay side by side for a few minutes. I heard her sniff and fidget, sounds that told me she couldn't fall asleep.

"You okay?" I said.

"I never thought Chicken Neck was the old-boys-club type. He keeps his in-box of job apps and résumés on top of his file cabinet. The detectives have decided that it's supposed to motivate us by reminding us that other, highly qualified people are waiting in the wings."

"Where's this going?"

"I can't figure out why, with all that talent scratching at his door, he hired Millican."

"Maybe he knows something about the man's talents that no one's seen yet," I said.

"I don't know. His main strength is blowing holes in the concept of teamwork. I see anything that makes it tougher to solve cases as a weakening of job security. If I lost my job, I'd have to leave the Keys."

"If that happened, I'd have to apply for a job."

"What do you mean?" said Bobbi.

"Your professional traveling companion."

"You'd follow me somewhere?" she said.

"Anywhere. Except Siberia. I've grown attached to warm weather."

Her hand went to my belly. "Maybe I can coach you on filling out your application."

"The painkillers . . . I might need some lead in my pencil."

"That was never your problem."

"What **was** my problem?" I said.

She lifted her hips, pushed down her panties. "I can't remember."

"Be gentle with me dear, I'm injured."

"Hah."

Bobbi woke me before daybreak. The only light in the room came from the bathroom. She was clothed, ready to attack her new day. She went to her car and brought in a candy box with a piece of clean plywood on its bottom.

"I'm still not sure I want you hovering around my case," she said. "I brought you a bribe to keep your distance. I hope it distracts you."

I opened the small box. A five-inch strip of

duct tape, sticky side up, was held away from the lid by thumbtacks stuck through to the plywood.

"From Kansas Jack's mouth?" I turned on the bedside lamp.

"The forensics people knew going in that they couldn't get a thing off it. Any imprints are fouled by the cross-hatching of the threads that give duct tape its strength. Then there's other crap to deal with, foreign objects like dust and sawdust and bug shit and sand. Anyway, the experts need four or five identifying lines in prints to call a match, to testify in court, and they can't pull nada with the web of threads. It's rejected evidence. I caught it before it hit the trash, and kept it cool."

"Chilled, like champagne?" I said.

"We don't want the adhesive to melt, do we? Might obscure the rejected evidence. This way, you have a project."

The phone rang. We looked at it. It rang twice more.

"Could only be Marnie," I said.

"Or Sheriff Liska," said Bobbi. "I'm out of here."

"I was afraid of that." I picked up.

13

I GRUNTED A FAKE-SLEEPY "Mmyeh?" into the receiver.

"How's your back?" said Liska.

I drew a star on my chest—a badge—to identify the caller. Bobbi rolled her eyes and held a finger to her lips. She hung back to listen.

"Lemme roll out and check for pain," I said. "My reputation is screwed, I know that much. The downtown buzz has me employed."

"Word got out?"

"I'm hardwired to the telegraph. Do I have to opt out of this mess in writing?"

"Think about it a few days, Rutledge. Look, the reason I called, you got a twin here in the Keys. I had the Rock Harbor surveillance video brought down yesterday. I looped it last night and, spooky as hell, I saw your face ten times in a row. I mean I know it wasn't you, but it was you. Millican made an honest mistake."

"So he's excused?"

"His suspicions are. Not his actions. There'll be a proper inquiry, punishment as the case warrants."

"Let me get this straight," I said. "You don't feel compelled to solve two or three murders, but you're hot on discipline procedures?"

"I'm hot on all of it. I have subordinates who follow through."

"Cool," I said. "Was I supposed to be one of them?"

"Why don't you forget I ever asked."

"Is that all you need?"

"Your back hurts?" he said.

"Raw torture."

"The reason I ask is a deputy drove though the lodge parking lot two hours ago on a routine security check. He spotted a certain Toyota Celica adjacent to your room. You still have one of my detectives in custody?"

I pointed at her. She waved both hands.

I said, "What color was that Celica?"

Lewis threw her hands up.

"Congratulations, Rutledge. You passed the physical. Pain or no pain, you're checking out of that two-hundred-dollar-a-night infirmary. Put her on."

I handed her the receiver and headed for the bathroom.

When I came out, she was in her car with the engine idling. I pulled on my shorts and went to speak with her.

"Get your stuff and get in," she said. "I'm your taxi, too."

My stuff was my shoes, six remaining pain pills, and the book I'd begun to read. Before I could slam the door, the phone rang again. I wanted it to be Tim calling from Homestead to tell me he was sorry and he'd left the Keys.

"Alex?" It was Tim's new flame, my ex-lover Teresa.

"You got me," I said. "I hear that I've become a distant, less recent unpleasantness."

"You hear out of context, but . . . yes, that's why I was calling."

"You've got your hands full this time," I said.

"It's more than that—"

"Please, no details. Is he there right now?"

"No, I'm at work," she said. "But I wanted to say . . . to tell you . . . I'm not trying to do something false to fuck with your head. I really like him. You two are very different, and I wanted you to know that. Am I confusing things or making sense?"

"If it makes sense in your heart, it's okay with me," I said. "But watch you don't pay for all the food and rent."

"He insists on covering his share. He'll start

doing drywall with a renovation group at six-thirty tomorrow morning."

"Are you calling to have me bless your union?"

"I guess so, but something else—"

"Consider it done. I gotta go." I hung up and hurried to the car.

We needed to go north. The Lower Keys rush hour had us stuck waiting for a break in both the south- and northbound traffic. Bobbi finally broke through. Face-front to the rising sun, I rejoined the world with which I'd been out of touch for forty hours. With the school zone at Mile Marker 19 and an accident cleanup across from the Sheriff's Substation on Cudjoe, it took twenty minutes to reach Little Torch. Thanks to the Celica's age-hardened shocks, I felt every bump of the journey. I contorted myself to get out of the car without summoning new agony.

Lewis said, "Straight question wanting a straight answer. What, beyond the davits, did you see at the Kansas Jack and Milton Navarre murder scenes that supports direct link?"

"The bottom end of the wealth spectrum and identical but mirror-image noose knots. What did your forensic people find?"

"Zilch, except for alcohol levels that would destroy you or me. No footprints, fingerprints, or drugs. I've got no leads, no trail to follow. I don't even have a damned forest to get lost in."

"They sure as hell weren't random acts of vio-lence," I said. "But here's your big question. Why would someone want to snuff two nobodys? Find out why they're dead, and who done it might come into focus."

Bobbi nodded, accepted my reasoning.

"I also figured a way to buy in to your suicide idea," I said. "Do you want a far-fetched concept, just for its entertainment value?"

"Please entertain me."

"Connect, somehow, Mason, Navarre, and Haskins. Then imagine that Lucky killed the first two and committed suicide out of remorse."

"When we start drawing diagrams," she said, "I'll post that one for all to see. Except you pro-vided the disproof for that one. If Lucky had made perfect noose knots for his victims, why wouldn't he show the same pride for his own demise?"

"Good thought," I said.

"One last thing. Did you apply for a home-equity loan or a refinance in the last few weeks?"

I shook my head. "Where'd you come up with that?"

"I wanted to see if Weedy Fields might be alive up in Michigan, just so I could follow up on his daughter's whereabouts. I went to the county to look up the deed and transaction records for your address, to find what city he was from. I couldn't help noticing that someone had checked out your records, I don't know, maybe two weeks ago."

"My records weren't there?"

"Oh, they never leave the records room. But they make you sign a cover sheet when you have a look. I couldn't decipher the signature."

"Sure as hell wasn't me."

Bobbi backed up to leave Manning's yard but stopped before reaching the street. She put her phone to her ear, became lost in the conversation.

I started up the outside stairway and remembered I had no keys in my pocket. A good start to the day: the Key Largo deputy had obeyed Millican and left the door unlocked. A moment later the Celica pulled under the house and its engine went quiet. I walked back downstairs.

Bobbi held a hand to her forehead. Tears smeared her cheeks.

"What's wrong?"

"Nothing," she said. "I've been laughing."

I took her words as evasive and steeled myself for awful news, a deputy or a relative dead or injured, Liska with a heart attack. She composed herself and got out of the car, weak-kneed, supporting herself against a fender, and began to laugh again. I had no idea how to console her, to diminish hysterics. I ran for a chair, brought it around, helped her aim for the flat part.

When she gained a semblance of calm, she took a deep breath and her face became stern. "You will not fucking believe this. Detective Millican . . ." The wide grin returned.

"Don't laugh," I said. "Too much of anything is bad."

"Fuck it. I needed this." She took a deep breath, began to smile, stopped, and set her jaw for delivering facts. "Millican was due for an interview at seven this morning, downtown, on the possible civil rights beef. He was a no-show and the feds were steamed. His attorney called around. His neighbors in Marathon thought they heard him leave after midnight."

"Cops know their life expectancy in jail," I said. "Stands to reason he hit the trail. By next week he could be driving a cab in Nicaragua."

"No, they found him on the road out of town."

"Trying to thumb a ride?"

"Picture a plywood star taller than you, painted gold."

"I'm with you."

"That accident cleanup across from the Freeman Substation on Cudjoe?"

"The one we just passed?" I said.

"Someone kidnapped Millican before dawn and drove him to Mile Marker 21. They bolted the star to the bus-stop sign post across from the substation, then pantsed him and tied his neck, wrists, and ankles to the points. When the sun came up, there was Millican, blindfolded on the star with his trousers bunched around his ankles, showing his butt to southbound traffic."

"They starified him?"

"It gets better. Remember the city's flap with the uniformed mannequin?"

"Beth Watkins told me that Matilda was stolen."

"Sure as shit, they found her, still in her uniform shirt but naked from the waist down. She was between him and the star, positioned to look like they were screwing. To make sure everything stayed in place, the kidnapper superglued his dick inside her. An EMT extracted him, and the stuff that neutralizes glue is not recommended for private parts."

"That's just wonderful," I said. "How long did he remain on display?"

"At least thirty minutes." Bobbi began to chuckle again. "The supervisor found him. He said he thought at first that Millican was a new species of tropical flower."

"Millicanthus?"

"Stop with that. I can't start laughing again. I have to go to work."

"A whole new concept for Art in Public Places?"

"Stop." She looked too wiped out from her jag to put in a full day.

"I'm baffled by the logistics of it all," I said.

"The star was hinged down the middle so it would fit in, say, the bed of a pickup truck." She took a breath, fixed her eyes on mine, removed the excitement from her voice. "We're not seeing this at the same level of humor."

"Where was he taken from? How was he kidnapped?"

She shrugged. "I wasn't told that. Apparently I didn't care enough to ask."

"What was he tied with?"

"I believe they said it was rope."

"Anyone think to save the rope?"

Her eyes hardened, moved away. "What do you care? It wasn't your revenge. Your alibi is tighter than Dick's hatband."

"My wild imagination paints odd pictures. I keep an open mind toward evidence."

"You're as bad as my ambitious new neighbor."

"Beth Watkins? I thought you liked her. Hell, you brought her to Lucky Haskins's place."

"She wanted to watch us work a county crime scene, to see if there were ways to improve her approach. Now it's like she's made these hangings her personal crusade. I can understand she might be bored in the city, but damn. All her questions and ideas . . ."

"Maybe that explains her visit on Saturday morning. She wanted to pick my brain."

Suspicion filled Lewis's eyes. "A visit here?"

"She was out riding her nifty motorbike. She came by to admire my Triumph."

"She knew how to find this place?"

"Drove right in," I said. "I assumed she got it from you."

"This was before Millican came and got you?"

I nodded.

"A lot of screwy shit going on," said Lewis.

"Aside from his klutz move," I said, "what did you think of Bixby?"

"He treated the Haskins death scene like it was his ticket to a Pulitzer Prize. Why do you care?"

"Watkins told me that he helped solve two murder cases while earning his master's degree. I would think he'd be sharp enough to keep from falling off a seawall."

"He was focused on glory more than results," she said. "That always kills cases."

"I'd love to know how a student put himself into a position to solve anything."

"Your phrase, 'put himself,' telegraphs your doubt. Maybe he got there first?"

"Exactly my thought. When will you get a report on Kansas Jack's fingerprints?"

"Maybe today," she said. "Wednesday at the latest."

"Has the Milton Navarre murder case been re-assigned?"

"I don't think so. It was a quick wrap. A man's in custody, and they've got a witness who claims he heard the accused threaten the victim. Fifty cents says Millican wrote his reports before he came to get you. The prosecutors can play with it now."

"Even if the man in custody didn't do it?"

She gave me a quizzical stare. "Don't even think about it."

Ten minutes later we ran a repeat of Bobbi's departure. This time she made it four houses down the street before stopping to answer the cell. I was putting the box with the duct tape into the fridge I when heard the tires crunch the pea rock.

I walked downstairs to greet her. "You don't look so gleeful this time around. Don't tell me Millican died of exposure."

"End of jokes, Alex. How long were you going to wait before you told me?"

Oh, shitstorm.

"Who called you, Teresa?" I said.

"No, your friend Beth Watkins."

"And what was so grim about her conversation?"

"Your ex-girlfriend has a new boyfriend?"

"It wasn't a priority," I said. "What's with the cloudy face?"

"Teresa asked Beth Watkins to run a background check on him."

Now I understood why Teresa had called the lodge an hour earlier. I'd hung up before she could 'fess. "Checking a man's past is a wise move for any woman—"

"You never told me he went to prison," she said.

"I don't know that he did."

"I bring sad tidings." Bobbi raised a notepad and read from it. "He stood thirty-one months of a five-year pull in Pennsylvania for armed robbery. He held up a dry cleaner in Altoona brandishing, of all things, a carpet cutter."

"How long ago?" I said.

"He hit the street fifty-five days ago. The State Correctional Institution at Greensburg is what they call medium-security, southeast of Pittsburgh. It's more like a fortress, full of hard cases. Your brother must have pissed off the sentencing judge. He probably did a lot of push-ups inside, fighting off potential boyfriends."

"I thought he looked beefed-up across his shoulders."

"That's your entire reaction?"

"What's to change?" I said. "His past is just that—his. I'm booked up living my own life."

"Eloquent. Watkins phoned the prosecutor up

there. He recalled the case. Your brother was seeing a sophomore in some local college. She had
him settled down, and she was the only thing
keeping him straight and narrow. Then, out of
the blue, she killed herself with pills. He rode it
downhill and hit the sauce. They caught him
shoplifting a few times before his holdup. If he
had used a gun instead of the knife, he'd be in for
another seven years."

"Sad chapters dominate Tim's story," I said.

"When you were still in the hospital—that
phone call from Liska—he told me Millican
matched your face to a credit-card scammer. Is
that why you kept his presence a secret? You re-
semble your brother?"

I shrugged. "Do you think Tim learned new
tricks in jail?"

"Don't they all? Of course, if you think about
it, we all know how to do crimes. Lucky for us,
we don't put our knowledge to use."

"So you're thinking . . ."

"I'm thinking your brother screwed up within
an hour of entering Monroe County."

"What's your next move, arrest him?"

She shrugged. "For now, I just want to talk
with him."

She backed in a half-circle and left Manning's
yard with her foot in the carb. Or in the kazoo,
whatever Celicas have. It sounded like a Waring
blender.

I reflected on Tanker Branigan's grand plan to help Tim get a grip, and whether the big gold star had been hinged to fit inside a Chevy Caprice station wagon.

I quit wondering.

I knew.

I could think of only one approach with the "rejected evidence" in the fridge. I wasn't sure what photos of the duct tape might glean, but I needed to talk with Monty Aghajanian, an ex–Key West cop who had saved my life before going to the big leagues. These days I asked few favors and never assumed he would grant them.

After Monty's basic training at Quantico, Virginia, the FBI had posted him to Newark. I dialed his direct number, hoping to reach his office answering machine. I wanted to pose my questions without having to answer any. The machine granted my first favor. I sent my best wishes to his family, told him what I needed, gave him my cell and Manning's home numbers with an okay for voice mail.

My '70 Triumph Bonneville and '66 Shelby GT-350H waited under the house. I had been reminded during my midnight horizontal therapy that my body still needed to heal. I chose the car because I didn't have to balance it. I could stop without falling sideways.

I sifted through boxes until I found the Shelby's distributor cap, carried it to ground level, and hooked up the plug wires. I tripped the electric fuel pump's hidden switch, pumped the pedal five times, then twisted the key. The Shelby's engine sounds like a boat explosion when it comes to life. To fans of muscle cars, the sound is pure symphony. To those accustomed to fewer than eight cylinders and the modern muffling of catalytic converters, the motor is raw threat.

Wendell Glavin, from across the street, fit the first group. Before the oil pressure peaked, he was worshipping at the altar of carbon monoxide.

"That's an old Hi-Po 289, isn't it?" he yelled, strolling across the street.

I shut it down and told him a lie. "It's a massaged 289, but not a Hi-Po."

"I hear those solid lifters." Wendell inspected the interior. "Looks like somebody in the old days tried to make a fake Shelby out of a Mustang. Too bad it's not the real thing. You'd have some bucks in the old beast."

His words struck an odd note. Glavin lived in a neighborhood where residents spent more for boats than they did for their cars. "Too bad I didn't buy this house in 1998, too," I said. "You have to live with what you've got."

Years ago I had opted for the opposite of

restoration and spent money to make my genuine
Shelby look unattractive to thieves. I had removed
its original emblems, bought a flat brown paint
job, stashed the original aluminum wheels in a
closet, and bolted on junkyard shoes with black-
wall tires. These days the car looks like any old
fastback on its last legs. But I can drive it without
being challenged, and I can park without having
it vanish. If it fooled a car nut like Wendell, the
money was well spent.

"I drive that old Buick over there," he said,
"but I always dreamed of owning a Shelby. Hope
you paid a right price."

"I paid for a Conch cruiser, Wendell, and
that's what I drive."

"Maybe so, but it sure sounds like an F-18.
You doing okay?"

"Peachy, Wendell."

"I didn't want to stick my nose where it don't
belong, but I saw that bullshit go down on Saturday. It just didn't look right, I mean, a friend of
Al's getting tapped by the man. I hope you didn't
mind I made a call."

"Not at all, Wendell. Matter of fact, thank
you. You a mechanic?"

"Machinist. I was in the tool-and-die business."

"You ran a lathe?"

"That's part of what I did." He began to edge
toward the road.

"Here in Florida?"

"Up north, years ago," he said. "I gotta go."

I couldn't believe I was getting off that easy. "Anything wrong?"

"I don't know," he said. "These random killings have the whole Lower Keys spooked."

"Consider yourself lucky. You don't have davits."

"Sure don't, Rutledge, but you do, so watch yourself. Glad you're not mad about that call I made."

"Keep it between the beacons, Wendell."

I drove to the highway, ran it through the gears. I couldn't believe my feeling of escape. There's something about being arrested, chained into the back of a cruiser, and beaten up by a cop that makes you appreciate the simple things in life. Like rolling down a window, flicking a turn signal, applying the brakes. I watched flags whip in the wind at Dolphin Marina, checked the wind direction in South Pine Channel.

I was back in the high life again. I was going to Marathon.

Traffic moved quickly on my side of the road. Typical of a Monday, southbound was more delivery vans and semis than cars and SUVs. I approached the west end of the Bahia Honda Bridge with my usual dread. Several years ago I was sent there to photograph a Jane Doe, and I recognized a former lover in her death mask. At that time a dense hammock and two lovely palms marked the beach. After Hurricane Georges it was one struggling palm and a patch of depleted shrubs. When the county finished sanitizing the scenic view, the hammock was history.

Score one more for turf farms and the pavers.

Such was the power of the county. It could sanitize a hammock and wrap up the Milton Navarre killing. It could do what it damn well pleased with an ex-con like Tim Rutledge.

14

THE MAN SMILED, THEN barely moved his mouth to say, "Hey, dude."

When I told him my name he narrowed his grin, told me he was Simply Bud.

"Great place you got here," I said.

"I don't make excuses," said Simply Bud. "Mac and Joe's is Marathon, Florida's prize dump." He swung his arm to present faux-neon beer ads, gray walls, grimy windows. It was a no-frills slopchute with the stink of a holding cell.

"At least we can soak up the air-conditioning," he said. "You're walking kind of stiff. Mind if I ask?"

"Police brutality."

"Are you the guy from the accident? The grapevine's full of you."

"I didn't know that," I said. "I didn't know that at all."

Simply Bud was in his late thirties, stocky and scruffy but sharp. I asked about the bar's name.

Mac and Joe were three owners ago. Mac went down to diabetes and Joe was doing hard state time in the Carolinas for selling Costa Rican weed out of a custom van in a KOA on the coast. Bud paid his ex-father-in-law four years' construction wages for the place. He never met Mac, saw Joe maybe once.

"This town's growing and I've got a plan. Some day this space will lease to Staples or Avis, or some other deep-pocket franchise. The rest of my life, I'll cash fat checks. I can cruise out in my yacht and catch innocent fish in the Gulf Stream. My first mate will work naked, and one of her jobs will be to bait my hooks."

I asked about Milton Navarre.

"Piece of work, that rummy-ass drizzle dick. Not to speak ill of the dead, but the fucker was a broken record. Every day it was ahoy, and abaft this, astern that, and decks and bulkheads and aloft. Like he was a swashbuckler out of a Patrick O'Brian novel." Bud looked for surprise on my face, and found it. "My one vice. I'm a bar owner who doesn't drink. I read books."

"He was a regular?"

"I regular kicked him out. Is that what you meant?"

"Is that what happened the night he bought it?"

"His pal, Rudy Downer, carried him out. Threw him on the hood of his car, their usual deal."

"Like a shot deer?"

"One time he tried to get him in the front seat, it was like putting a drunk hooker in a paddy wagon. Somebody said booze made Milton claustrophobic. After that incident Rudy would push him onto the hood. What did they have, three hundred yards to get home?"

"Maybe Milton fell off the car, was killed by mistake. The hanging was a cover-up."

"No way," said Bud. "They were a well-tuned act. Milton was too big for Rudy to heave up there without a little cooperation. He was never too drunk to hold on to the windshield wipers. Some nights he'd ride home that way close to sober, after only six or eight beers. He didn't fall off."

"Did Milton get into fights?"

"Only with his mouth. Some big deal about not being second-class. He wanted first-class respect. He'd tell other drunks not to call him sir, but to treat him like sir. Twice since the first of the year he was run out of here by Deputy Hard-On."

I caught myself before I asked. He meant No Jokes Bohner. "You call the deputies on many customers?"

"Once, since I bought it," said Bud.

"Which means one of those times Bohner was already here."

"Right. He likes the stool where you're sitting

now. When he comes in to drink, he's not in a good mood."

"In his civvies, I assume."

"Yep, strictly on leisure time. But that doesn't diminish his power trip."

"Why did he need to run Milton out?" I said.

"He'd kick him to the curb when he'd heard enough of his fo'c'sle-and-blimey hogwash."

"Man named Millican ever come in here?"

"I don't know the name," he said.

"Bohner always come in alone?"

"Once, no, twice with an older guy," said Bud. "A guy with a crew cut and an attitude."

"Any idea where Milton earned his drinking money?"

"Odd jobs, handyman shit like plumbing and wiring. I guess he did magic tricks for the water bills in that trailer park. People down there don't want it talked about. They can't afford rent and utilities to start with."

"Or basic vices?"

"Right, cheap bourbon. They can't even scrounge haircuts for their kids. They got a hard-times monkey on their backs, they don't need the meter police on their asses. Can I sell you one?"

"You got ahead of me."

"I ain't selling meter police."

I tossed a five on the bar. "Pretend you sold me a six-pack?"

He palmed the fin. "Throw a sawbuck, I'll pretend I sold you the bar."

"You stock Amstel?"

"An import? Don't be foolish."

"You pick."

He grabbed a bottle of Bud Light, twisted the cap, and put it down. He made change in a cigar box, handed me back three ones. "The county's got Rudy now. I guess they didn't buy his alibi."

"Did he come back here after he took Milton home on his hood?"

"Oh, man. I'd have to think about that. We're talking four, five days ago, they all start to blend together. I'll say this. It wouldn't have been unusual."

"He's done it before?" I said.

"Rudy calls himself a recovering sleazeball. He's one to stay late, sniff out the action, hit on a straggler or two. I don't believe age or size matter to him. He hangs in, specializes in the late harvest. No woman is too ugly for Rudy."

"What time do you close?"

"Depends on the crowd. Also, whether I can keep my eyes open. I never lock up before eleven. Most nights it's close to one-thirty."

"Rudy get lucky with any regularity?"

"You'd be surprised," said Bud. "He was probably exaggerating, but he once said his batting average was right up with Sammy Sosa's."

"He'd take them back to his trailer?"

"I never asked. I know which trailer it is, but I've never seen inside. Why all this shit about him?"

"He told the deputies that he gave Milton a ride, came back, and took drunk himself, too drunk to walk. He told them you drove him home."

"They forgot to tell me I was his alibi."

"I think you're it," I said. "Who called you from the Sheriff's Department?"

"Some lady. I told her what I told you. It's only four or five nights ago, and I might have done that, but I can't exactly recall. What time did I drive him, supposedly?"

"Real late."

"That's about as likely as him killing Milton. But if it would help get him out of the clink, I'd remember him wearing pink tights and a tutu. Pain in the ass that he is."

"Even the next day, after you heard about the murder, nothing from that night stuck in your memory?"

Simply Bud wiped sweat and shook his head. "Gimme a card. I'll call you if anything unsticks."

I didn't have a card. I wrote my name and number on a bar napkin.

I drove into Florida Straits Estates, eased past the turquoise dolphins with their smiling cherry lips.

Another artist had logged a visit, painted an X over each dolphin eye. I decided to park near the road, faced outward for a quick departure, just in case. I also tripped the hidden fuel-pump shutoff switch.

I wasn't sure where to start. Going trailer to trailer would get me a fist in the face before I found useful info. Finding someone outdoors in the midday heat also would be a challenge. I hadn't walked fifty yards before getting the sense that I had entered a foreign country. Discolored homes and fractured concrete mocked the perfect blue sky. No vehicle in sight looked capable of making it to Miami or even Key West, but that was not their purpose. There was a chance I spoke the local language, but no guarantee.

I aimed for the ratty seawall where the davits stood, passed a slender woman in a plastic chair facing outward from three feet inside her mobile home's door. Her setback limited her peripheral view, though I doubt she cared. Her eyes clicked onto me, her expression didn't twitch. I didn't see her as a hot source of intelligence. If I skunked, I always could check back.

Forty yards later I waltzed through a pot cloud riding the sea breeze. I took it as a stronger sign of life than the seated woman. I heard a **thwock,** then a quiet, urgent man's voice said, "Point, point!"

The seven-foot chain-link fence was lined with

a cheap rattan screen, the trailer's yard shaded by an awning made of four bedsheets knotted at their corners. Someone saw me through the rattan.

"Say your name, or I'll shoot your ass," said a man with a gruff voice.

"My name is Rutledge. Looking for Rudy Downer."

"He's one mile north, behind where you get your driver's license."

"Talk to you a sec?"

"Fuck off. We ain't nothing but registered sex offenders. You might be our next victim of love."

Someone else in the yard drawled, "Or rectum of love."

"Bullshit," I said. "If you had a hammer that big hanging over your ass, you wouldn't smoke dope in the open air."

A section of rattan fell away. First came the nose of the pistol. Next, the nose of the ex-linebacker type. It was the mullet-cut I had seen at the trailer court entrance on Thursday. The panther still crawled his shoulder, under a tank top's strap. Behind him sat a small dude with a thorny rose tat on his upper arm, a longneck in his fist. Stringy hair, a dirty goatee, an anchor earring, a one-inch roach clamped in his teeth like a cigarillo. Next to him, slouched on a rear seat from a minivan, was a skinny boy with slicked-back blond hair and a thousand-yard sneer. He was the smart-looking one. He held a five-foot length of inch-thick PVC pipe.

"Saw you with the badge man." The mullet breathed through his mouth, wiggled the pistol. If he was going to shoot me, he'd have done it before I scoped the panorama. "You rode in with the fat shit to see the dead man swing."

"They dragged me up here from Ramrod. They thought I knew Milton, which I did, a little. But I didn't tell them that. I came to see Rudy Downer, see what he knows about all this."

"Which means?"

"I'd like to know who it is that needs to be hanging people I know."

"Which also means you want first shot, before the cops?"

"There's your criminal mind at work again."

"And you know all about that?"

"I never did a day behind the door."

"Oooh-wee. You use the word **door** like that, you done seen it."

I had passed a secret test. I was now okay. The pistol went out of sight.

The skinny boy behind him raised the PVC pipe parallel to the ground and blew through it hard. It was a blowgun. His homemade dart pinned a fat cockroach to a trellis hung from the trailer. "Point," said the boy. He lowered the pipe and lifted a can of Bud. "Four for seven."

"You want to buy in to the game?" said mullet.

"I'm on a mission," I said.

"From God or the devil?" said the mullet.

"Depends how it ends," I said. "You hear that davit creak in the night?"

"I did," said the skinny sharpshooter. We looked at each other. Neither of us said a word.

"Around here," said mullet, "we don't go outside for noises after three A.M." He paused for my reaction, then said, "We ain't afraid of shit. By that time, we're too fucked up to get off the couch."

His teammates laughed their approval.

"Check that puke-green Argosy house trailer." He wagged his head to his right. "See if the queen of darkness will give you two minutes of her time. If you get past three minutes, fuck her for me."

15

THE WELL-MAINTAINED FORD ESCAPE looked out of place alongside the Argosy trailer. I knocked on an aluminum door that was missing its screening. A woman in her mid-twenties appeared. She looked like a five-three goth girl with a Lands' End account. Black polo top, khaki tennis shorts, red high-top sneaks, jet-black short hair.

I said, "Is this the former residence of Milton Navarre?"

"It's where he crashed when he could make it home. If you're a bill collector, his net worth was a flat piece of bug-holed driftwood with a shrimp boat painted on it."

I peered inside and saw negative net worth. She would have to pay someone to haul it away. The wall paneling had been scavenged from numerous scrap heaps. Wet weather had attacked the sofa before its current installation. The arm-

chair, with its stained bed-pillow booster, confirmed that curb shopping paid off. The room
smelled of cat piss and a stale AC filter.

I refocused, checked out the young woman.
Tough, with a pixie face.

"What did you expect to find?" she said. "A
crack whore?"

Yes, I thought, with runny eyes and crappy
clothes. I held out my hand. "My name is Alex
Rutledge."

A surprise punch: "The photographer?"

The look on my face must have been affirmative.

"I've seen your work in my dentist's office
and my lawyer's," she said. "How did you get
to photograph Jack Hemingway with Gregorio
Fuentes?"

"Lucky timing, I guess."

"It made for a great picture. I'm Gail Downer."

"Rudy's daughter?"

She squinted with puzzlement. "I'm not trying
to be unfriendly, Mr. Rutledge, but can I ask why
you're here?"

"I had to photograph Milton Navarre while he
was still in the air. I sometimes do that for the
county. I also was here when they put Rudy in
the squad car."

"So stupid," she said. "I guess they needed an
instant scapegoat."

"Well, it probably made sense to question him. But he shouldn't still be in custody."

"I'm glad someone agrees. Technically, I'm his stepdaughter, but I was too young to know my real daddy. He went to Jamaica on a drug scam and never came back. Rudy was a good replacement. He was the first mate on a charter yacht and kept food on the table and shoes on our feet. My mother left him for a lesbian."

Gail let that news hang. I said nothing, soaked up scenery.

"I'd offer refreshment," she added, "but there's nothing here you'd want in your stomach. I was just about to go around back to defrost the bait fridge."

I followed her to the postage-stamp fenced yard. "Do you live in Marathon?" I said.

"My husband and I are on Grassy Key, but I keep an office here in town. I'm a tax accountant. Rudy and I keep our distance. I get calls on my birthday and Christmas and whenever he's in jail." She rapped on the ice that clogged the top section of the bait fridge. "I'd pry this out but I don't want to puncture the cooling coils."

"I take it Rudy stopped working charters."

"Rudy fell in with a crowd of losers, started staying out all night, sucking the sauce. His job went south inside a month. That was two years ago. Now he's locked up because somebody put a crazy idea in a detective's head."

I wasn't about to admit that I was that somebody.

"We must've just missed each other on Thursday morning," she said. "I arrived just as they brought Milton down." She looked off in the direction of the davits. "Something about the cable made him spin slowly. He did this macabre pirouette, then he lay on his side as if he'd wanted to be in that position all morning. The dumb-ass who let down the davit forgot to shut off the switch. The metal block hit Milton on the forehead, and his legs kicked up."

"His last complaint," I said.

"I hope so. What do you think happened before sunup?"

"I think it was planned in advance. You can't turn a perfect noose in a hurry in the dark. What do you think?"

"Someone he knew." Gail pointed at the trailer. "He could've been beaten up inside, but the police didn't look for bloodstains. His face was dog meat before that block hit him, so someone hit him with a hard object." She reached inside the freezer, pulled out a long piece of ice, mimicked a downstroke. "Then, for whatever sick reason, his killer dragged him to the davit and made a display of the poor man."

"I think you're exactly right."

She flipped the ice into the weeds. "Hello. It doesn't take a genius to agree with perfect reasoning."

"No, you're double right. That's why there's no murder weapon."

"I just said, a hard object."

"Right. And if it was a chunk of ice, and the killer tossed it aside like you did, then it melted."

"Not bad. Do you agree it was someone Milton knew?"

"It's a start," I said, realizing that our combined words suggested that her father was implicated. If our speculation kept going, I wanted her to take the lead.

"Did you con me into talking a circle?"

"I'm no cop and I hope no con," I said. "We're just tossing around ideas, right?"

Gail bit her lip, quit messing with the fridge. "The Rudy and Milton Show. This is not saying much for either of them, but each was the brother the other never had. They were a mutual enabling society."

I decided to step in shit. "Plenty of best friends have drunk too much, let a nothing argument escalate to violence."

"I've read about those, too. Wait till you see my father. He's my size, but I outweigh him. He couldn't have dragged Milton five feet without a helper."

"A helper fits the planning aspect," I said.

"But planning blows apart the spontaneous violence."

"Now you've conned me into a figure eight."

She sprayed 409 on the inside walls of the ancient refrigerator. "It was a mistake, but I'll take credit."

"Tell me about Milton."

"His specialty was splitting water mains," she said. "Milton could run lines to five or six trailers off one main. His talent became more important after the Aqueduct Authority started that arbitrary ten-dollar-per-month fee. Back here, it doubled everyone's bills. His customers claimed to be seasonal residents. They had their water turned off eight months a year."

"How could he make money doing one-shot jobs like that?"

"He got referrals and favors in return. Rudy told me once that Milton lived like a bum but always had a five or a ten in his pocket. I mean, hell, he owned the trailer. I don't know what'll happen to it now, or where Rudy will live if he gets loose of this nonsense."

"You ever meet a man named Jack Mason?" I said. "They called him Kansas Jack."

Gail shook her head. "The man murdered on Ramrod? I read about him."

"His murder and this one were similar."

"All the more reason why Rudy's innocent.

How the hell would he get all the way to Ramrod?"

"Do you know if Milton was ever in the military?"

Gail shook her head. "He talked like some old pirate, but everyone took it as wishful thinking. Somebody once gave him an eye patch as a joke, and he wore it for weeks. Why do you care about this crap? You're not a cop, you didn't know these people."

The question came from a young woman who knew perfectly well that you can't pick your relatives. I hadn't wanted to discuss Tim with anyone, even Marnie. This felt different. Perhaps because she was a stranger, I could vent without drawing judgment. Maybe I'd become tired of my own silence, wanted to let go no matter who listened.

"My younger brother has been stepping in shit all his life," I said. "He hasn't been in the Keys for years, but he got here a few hours before the crimes. The first thing he did was buy gas with a bad credit card. They know he did that, and the detective who arrested Rudy came up with a harebrained idea. Anyway, when they spring your father, they might want to make Tim their next suspect of choice."

"You want to prove him innocent?"

"It's not that simple."

Her face went to sympathy. "He could be dirty

or clean, and you want to know they made a right decision."

"Kind of like that, yes."

"It would be great if my shitty old dad was innocent. Not that I'll miss Milton. I think he had a few secrets of his own."

"Secrets that could bring about his murder?" I said.

"Somebody down there at the sheriff's office ought to look into his background. I'm not saying the victim caused his own death, but Rudy once said that Milton bragged on a felony he ducked years ago. Bunch of people in on it. Deals like that sometimes can bring resentment and strife."

"Especially if someone goes to prison and someone else doesn't," I said. "Or if somebody blabbed and others suffered."

"With Milton and that murder on Ramrod, do the police know which man died first?"

"I haven't heard them discuss it."

"Because, what's Ramrod, Mile Marker twenty-something?"

"Twenty-seven," I said.

"And this is forty-seven and change, so call it twenty-one miles with the slow zone on Big Pine, a half-hour maximum . . ."

"Plus the time it takes to kill two men."

"Okay," said Gail. "It could be one killer, no stretch. Except for Rudy, of course."

"And just as easily two."

"So maybe the dead men were snitches and the murderers did time in jail."

"Clean logic," I said.

"Speaking of clean, I need to go shower. I have to sit with a client at four-thirty."

"Did you already start cleaning the trailer?"

"A little. Those two men never washed their hands. I can't spend more than ten minutes in there without having to wash mine. I've Windexed the doorknobs two or three times. Are you thinking I might be messing up evidence?"

"It's possible," I said.

"Nobody told me not to do it. There's no crime-scene tape. Can I get into trouble?"

"No, but you may want to put it off until we're sure. Do me one favor, though."

"Tell me what it is."

"No matter how grody or disgusting it all might be, please don't throw away any of Milton's belongings."

"I might have to triple-bag it," she said.

I wrote my cell phone number on a Winn-Dixie receipt and thanked her for her time. "One last thing," I said. "Do you know the man who owns that bar up on the road?"

"Simply Bud?"

"He seemed okay to me."

"His charm works every time," she said. "He's

a known truth-expander with a line of hooey a mile long. He should call himself Mostly Bull."

"He told me he bought the place with construction wages."

"You ought to hear his ex-wife's side of the story. The court ordered him off cocaine, and I guess it's to his credit that he went straight. But I think drugs scrambled his eggs for the long haul."

"Not your most reliable witness, then."

"In this county, he's a wizard," said Gail. "Good luck with your brother."

"And you with your dad."

She looked away and forced an unamused laugh. "We may be the only two who can hope for it. I'm afraid I'm dealing with a man who's hard-boiled his luck for good."

Before leaving Marathon I stopped back at Mac and Joe's Bar.

Simply Bud was pulling onto the highway in a ten-year-old pickup truck. I waved him back, so he executed a 360 on U.S. 1 and wound up parked next to me. He leaned on his truck door's windowsill. "What's up?"

"When I first walked into your bar, you acted like you recognized me."

"Right, I did. Wasn't your picture in the paper?"

I shook my head.

"Well, I sure as hell . . . no, wait." He focused on my eyes, then pasted an expression of disbelief on his face. "Fuck, man. What are you up to? You were in the bar that night."

"What night?" I said.

"The night Milton got whacked. You were in there drinking Michelob like water. And here you ask me all these questions like you'd been a million miles away."

"What was I wearing?"

He shook his head. "No fucking deal, dude. I said I'd be Rudy's alibi, sure as shit, but I ain't going to be yours, too."

Simply Bud popped his clutch, whipped the steering wheel, and shot into the line of northbound traffic.

I drove away fearing that Tim, too, had hardboiled his luck.

16

THE TAILGATING ASSHOLE IN the Chrysler van
finally passed me. NASCAR numbers on his back
window, as if you might ever see a family minibus
on the high banks. This moke was a dreamer on
all fronts. He had an American flag decal and
stickers that said BLESS THE WORLD, and I SUP-
PORT OUR TROOPS, and BLESS AMERICA. Meanwhile he was clocking seventy in a crosswind on
the Seven Mile Bridge, two feet off the next guy's
bumper. He didn't want fellow-citizens slowing
his patriotic rush to Key West. He needed to get
started on his vacation drinking.

I wasn't in his hurry.

Twenty minutes later I passed the Little Torch
turnoff to Al Manning's house. I floated the
cheap rationalization that my throat felt scratchy
from cat spray and mold in Rudy and Milton's
aluminum palace. Cold beer would fix it, and I
had my choice of two saloons. Bobbi had said
Friday that no one at Boondocks knew Kansas

Jack. I parked in gravel in front of the Looe Key Reef Resort's open-air Tiki Bar.

Seven ceiling fans spun above nine men on tall PVC-web stools, most with sixteen-ounce plastic draft-beer cups in front of them. I sat where I wouldn't be downwind of cigarette smoke. Thin Lizzy's "The Boys Are Back in Town" came from overhead speakers—Tim's favorite song when he tuned in to rock and roll, bought his first Camaro. The song was his rally cry, his call to lunacy. He wanted that rock star's lifestyle, with hash pipes, bimbos, vials, late nights, and limos. With that life he could boogie till eternity, gain the admiration of manic crazies around the globe. Popularity would cease to be a problem.

Years ago I heard that Thin Lizzy's lead vocalist had died. His opinion on popularity is not currently known.

I wanted to blend, not draw attention to myself by ordering an import. I asked for Bud Light in a bottle, leaned back, listened. Four housepainters under the Marine Corps banner could have been finalists in a Keith Richards look-alike contest. A man on my side of the bar studied the TV section of the **Herald,** marked with a pencil his hour-by-hour plan for the evening. Two outboard-engine repairmen discussed prop-blade pitch. A woman of forty-five or fifty, her sunglasses perched on top of her head, sat two stools away from me and drank what I hoped was a vodka and cranberry. An insistent man four seats away bragged about turning down a ride home two nights ago. "They were idiots," he said. "I would've had to chug a bottle of Jack to catch up, just to get in the car."

The crowd kept the server hopping, treated her well. She popped tops, called the men by name, collected from stacks of singles, doled out reserved smiles like stingy approvals. A surly senior with a square of black cloth tied over his skull—perhaps the oldest biker in Florida— tugged his long white beard and fought a grin when she put a fresh draft in front of him. She patted his money stack, took nothing. It was a freebie.

I was soaking up atmosphere galore, getting nowhere. I motioned to the server.

She pivoted, stuck her arm toward a cooler. "Another one, honey?"

"Ask you a question?"

When she came closer, I said, "Did Kansas Jack come in here much?"

Her eyes wandered, caught on the house painters. "Not much on my shift." She pointed at the woman two stools away.

The woman turned, sized me up. "You talkin' the dead electrician?"

"I guess I am," I said. "Horrible way to die."

I'd found an info-compulsive, and this put her into gear. She shifted sideways, moved her fringed purse, drink, and coaster, sat next to me. "He didn't live too beautiful, either." She offered her hand. "I'm Lally Mattox. Eighteen-year resident of the Florida Keys."

I told her my name, signaled the server for two refills. Lally had a dark tan and thin, long dark hair. She had been attractive in her day. Inflation and deflation had done her no favors. The old "Mother-in-Law" soul singer, Ernie K-Doe, on his WWOZ radio show in New Orleans, used to call such bar women "Naugahyde doves." This one had perched and was ready to talk. The server slid away.

"I saw him once," I said, hedging the truth. "Didn't get to know him."

"He was your typical fifty-two-year-old playboy. You mind if I smoke?"

I hedged a lie, told her to have at it.

"Jack was handsome as hell but broke," she said. "He did a good job of covering his lack of cash. He knew people's names, always laughed. He tried to make up for his shortcomings by being positive."

I took a chance. "He didn't live too well? You saw his house?"

"You mean, did I ever shack up with him?"

"I don't mean to pry."

"It's okay. We were teammates. The party troupers versus party-poopers. We hardball hitters stick together. I went home with him twice."

"Why not a third?"

"You just said you didn't want to pry."

"Sorry. Forget that one."

"It's okay. I've had three husbands and I've been divorced four times, if that makes any sense. I've never kept my pants on too good, and I'm long past keeping secrets. The second time I went back was to give him a second chance. He literally begged."

"The first time?"

"He was a diving champ, so I got mine. The man knew how to make a girl happy. I don't think he reached the same plateau, if you know what I mean. I got blisters, but he never got wood. I expect the years of booze had wilted his Johnson. Plus he was running a double whammy. He was needy and weird. I got rid of one of those two years ago after they found my old man on Big Pine, facedown in Lake Winn-Dixie."

"I hear they tried to drain that parking lot," I said.

She laughed. "They tried to elect Al Gore back in 2000, too."

"Did Kansas Jack ever talk about his past?"

She stared at the ashtray, pulled back into her memory. "He had lots of friends. They were from everywhere. He kept telling stories about his pal from Cleveland with the car dealership, the old friend from Buffalo who went to work for Customs. Another one tight with the mayor in San

Diego or San Francisco. But now that I think about it, he never told me about himself. His stories were always about someone else."

"Like he defined himself by the people he knew?"

"Maybe so. But also like he'd blanked himself out of the past. He was a man without a yesterday. Or one that he wanted to share with me."

"Can I buy you another drink?" I said.

She looked at her watch, shook her head. "Thanks, but I've hit my limit. My party days are winding down. Like now I have to meet a school bus. My grandson goes to day camp, and I got the duty till my daughter gets home from work."

The server had drifted back into earshot. "Or gets home from here," she said.

"She shows her sorry face today," said Lally, "you send her home, tell her I said so."

Lally left the bar. I heard an engine start out front, looked up to watch a small Japanese pickup go north on the highway.

The server asked, and I declined another beer.

"I was you," she said, "I wouldn't ask none of these boys about Kansas Jack. Most of them, over the years, got burned, they dealt with him."

"But not enough to kill him, right?"

"You make a good point. You're looking at fifteen attitudes and no motivation. These guys are your workers who swear quitting time is right after lunch. They talk bad all day, but I'd bet my britches they all, every last one of them, sleep with stuffed animals."

I gave her a look of disbelief.

"On the other hand," she said, "you're right. They might all kick the shit out of you."

"Was Jack in here the night before he died?"

"Not my shift."

"But, you know, people talk." I put a five on the bar.

"I heard they ran him and another guy out at closing time."

"You remember whose shift it was?"

She stared at my five. I took it away and dropped a ten.

"Her name is Shari. Her old man has a white ponytail and a black goatee. Don't talk to her when he's in the bar."

"I appreciate that," I said.

I walked out to the brightness and grabbed for my shades. Six hours of pain denial were starting to catch up with me. A man climbing out of a rusty Valiant offered me four hundred for my "Stang."

"I need the car more than the money," I said.

"You're a lucky one."

I wasn't so sure about that. I waited two minutes for a hole in traffic and fought a mental picture of Kansas Jack and Lally Mattox trying to figure how to do what and with which and to whom. Jack Mason was a broke stay-at-home

who died wearing Navy-style shoes. Bobbi Lewis
had found Navy flashlights in his house. Lally
Mattox knew that he had friends "from everywhere," as an ex–military man might. Milton
Navarre was a pain in the ass for all his swash-
buckling bar talk. He made a big deal about not
being called sir, a timeworn point of honor
among enlisted men. He wanted first-class respect and didn't want to be second-class. As in
first-class versus second-class petty officer?

I had all the confirmation I needed. The link
between Kansas Jack Mason and Milton Navarre
was as vast as the U.S. Navy.

Not too damned specific, I thought. It was like
saying that the killer had once been in Florida.

17

I TURNED ON AL'S ceiling fans and opened windows, then triggered an avalanche by dialing my voice-mail access code. Seven missed calls spewed out, the newest first.

Connie at the Naples ad agency: "Alex, please get back to me on that furniture job in Georgia. If you get this, I need to hear from you today."

A small, rational region of my brain told me to call back and accept the gig.

Monty Aghajanian, in precise FBI fashion: "Monday, one-seventeen P.M., following up your duct-tape request. I asked around and struck gold. Touch base with Dave Klein. He's a Broward Crime Scene Unit forensic analyst, and he's been working to get digital images admissible in federal courts. I hear he's great with difficult evidence, bringing out details in Photoshop. If anyone can help you, it's him. I worry about you, old pal. I thought you were going to keep your nose out of the fuzz biz for a while."

Marnie: "I'm pissed at myself for backing off my Millican story. They pushed through his arraignment and he bonded out this afternoon. He told the feds that a man and a woman abducted him, but that's not public, so hold it tight. Sam says he's not drinking beer and not catching fish. Also, I followed your advice the other day. The last nonsuicide hanging in this county was in 1973."

Teresa Barga, the city's media liaison and the future ex–Mrs. Tim Rutledge: "I might have opened my mouth once too often. I mentioned your brother to our new detective, Beth Watkins. She got a very strange look on her face. Is there something I need to know about him? Call, if you want to."

Liska came next: "The FDLE, the feds, and **The Miami Herald** wanted to swarm your butt for this new Millican fiasco. So as not to divulge personal info about my best detective, the fact she was in your bed at time of abduction, I vouched for your whereabouts. I told them you had no connection to the Big Gold Buttstar, as the **Herald** reporter called it to my face. For all this, you owe me."

Duffy Lee Hall: "One more thing on those noose knots. To you and me and fifty regular observers, they were tied by two people, a righty and a lefty. But I blew them up a few hundred percent, and guess what. The tips of the ropes were burned so the polyester wouldn't fray. The burn marks and melted curlicues are the same color and size. I want to blame it on technique rather than the composition of the rope."

The last one from Carmen, I assumed from Sunday: "A problem with your tenant. The noise pissed off my father at two A.M. last night. Bunch of people in your front room, reggae music rocking the lane, a couple girls with shrill laughs. Hector didn't want to confront the crowd or call cops because it's your place. He sneaked across the street and into your yard, opened the breaker box, and threw the master power switch. The idiots looked outside, saw the lane was dark, and assumed it was a typical Key West electrical failure. They broke up the party and the neighbors got some sleep. You owe me two extra bottles of wine, because of the mess I know I'll have to face."

Carmen's parents, Hector and Cecilia Ayusa, had lived across from my Dredgers Lane home since long before I arrived. A few years ago, Hector retired from City Electric, then sat on his porch for a while, fondling the cigars he no longer was allowed to smoke, staring at his overgrown yard. He'd become our private Neighborhood Watch, and he'd saved my house twice from intruders. I hadn't thought Johnny Griffin would ever make trouble, and Hector was the last person I wanted to piss off. I made a mental note to fix the situation.

———

Age-dating or not, the Tiki Bar beers had left a stale taste in my mouth, so I opted for the most effective solution. I opened an Amstel Light, swallowed a pain pill, and put away half the bottle with my first sip. I needed solids, too. I found a chunk of cheddar cheese in the fridge and a box of Wheat Thins in a cupboard. The energy I gained from my first three bites of snack food cleared my head, reminded me to set priorities and pace myself.

I called 411. A digital voice gave me the Broward sheriff's main number. I dialed, and another digital voice began to recite a list of options. I took a chance and hit zero. A human connected me to the forensic lab. Let's hear it for us humans.

"Dave Klein, Crime Scene Unit. How can I help you?"

I told him my name, my location, and how I had gotten his name.

"So far, so good," he said. "What do you have?"

I described the duct tape, told him why it was important.

"Can you e-mail me a high-resolution digital image?"

"I haven't photographed it yet," I said.

"Is it stabilized?"

"I don't know what you mean."

"Treated to neutralize the adhesive," he said.

"All I have is the piece of tape, boxed so it won't stick to anything."

"My only open slot is noon tomorrow," he said. "I need to catch a two forty-five Atlanta flight, so the most I can give you is forty minutes. If that doesn't work, we could wait till Thursday."

"Tomorrow's my best day," I said.

He told me to ask for him at the Broward County Court's main desk. He would pull a pass and escort me to his office. "I'll be giving up my lunch hour," he said, "so this will cost you. Tuna on whole wheat, no cheese, from Subway."

I hung up, congratulated myself for getting that far, then told myself to chill. I wanted to hand Monroe County's trash to a Broward scientist and ask for his help in my personal campaign to disprove my jailbird brother's guilt. I was making it incredibly easy for Klein to shove me out his door and slam it on my vigilante ass.

I called Cape Air and waited for an airline clerk to check for space. I would have to drive if I couldn't get a flight, but the clerk found me a seat on a 9:25 A.M. flight with a 10:20 arrival. The return would leave at 2:45, the same time Klein would be leaving for Atlanta.

I made one more call, to Marnie, but it was my turn to reach an answering service. I said, "The solid link in the hangings is the U.S. Navy.

The second-most solid link is the fact that neither Kansas Jack Mason or Milton Navarre have
histories, so it's possible they've been living under
fake names. You might try to find what you can
about Bixby, the city's new photographer. He
helped solve two murders in college. My cynical
side wonders if he isn't one of those glory hounds
who creates problems so he can be first on-scene.
His connection to the Navy, I don't know."

I took the Wheat Thins and cheese to the
porch to stare at the canal, to count ripples in
the water. I caught myself humming "The Boys
Are Back in Town" and forming a mental picture
of Tim knocking back Michelobs in Mac and
Joe's during the several hours prior to Milton
Navarre's death.

That evening I drove to Mangrove Mama's for
a supper on the patio. Crusted snapper, carrots,
and cauliflower. Anne, a lovely server with a
British accent, asked me how long I had lived in
the Keys.

I told her, then asked how she knew that I
lived here.

"In summer months, only locals eat out here
on the patio," she said. "All these visitors save
their money to come to the tropics. Then they
insist on air-conditioning. I don't get it."

My only worry, as I drove from the restaurant
to Little Torch, was that I would draw Wendell
Glavin from his lair and have to endure motor-

head talk and tropical philosophy. His house was dark, but the eerie silhouette of his wet suit spooked me for a moment.

Three too many hangings had brainwashed me.

I watched the sun rise fat and red. It was just me, my Cuban coffee, and the waking world until howling doves and barking dogs broke the peaceful ambience. The brochures never mention bugs and noise. I went inside to shower and dress for the big city.

My wardrobe had taken a hit in the move to Little Torch. All my Levi's were dirty and one pair of khakis wrinkled. I figured bureaucrats would take to wrinkles better than to fishing shorts. Tropical logic told me that an ironed button-down would still their judgment if I wore loafers instead of my deck shoes. It took me ten minutes to find a matched pair of socks.

The box with the duct tape went into my canvas attaché, along with some business cards and a paperback I had bought for porch reading. Its title was **Black and Blue,** like the old Rolling Stones album. I had yet to see page 1, but I hoped for the best.

I started the car, saw Wendell Glavin in my rearview loading his boat for a day on the water. I wanted to back out and go before he crossed the road to quack nonsense and ogle the Shelby. But

I skunked myself by forgetting my cell phone. When I returned to ground level, Wendell was hovering.

"You must have a king-hell starter motor on that monster," he said. "It cranks up almost before you turn the key."

"One time it did, Wendell. I got in one night and looked at the ignition switch. Damn thing came to life, put itself in gear, and drove me home."

He was quick on the uptake: "From which bar?"

"The Full Moon Saloon."

"Oh, right there on United." He gazed across the canal. "That place was before my time, but I heard about it. Look, get a message to Al, the next time you talk to him. I seen a bunch of wild iguanas in the neighborhood. They'll eat every plant on the island. All these shrubs, he paid through the ying-yang, he may want to think about a fence."

"I'll let him know. You going diving today?"

"The **Adolphus Busch** wreck," he said. "I been doing that lately."

"Why the wet suit, Wendell? Isn't the water temperature like bathwater this time of year?"

"It's warm at Looe Key, but the **Busch** is deep and cold. Shit, I felt a raindrop."

"So much for your trip," I said.

"Hell you say, bubba. It doesn't rain underwater. Even if this was big enough to build up seas, the waves don't mess with you sixty feet down. For kayak boys like Al Manning, it's a different story. It's dangerous on the surface."

It came on us fast, a strong one-clouder. An east wind rose and blew the wet almost sideways.

"This can't last," said Wendell. "I'll stand under here, wait it out."

"I gotta go." I slammed the car door.

Wendell had been right about it not lasting. South of Ramrod Key I found a dry highway and blue sky. Traffic was light—gravel trucks, pickups, rented convertibles, and motor homes. As I drove across Sugarloaf Key, the bastard rang. I hate to talk while driving, not for safety's sake as much as not being able to hear inside the Shelby. The window showed 973—Newark. I took the call.

Monty Aghajanian, my FBI pal, could hear the car's engine. "You going somewhere? I wanted to follow up, see if you called Dave Klein."

"I'll be in Lauderdale by noon. Thanks for the tip."

"Driving your hot rod?" he said.

"Only to the airport. I'm flying a puddle-jump."

"The grapevine has it that our man on the island had to bust a deputy on a civil rights squabble. You know anything?"

"His name is Millican," I said. "He's a detective in touch with his inner thug. As it happened,

I found myself on the receiving end of his bad mood."

"No shit. It was you?"

"I'm afraid the newspaper will print details of bruises on my testicles."

"What will you do about it?" said Monty.

"Make the county buy me a hot tub and a boat slip at Ocean Reef."

"When it boils down, don't press the criminal case, Alex. The boys will get into your life more than you ever imagined."

"A nightmare, right?" I said.

"You want my advice, suck it in and tough it out. Settle quick, small, and quiet. Don't talk to the media."

"Consider it taken," I said. "Can I play off your sympathy?"

"I'm granting only partial favors these days. We have a history of your mangy dogs biting my lovely ass."

"This won't require an NCIC search. It's more a gossip request."

"No promises," he said. "Give me a name and town."

"Our new city detective, Beth Watkins, last employed in Marin County."

"Do we wish they all could be California girls?"

"No way. I'm having a hard enough time."

He was quiet a moment. "I'll see what I can do. You may not hear back."

The bastard beeped as the line went dead.

The Shelby surfed pavement undulations across the Saddlebunch Keys as south-side phone poles ticked by like passing time. In my youth I would have wanted that roadside clock to conform to Einstein's theory: the faster you travel, the slower time goes. My two-bit corollary was the faster you live, the longer you live. It was proving less true as I aged.

Perhaps Tim was learning a similar lesson.

I ran a slalom to dodge rough pavement around the long bend of South Roosevelt. Joggers and skaters and walkers wove their paths like braid strands toward Smathers Beach, and shorebirds floated in slow motion above heat in the shallows. A man in dreadlocks on a smoking moped passed me. A small dog rode his handlebar.

I felt a twinge of doubt about flying north. Not that I have a conscience, but something whispered that I should live my life and no one else's.

Forty minutes later, I was in the air.

Air terminals, with their lines, security, everyone staring at each other, tend to shut down my brain. Being aloft wakes it again, churns my thoughts, gives me perspective as well as relief. But my doubt returned. I worried that I had invested too much hope in the duct tape. Lop-sided odds held that the price of my ticket plus seven hours would yield no clues. Professionals had deemed the tape useless. I was a rank amateur with no stake in the outcome, or none that I wished to share. Tim had a stake but no idea how to fight the fight.

In high school, when I heard about mischief or vandalism, cars shot with pellet guns, school bus seats slashed, empty beer cans dumped on a neighbor's lawn, the story almost always found its resolution with the kid in the next bedroom. It worked out to one minor crime per semester. Practical jokes gone wrong, all the time. He was a crap magnet. Guilt ruled his body language. Blame stuck to him like wet leaves to a heel.

I recalled two open windows, a warm breeze, afternoon sunlight in my bedroom. The smell of a neighbor's power lawn mower. I was seventeen, a senior in high school. I had just finished reading **Somebody Up There Likes Me,** an "as told to" autobiography of the boxer Rocky Graziano. Two things intrigued me as I stared at the photo—a movie still—on the paperback's cover. I felt amazed that the man had survived a childhood so different from mine. His months in adult jails, his scramble to survive ugly streets. I wondered about the "as-told-to" process of writing the book, then pondered the idea of writing a book myself. It wouldn't be the same kind. My life up to that point would put a reader to sleep. But fiction would be different. I could invent heroes and jerks, give them odd and dangerous jobs, make up friends and families for my characters. I wondered how I'd describe the mother of a hero or the father of a loser. I imagined having a champion for a sister, an asshole for a brother.

That's when it struck me: I was, indeed, the brother of an asshole.

Before that day, I'd never dared to describe Tim, even to myself, by that term. So much made sense behind the definition, but much more alarmed me. For the first time I projected my brothers into the future. Raymond, the oldest, would find his boring way through life. I would strive to evade boredom, play it straight, enjoy my days as they came. But each time I tried to imagine Tim's destiny I heard the solitary, echoing clank of a cell door. The same sound that had rung so often through the story of Rocky Graziano's delinquent childhood.

I recalled walking down the hall, looking into Tim's bedroom. He was off with friends, so the room was empty. He had only two decorations, both on the wall above his bed. One was an award certificate for a science project, hung upside down with a small bird feather jammed between the frame and the glass. The other was a photo torn from a travel magazine, a serene beach with tall palms, white sand, calm water, and foot-prints at the tide line.

At the Broward County Courthouse on South-east Sixth, I passed through the metal detector, gave the guard a responsible, patriotic "Good morning."

A male receptionist called Dave Klein to escort me inside.

Six minutes later Dave checked my tan, my head wound, then my clothing. He didn't miss a wrinkle. He took the sandwich bag and asked me for a business card.

I dug one out of my canvas attaché bag, handed it to him.

"You're a civilian? I don't believe that fact registered with me."

"I work with the Key West PD and the Monroe County sheriff."

"So do their floor sweepers. Tell me again, who gave you my name?"

I explained Monty, then pulled the candy box from my canvas carry-on. He opened it, sneered at the duct tape.

"You know you've lost chain of evidence, don't you? This is dead info."

"I figured as much. But I thought, if it can't be admissible proof, it could give us a lead, a direc-tion to look for clues the court might accept."

"Well, that's wonderful except it's bullshit," said Klein. "This is from outside Broward. I can't even hold it in my hand without an okay from my supervisor. I need a Monroe case number so I can draw a new Broward tracking number. I need to know where it came from, date, time, all that, and who's handled it. What the hell are you up to, anyway?"

"Just trying to stop crime."

"Here's how we do it. We collect enough valid evidence to convince a tough-minded prosecutor that he won't waste time he'd rather spend at his kid's Little League game. We make a legal arrest, with speeches, procedures, protocol, and tender care. We attempt to send bad guys to jail. It backfires too often. Sometimes it gets twisted by citizens who want to do the right thing. The thing for you to do, now, is go for the door. Take your piece of stickum with you."

"So we can have another sunrise murder tomorrow?" I said. "You have any relatives or friends in the Keys?"

"I have a workload that would blow your mind," he said.

"I don't doubt it. My FBI friend said you get calls from all over. He said you helped the Royal Bahamas Police with a DNA review. You told me you would give me forty minutes. Could you make it ten and see if there's anything here?"

My flattery failed. Klein looked at the Subway

bag, his watch, then pulled out his wallet, extracted a five, and handed it over. "We go by rules in our business for a hundred good reasons. If you had a badge plus proper paperwork, we could approach my supervisor, go for the long shot. Under the circumstances . . . I got to go."

"Thanks for your time."

I had two hours to kill and I wasn't hungry. I was frustrated, but I wasn't ready to start drinking at twenty after twelve. The sit-down lunch at Subway had given me a calming hint. Why not sit in the airport's cool air and read a book?

Who said that the road to hell is paved with good intentions?

I taxied to the airport, went straight to the bar. I looked at the glass after my first sip; it was two-thirds empty. Or, if I wanted to be an optimist, it was one-third full. I hypnotized myself by concentrating on CNN's bottom-screen rolling banner. My second beer was half consumed when someone tapped my shoulder.

Dave Klein stood there, a neutral look on his face. "I started thinking, your name was familiar . . ."

I caught on fast. "I was here three months ago."

"From Monroe County. Okay. We had that situation with a rotten detective."

"You sure did."

"It ended in Monroe," he said. "Did you help bust him?"

"I picked up on his scam. Someone else brought him down."

"I read that summary. Brought him down with a bullet, right?"

"Two crimes collided, yes."

Klein thought to himself, winced once or twice. "Look, we hated the stain that man put on our department. I, for one, appreciate what you did. Maybe I can do you a favor. Truth is, I wish I could do fifteen of them. But there's one catch. So it doesn't come back to haunt me, I need to send my report to an enforcement agency."

"My friend at the FBI?"

"You got it." He held out his hand. "Let me see what I can do. Get me his phone number and address." He put the candy box in his briefcase. "How's that slow and easy life in the Florida Keys?"

"This week it's a big fat lie."

18

FIVE OTHER PEOPLE WAITED to fly south from Lauderdale. I knew the owner of the Goon and Whale gift shop; Sam's friend Captain Turk, who had gone to Titusville to order a new skiff; and an attorney wearing a black suit in summer heat. A muralist had painted a shark's nose, an eye-patched pirate, a parrot, and a reef scene on the Cessna 402 that would wing us home. I loved the idea of commuting in a twin-engine Hawaiian shirt.

After takeoff I again pretended to read and pondered the murder puzzle.

Kansas Jack and Milton Navarre had left the Navy long ago. What, besides their love of saloons and near-simultaneous deaths, had linked them in recent years? For that matter, had they known each other in the past? Who had stood in Dredgers Lane and taken that picture of Pokey Fields? Had Kansas Jack stolen Pokey's teenage heart, or been the hard-on who came later with verbal abuse? Or had he been a family friend or relative? If he and Navarre were connected, as I believed they were, had Pokey known Navarre under a previous name, too? Was he the lover, friend, or relative?

I thought again about the day she walked nude across my living room to kiss my forehead. Had my gentle rejection of her proposition, my words to bolster self-worth, changed her life as I had hoped they might? Had the books I'd loaned informed her of life's positive side, its possibilities beyond the path of perennial victim? Had she lifted herself from the lost existence of swapping sex for approval, learned from mistakes, passed lessons to her own children? Or had she undressed without ceremony and paraded across a hundred rooms to kiss a hundred other men?

Perhaps she recalled our friendship as a turning point.

Or maybe it was a short, forgotten phase in a sad life.

And how did Lucky Haskins fit in? Milton and Kansas Jack had lived at subsistence level while Lucky, a younger, married man, lived in plush comfort. No matter how many details I sifted, only Lucky's davit connected his death to the other two. After discounting my odd theory about Lucky having killed the other two, I had to ask who had been the copycat, Lucky Haskins or his killer?

Finally, one last question begged an answer. With the deaths of two men she might have known, was Pokey now in danger?

The woman across the narrow aisle said, "Enjoying your book?"

I turned my head as little as possible. A red tint to her short brown hair, a pair of half-moon reading glasses perched on her pointed nose.

"I read that one last year," she said.

I checked the cover to remind myself of the title. "It's great, so far."

"I wondered because you haven't turned a page in six minutes."

"Has it been exactly that long?" I said.

"I don't own a stopwatch, sir. It might have been longer."

"I guess my mind escaped the story on the page."

A screwy look crossed her face, perhaps a reaction to my breath. "Mine goes away all the time," she said. "If you want me to stop talking, say so."

"Thanks," I said. "Let's give it a try."

The offended queen: "Is that like shut up?"

I let my silence answer and thought back to my conversation with Gail Downer in Marathon. According to her father, Milton Navarre had bragged on a felony charge he'd dodged in the past, probably under a previous name. Milton had suggested that others were involved. Had the felony gone down in the Keys? Had Kansas Jack, under another name, been a coconspirator? Had Pokey known of the crime, been a bystander or an innocent common-law spouse? Or had she been a felon?

The pilot announced our approach, banked to avoid a huge thunderhead above Calda Channel. I glanced sideways as the woman next to me closed her notebook and saw the word "Information" at the top of Federal District Court letterhead. An indictment in the making. She shuffled the page before I could search for Millican's name.

I paused for a last look at Florida Bay, its small mangrove clumps polka-dotting pastel channels. Brilliant, I thought. I had just spent an entire flight, a transit over some of the most beautiful land and water on the North American continent, dreaming up questions that only dead men could answer.

Each time I fly into Key West, I see something new. A radio tower near Southard and Simonton caught my eye. The spindly one had been replaced by a proboscis that looked like the world's tallest silo. You wonder why Old Island Restoration bothers to dictate historic district standards. If they tried to paint old wood shutters on it, of course, or palm fronds, it would be like dressing R2D2 in a Pilgrim costume. Maybe a barber-pole motif would bring a laugh or two.

Yes, I was carrying a cell phone. We blame

electronic progress as we become addicted to it, though we secretly pray for a storm with selective tornados.

Our landing went quickly, with a short run to the gate. At four o'clock in the heat of summer, a fuselage turns into a tubular oven when the engines stop and the air-conditioning goes away. I paid the price for my rearward seat. The lawyer split first, hurried his dark suit to the cool terminal. By the time I filed off, last in a bumbling line, I had sweated out my shirt.

Walking to the car, I turned on the phone and found two messages.

Monty Aghajanian said, "Expensive gossip for you, bubba. Beth Watkins, real first name Elizabeth, middle name Ann, last employed San Rafael Police Department, Marin County, California. Not popular with her coworkers, a hard-nose, strict rules follower, but reported only two infractions to internal affairs, both egregious. She was nicknamed "the Finger," but not for what you might think. She and her partner were facing down a hyper nutcase. The perp surprised her partner, lifted a pistol to the cop's forehead. Watkins reacted, shot once at the perp. No one fell down, but the perp started shaking his gun like he was trying to unjam it. She couldn't figure out why her shot hadn't hit the bad guy, at least in his neck or shoulder. Her partner got his shit together and jumped the perp, and the two of them got him cuffed. She had shot off the crazy's index finger as he pulled his trigger. Her shot saved her partner's life. She thought the harassment would ease after that, but it didn't. Being a hero didn't change her status. That's why she went job hunting, and she found the Key West opening. Does that help you? I love leaving messages. When you're not there, you can't ask more favors."

The second voice was Gail Downer. "Alex, I cleaned up the trailer a bit this morning, and I found an old Zippo lighter. It's silver and engraved with a date, the word **Nevada,** and four or five sets of initials. I don't know if this interests you, but I thought it weird that a drunk like Milton would own a keepsake in the first place, and especially one that nice." She left me her work number.

I called Bobbi and listened to a recording. After the beep I advised her not to close out Millican's file on Navarre, told her we had a connection stronger than davits, and asked her to call back.

The instant I clicked off, the bastard rang.

"Hey, Alex, Connie in Naples. Touching base with you on that furniture store shoot in Blairsville, Georgia."

"Thanks," I said. "I'm jammed up down here. What's our time frame?"

"The client wants us early Thursday, which

means we both catch flights tomorrow afternoon. I warned him I wasn't sure I could get reservations."

"Us meaning I work with an art director?"

"Us meaning we—you and me," she said. "Objections?"

"Just a massive respect for your husband's gun collection."

"He sold it. Now he's into butterflies."

"Blairsville nice this time of year?"

"Hot days like Florida," she said. "Cool nights like everywhere else."

"Honey, I know what you really want."

"You're so right, Alex. I can't wait to get into a motel room."

"If can't do it tomorrow, is there a rain date?"

"The client wasn't sure about next week."

"Can I call you in the morning?"

"By nine A.M., please."

"I promise."

The woman lived for business trips. For some odd, misguided reason, her husband did not allow television in their home. When we did agency jobs together, she would do the gig and eat meals with me, but that was it. The rest of the time she would hole up in her room with bags of Pepperidge Farm cookies and a **TV Guide.** I once warned her that she might get blisters from clicking the remote. She'd said, "I live for the day."

I didn't want to call Marnie Dunwoody

through the **Citizen**'s switchboard. It took me a minute to locate her number in my phone's list of received calls. She grabbed the second ring but also checked her caller ID. "We can't accept flowers over the phone."

"If I give you a connection between the first two hangings, can I get a favor?"

"You already told me. The solid link is the Navy. And I don't make deals with chronic holdouts who ask me to fly below imaginary radar. Is there a hint of a story in it for me?"

"Yes," I said, "but it's like before."

"Oh, where you don't tell me shit?"

"No, I tell all, but you sit on it until the clues make sense."

"I'm working at home. The gate key's in its usual hiding place."

I drove past Smathers Beach where boardsailors, paragliders, and ultralights mocked laws of physics. It wouldn't surprise me to see some holy fool with Icarus wings coasting above the 1800 Atlantic luxury condos, though not in the heat of late June.

A tall fence and shrubs hid Marnie and Sam's house at the south end of Elizabeth. I parked in front of the small gatehouse, set the fuel shutoff, and brought my shorts so I could shed the khakis. The key was not in its usual spot behind the fifth slat in the fence.

I used my cell to call her again.

Marnie met me at the gate. Her gray T-shirt read LEAVE ME ALONE. I declined coffee so she offered a beer and led me to her first-floor office, the private turf that I'd never seen before. It housed computer gear on a desk module, a swivel chair, a beat-up rattan chair, an overflowing bookcase, and four filing cabinets.

She offered me the rattan chair and plopped into her seat. "Speak."

"Odd, identical objects owned by both Kansas Jack Mason and Milton Navarre."

"Please describe said objects."

"Bobbi found a silver Zippo lighter when she searched Mason's place. It was engraved with a date, several groups of initials, and the word 'Nevada.' I drove to Marathon yesterday and met the stepdaughter of Rudy Downer, the accused man and Navarre's roomie. She was cleaning their trailer, so I asked her to look for anything unusual. She found a Zippo with the same engravings."

"Souvenirs?"

"Maybe so. They could be from Vegas or Reno."

"Does Lewis know about Navarre's lighter?" said Marnie.

"I left a voice mail," I said. "I told her there was a connection, but not what it was. Once they find out, the deputies will probably ask you not to make it public knowledge."

"Tell me more about these dead men with no histories."

"They were handy with tools. Kansas Jack did odd jobs on referral, and Milton Navarre had plumbing skills."

"Anything else?" she said.

"When I talked to Bobbi I held back something. You have to promise—"

"I'll tread lightly, okay?"

"She found a photo in Kansas Jack's stuff. An old picture of a teenage girl standing in front of my house, maybe five years before I bought the house from her father. By then she was living with a Navy man here in town. I spoke with her a few times. Her nickname was Pokey, last name Fields, and Bobbi Lewis knows that."

Marnie wanted to scold me in advance. "Did you do more than speak with her, Alex?"

"I befriended her for a short time, and it wasn't what you're thinking. I don't know her connection to Kansas Jack. He could have been the man she lived with, or a friend of that man, or an enemy. Whatever the relationship, Pokey might provide some background info, even a real name for Kansas Jack Mason. She would have been a student at Key West High in the early seventies."

"If Lewis has her name, she's already ten steps ahead of me. Is that everything?"

I thought again about Gail Downer's recollection of Milton Navarre's not-too-secret felony charge from years ago. "Can I ask you to do some newspaper-type research? On company time, of course."

"The word **research**," she said. "I assume you want ancient history."

"Thirty years ago, give or take. I'm curious to see if any Navy men were arrested by the city or county."

Marnie sneered. "That's like asking if high school kids got caught with cigarettes and gin."

"I don't mean bar-brawl stuff," I said. "I mean felony-level theft or conspiracy."

"So I'm looking for multiple arrests?"

I nodded. "Three or more."

"Are they connected to that last hanging in Monroe County?" she said. "That dead sailor on Truman Annex?"

"You didn't tell me he was a sailor."

"You didn't ask. But I picked up on it when you mentioned the Navy. He was a petty officer assigned to the submarine tender, hung from a flagpole."

"The **Bushnell**?"

"I don't think so. I think the **Bushnell** had been relieved." She shuffled a stack of notes on her desk, found a sheet of yellow paper. "Yes, the **Bushnell** was gone by then. It was the USS **Howard W. Gilmore**."

"A sub tender would be wall to wall with men

who possessed the skills of Kansas Jack and Milton Navarre. Any more details?"

"Let's see . . . last name Evans . . . first thought to be a suicide . . . despondent . . . bad love affair. AWOL at time of death. Oh, hell, I didn't read this far. Several of his fellow crewmen experimented with weights, and proved he couldn't have hung himself alone. It's still on the city's list of unresolved cases."

"Shit."

"What?" she said. "You think the flagpole was connected to these old crimes you want me to find?"

"What year was that hanging?"

" 'Seventy-three, in late January. What date is engraved on those lighters?"

" 'Seventy-three, early January," I said. "Who were the investigating officers?"

Marnie flipped another page, ran her finger down lines of print. "Shit's the word, Alex. Key West Detective Sergeant Chester Millican and Lieutenant Fred Liska."

19

I stood at Marnie Dunwoody's office window and absentmindedly watched a lizard patrol the outside sill. "Chicken Neck must have been in his mid-twenties," I said. "That's young for a lieutenant."

"Maybe he was on a fast track to detective," said Marnie. "Or an old version of that."

"Which forces me to ask why the great detective would be so flaky on Ramrod and refuse to go to Marathon? That morning you came to my house, he was depressed. Hell, he's seen his share of death over the years."

"Hangings are rare," she said, "and the flagpole death is still labeled a cold case. Some detectives see unsolved cases as black marks on their careers. Maybe Kansas Jack reminded him of his past failure."

"But it was Millican's failure, too. Now we have Chicken Neck depressed and Millican defensive at his crime scene, then, two days later, pounding on me and jeopardizing his job. Millican's hyper while Liska sulks."

"Maybe that's how they approached the dead man on the flagpole," said Marnie. "Or better yet, maybe that's the opposite of their actions back then. Liska was eager to solve it and Millican withdrew. Was that about the time Millican left the Keys?"

"Could've been," I said. "But let's not get trapped in overanalyzing."

Marnie tapped the paperwork on her desk. "Reporters love to get hypothetical, Alex. If I take identical lighters with engraved dates coinciding with the flagpole suicide or murder, whatever it was, the Navy connection, and three hangings, something smells like low tide. I've got a page-one story."

"I can see the headline," I said. "THIRTY YEARS, THREE HANGINGS, TWO COPS."

"Can I have that?"

"It would sell one day's newspaper, and you'd never hear another peep about any of it."

"Bullshit," she said. "It would break open the hornet's nest. The rest of the story would tumble out of the palm trees."

"Not in this town. Mouths would slam shut, records would vanish, and your boss would never trust you again."

"The early bird gets the word," she said. "It's a reporter's rule."

"Except this story exists in our minds and nowhere else."

"Don't forget the murderer's."

"Okay, but that makes it almost certain that you won't get scooped. Take a couple more days. When it grows into a real story, the exclusive by-line will be yours."

"Good old 'Watch-and-Wait' Dunwoody."

She joined me at the window. We listened to mopeds on South Street and said nothing for a minute or two. A bunch of Cuban Conch kids in the next yard attacked a Spanish lime tree. One was in the tree, tossing down fruit. Three others stood below, catching it with an upturned umbrella.

"What if it's all bogus and I strike out for the week?" she said.

I shook my head. "Liska's been here all along. He may be your best source, but he's not the issue. Millican left the Keys after investigating a hanging. He comes back to this county where no hangings have occurred in thirty years, and the hangings start again?"

She went to her office chair and plopped down. "Damn."

"I'm the one with sore ribs and back muscles," I said. "Why are you walking funny?"

"They had us kicking a hard bag last night in karate," she said. "The bottoms of my feet are still numb."

"You won't be doing the jitterbug this week?"

"Alex, I couldn't even do the funky air dance. Have you found anything to help your brother with an alibi?"

I shook my head, deciding not to reveal that Tim had been drinking in the same saloon as Milton Navarre the night Milton died.

We agreed to keep digging without spooking Liska. Marnie would research the 1973 hanging, and I would concentrate on my campaign for Tim's innocence.

Possible innocence.

The half hour with Marnie energized my thirst. I started to walk to Louie's Afterdeck but decided I needed a fish sandwich at B.O.'s instead. I parked in the Caroline Street lot and was locking the Shelby when Tanker's friend Francie called to me. She wore spray-on biking shorts, a sleeveless top with a puppy's face on each breast, and two-dollar flip-flops. She hugged me like a lost lover, with a little hip-bump and a smooch on the cheek.

"Stay clear of Tanker," she said. "He's in the Turtle Kraals in a mopey fuckin' mood."

"In the restaurant?"

"Up in the Tower Bar. He thinks he's Dylan or Darwin or some damn intellectual. I gotta go find a twenty-year-old who treats a girl nice."

My curiosity won out. I climbed the stairs. Seven people sat around the bar. At a table near the railing, overlooking the harbor, Tanker Branigan had his feet on a chair, the sun on his face, a shot and a beer next to his huge arm. He saw me arrive and pushed a chair my way. "Welcome to join me in my max-overview, Rutledge. It's a three-screen drive-in and this feature's called **Key West Bight.** One of those skies, if you don't like what you see, turn your head."

I wanted shade but the low, late-day sun rendered the broad umbrella useless. The bartender delivered two beers and two shots and took Tanker's empties. I sniffed the tequila and put it back on the table. "I ran into the little wild one on her way out."

"We're a gang, not a team. Same toilet and separate ways." His voice sounded like a broken bottle scraping on a concrete wall. He pointed northward, beyond the dinghy corral. "What was that building over there?"

"Fish house, sponge shed, fuel dock, bait shop," I said. "I've seen pictures of it back to 1906. When I hit town it was Young's Diesel Repair and Admiral Busby's charters. A boatbuilder was in there for years. A few years ago it was an art gallery. That old crane hoisted turtles off boats, back when catching was legal."

"Who owns it?"

"The city."

" 'Bout time for them to rip it down and put up a Mickey D's, isn't it? I mean, the last known fishnets on the island are decorations at Schooner Wharf."

"Did I interrupt a bad mood?" I said.

"The biggest one in a while."

"You pissed about progress?"

He shook his head. "My genius idea to boost your brother's self-esteem? I blew it."

"It already happened?"

He tossed back his shot, waved the glass at the bartender, waved two fingers with his other hand. "Please don't play dumb. I get enough of that from Timmy."

"After our talk on Sugarloaf, I wondered . . . You put a lot of creativity into it."

"That's just it. I was too interested in my own fun, my set design, to leave an obvious trail back to Tim. I used his car and drove it into the road-side dirt. As if anyone wanted to bother with tire tracks."

"If it's any consolation, I heard that a couple of deputies saw Millican on the star and kept on going. They pretended not to notice him."

Tanker wasn't cheered. "Anyway, I was hoping they'd bust Tim so he'd have to work his way out of it. Now, no news is bad news. There's nothing in the **Citizen,** so they aren't going to pursue it. I haven't been around long, but I know how it works."

A server put fresh shots of tequila in front of each of us. I hadn't touched my first one, so I drained it and let the kid take the empty.

"Wasn't your plan not to get him arrested?" I said.

Tanker hissed an exhale. "No test, no loss of esteem, no lesson learned."

"You can't dream up another one? Maybe a bit lighter than kidnapping a cop?"

"Easy to say, tough to do. With that one, I put revenge motivation right in his hand. If I come up with something else, it can't be contrived."

"Did cute little Francie help?" I said.

"The superglue was her idea. I let her handle it, so to say."

"The blow-up doll was brilliant."

"Ah, Matilda. Sweet Matilda. She cost me a hundred dollars. Three winos clipped her, and I suspect they each had a few dates with her. They had her hidden under a bridge, but they were scared of getting busted."

"She was back on the job yesterday."

"The past tense is perfect. They left her on Flagler, like no one knows how to slim-jim a cruiser's rear door. I got her at the house, sitting on top of our TV, wearing a grass skirt and coconut boobs. Saved myself a hundred bucks."

"Taking all these risks, it's like you're testing yourself," I said.

"Just honing my street skills. Some people

worry about the difference between right and wrong. I worry about the difference between wrong and fun."

"I believe P. J. O'Rourke said that first."

"Whatever." He grabbed my tequila and shot it down. "It proves I can read."

We listened to a recording of the military's call to colors, then watched sunset. I wondered about this man who collected old postcards, revered the past, disliked change. I wanted to ask him where he was from, what he had done, how he made his living. The kinds of questions you don't ask in Key West. From the look of him, I thought construction or factory work. I saw no reason why a laborer couldn't become absorbed in history. Or practical jokes on the police.

"You mind if I ask you something?" I said. "It might put me over the top for Key West rudeness."

"How can I afford to live here and not work?"

"My exact words."

"I proved inside of seven years that the definition of 'entrepreneur' is a lazy schmuck with one brilliant idea."

"Not so lazy that you didn't take action?" I said.

"True. The ugliest part of a University of Michigan football scholarship is you have to do menial campus jobs to pay back the administrative wallet. I slung cafeteria chow for my whole second freshman semester. Then I started walking the streets of Ann Arbor, wondering if there wasn't a better way. I befriended a drunk in his mid-thirties who owned a tow truck. He'd lost most of his best clients, the ones who own those permit parking lots where violators are towed. I quit school, became his partner, busted my ass, rebuilt the business he'd almost destroyed, and put us both in the money. Two years into it, he was a worse drunk and not a bit grateful, so I bought him out. I became a tycoon by mistake. Crowded streets, not enough legal parking, kids with give-a-shit attitudes and Daddy's credit cards. I lived on the cheap, didn't piss away my bread on booze and drugs, paid most of my taxes, and made a bundle. I sold the business to a national outfit that started to specialize in college towns and more than tripled my fortune." He pulled a plastic bank card from his front pocket. "Now me and Mr. Schwab are loose in the world. Even if I make a pig of myself, I won't have to go back to work for at least six or seven years."

I looked around the bar, now full. The woman I'd pissed off on the airplane sat there, bobbed her pointed nose at two men who looked straight and hard. I pegged them as FBI. They all wore upscale sports clothes, like dress-down day at the office. The men drank from rocks glasses, and she sipped an up martini.

"You're a towing tycoon," I said.

"Yep, was. Now I'm a sit-on-my-ass tycoon, but that'll get old. Maybe I'll get into the boat-building business." Tanker waved again at the bartender.

"I gotta go," I said. "Long drive to Little Torch."

"Fuck that," he said. "You got this beautiful view, and you want to go up where they're murdering people? Hang here, get your head right, you can crash on the couch. Tim's never there."

"Was he with Teresa last night?"

"All I know is he wasn't sprawled on my sofa," said Tanker. "The house smelled better than usual this morning."

"Thanks for the offer. I need to be up the Keys."

"What's with need?" he said. "Did you join a vigilante group?"

I shook my head. "Zip for clues, zip for motives. Everyone's waiting for another snuff to happen. I'm curious enough to wonder who and why."

He tilted his beer to straight up and down, then said, "I'm glad somebody's on duty. I got the check."

Ten minutes later I was outbound in light traffic. The bastard rang.

Bobbi said, "I can tell by the noise that you're

in your hot rod. Where are you going, to snoop some more?"

"I'm two minutes from your house, behind a slug with his ball-cap biography on his back-window package tray."

"Tell me why I shouldn't have your ass grabbed for obstruction of justice."

"Wait a minute," I said. "You gave me that duct tape. Does that make you my accomplice?"

"I'm not talking duct tape. I'm just leaving Marathon."

"So you took my advice?"

"You were right about Millican," she said. "He closed out the Navarre case on Saturday morning. Liska told me to reopen it. I drove up and found Gail Downer. That's why I said snooping."

"That takes me off the hook. It was a closed case when I found her first. All I did was ask her not to throw anything out. She called me about the Zippo."

"I don't know whether to bless you or curse you."

"Split the difference," I said. "Stop by Little Torch and jump me."

"Not tonight, dear. I have pain-in-the-ass reports to write."

"That's a disappointment but a relief, too. I was afraid my brother's situation had come between us. Did you ever learn the details of Millican's kidnapping?"

"That's a weird one, Alex. He hasn't shared particulars with either the feds or Internal Affairs."

"Was Lucky Haskins ever in the Navy?"

"It's another good question and I don't know the answer. I will say this. Guys his age, you don't find many with military backgrounds. They didn't have a war to fight."

Wendell Glavin was raking pea rock around his mailbox when I turned in to Manning's driveway. I loaded my arms with groceries so he would take the hint, allow me to lug them upstairs rather than stand and chat. The ploy failed. "Ahoy!" he shouted from across the street.

"Humid day today, Rutledge," he said.

I didn't want to say, "Duh."

"I know, it's always humid in the summer."

I nodded and thought about "ahoy."

"But when the air smells like fish," he said, "it's really humid."

"Wendell, were you in the Navy?"

"Almost, bubba. I grew up in Green Cove Springs, near St. Augustine. We had that mothball fleet, World War II ships harbored in the St. Johns River. My pals and me, we'd sneak aboard the ghost boats and play Okinawa Attack every summer. Hell, we found parts of uniforms, manuals, and what all. We were swabbies and commanders and gunners. We dreamed of going to sea, and for us poor kids, it was like a free summer camp."

"Expensive playground," I said.

"They should've turned it into an amusement park. Who were they fooling with that mothball ridiculousness? In the end they torpedoed all those ships in sub exercises. Sent them to that big trash can and toilet that poses as a major ocean."

I started up the stairs. "Sounds like the catch-22 of retirement, eh, Wendell?"

"You bet, Rutledge. You think you're parked and then you're sunk. I'm not going to fall for it. I'm a true believer in 'Use it or lose it.' You won't ever see me slow down. My dream is to die in the saddle."

Or choke to death on clichés.

Tim did me a favor when he rapped on the kitchen door at two in the morning. I had zonked on a sofa with all the lights on, my head jammed at an angle to my spine and my face wedged into a rank throw pillow. By morning I would have been a walking, wheezing hockey stick.

Behind his watery-eyed version of Lost Black Sheep, Tim looked more stoned than drunk. "Gotta put paradise behind me," he said. "I wanted to say good-bye in person."

"So the new girl and new job . . . down the dumper?"

"Maybe someday I'll come back under brighter clouds."

"Or no clouds at all?" I said.

"Too much to hope for."

"You okay for gas cash?"

"I'm set."

"Anyone expecting to be paid back?"

"Let's end this on a high note. Tanker said he never wanted to hear about it again, but he'll get a money order inside a week."

"Where to next?" I said.

"Ten feet the far side of the Florida state line. From there, the idea of sawing wood and pounding nails appeals to my stress-repellent nature."

"You want one piece of nonjudgmental brotherly advice?"

"I'll risk it," said Tim.

"Top of the Keys, go left on 997. Take it to U.S. 27 and take 27 past Ocala before you get on I-75."

"There's got to be a reason . . ."

I nodded. "Not a single toll booth."

"I can afford a few—"

"They use cameras these days," I said. "Not a single picture of your car."

He started down the stairs. "I never would've thought of that."

There but for a shake of chance went I.

Ahead of the qualifiers I always used to describe him, the anger, his ratshit luck, his hollow self-respect, I loved my brother. If you told me he could kill a man, I might punch you in the nose.

Then I would think about it.

20

AT 6:55 WEDNESDAY MORNING a trash-collection truck's squealing brakes hauled me out of a dream. I tried to rewind it, but saw only sea grass and pinfish without clear blue water or the nude woman. I concentrated on the underwater hum for maybe a minute, then the truck, having U-turned at the deadend, rumbled the length of Keelhaul Lane, rattled the headboard, and that was it.

As I carried my coffee to Al's porch for a blast of sunlight, I heard a vehicle stop under the house. A car door slammed shut. I pictured a mob of people climbing the stairs, coming to me with bad news, threats, problems, horoscopes for all I knew. Millican with a ball bat and reenergized attitude; Tim with a twelve-pack, a changed mind, and a two-hour apology; even Bobbi Lewis looking for just the right morning man. For the traffic I drew, I could have built a booth near the pavement and peddled lemonade, grubstaked a calming career. Better, I should have built a guardhouse.

With all the possibilities, the last person I expected was my ex-lover, Teresa Barga, but I knew the top of her head before I saw her face. I opened the door and sensed that she was leaning inward for a hug. I didn't know why she had come, but it sure as hell involved Tim and a comfort hug wasn't in me.

The look on her face prompted me to say, "Is he dead or alive?"

"He's alive and unhurt so far," she said.

I stepped back to let her in. She had dressed in a hurry, not for work. She wore nylon shorts, tennis shoes, and a gray T-shirt. Her hair was tucked under a Panama Jack visor.

"Did he really stop to say good-bye?" she said.

"Yep."

"He didn't make it off the Keys. His car quit running in Tavernier at four A.M. A deputy stopped to help and ran his tag."

"The computer had him for the credit card?" I said.

"It went in yesterday. They called me three times looking for him. Bobbi Lewis didn't tell you?"

"Must have slipped her mind," I said. "Tim loved that old Caprice wagon, but he said it would break down when he least needed it to happen. Coffee?"

"It wasn't because he was your brother."

"That the deputy ran his tag?"

"You know what I mean."

"That he passed bad plastic and his car broke down?"

She shook her fists with frustration. "That I slept with him, goddammit. You're making this harder than it has to be. I liked him for being him and it had nothing to do with you, which is not to say that I ever disliked doing it with you."

"Draw your brakes, Teresa. Coffee?"

"Whatever," she said. "I blew our affair, I admit it. And I apologize—if that makes any difference. But being with Tim wasn't some freaky attempt to substitute him for you."

"We went through this two days ago." I filled a cup for her and topped off mine. "Were you his phone call from jail?"

"He didn't know any lawyers' names," she said. "He asked me to pick one and call."

"Did you?"

"Not yet."

"Did he want me to post bond?"

"He said not to tell you. Or not to bother asking. Something like that."

"Did you have a specific reason to look into his past?"

She bit her lip. "I was afraid you'd hear about that."

"I'm not saying it wasn't a smart move."

"He spoke English like a college grad and Spanish like a punk," she said. "I wondered where he'd picked up his second language."

"Or else you knew?"

"Or else I knew."

"Did your feelings change when you learned about his jail time?"

"Even more than before," she said, "I wanted him to be happy."

"I wonder if he's ever felt that."

She fiddled with her coffee cup, then looked at me intently. "Are **you** happy?"

"How do you define the word?" I said. "It's like 'handsome' or 'rich.' At best it's an estimation. Outside of recent complications, I think I'm content. But isn't that a question most often asked by unhappy people?"

"I don't know," she said. "It's asked by me right now and I'm pretty damn unhappy. I want him back in my house."

"You might have to wait a while," I said. "If he's on parole, they won't let him post bond. They'll nail him for a violation and take him back to Pennsylvania to serve out his sentence. Watkins said that he'd knocked down thirty-one months of a five-year boogie."

"Which leaves two years and five months," said Teresa. "For using a bad credit card?"

"No, for the parole violation. It comes before he gets tried in Florida. Come to think of it, I never got a clear idea about that card, whether it was stolen or counterfeit or whatever."

"Can Liska stop the violation process?"

"I doubt it. If Tim didn't tell the arresting deputy that he's on parole, maybe his lawyer can make the credit card disappear before it snowballs."

"Like get the charges dropped?"

"Something like that. This county's pretty slick when rules need readjustment. Are you on good terms with the county's media liaison?"

"We're both called public-information officers."

"Perception management has many titles."

"I know, it's word spin. The Tiltin' Hilton is now the Duval Inn."

"Can you get Detective Millican's home address?"

"She'll give it to me in a heartbeat."

"Heartbeats are good."

"I saw you noticing," said Teresa. "I left home so fast, I forgot a bra. Since I'm getting the address, can I come with you?"

I weighed my desire for a witness against the improbability of danger.

"Alex, I'll drive."

"Before we leave," I said. "I'll loan you an overshirt."

But for two upended garbage cans near the road-way, and in strong contrast to the late Milton Navarre's dumpy trailer less than four miles away, Chester Millican's elevated home on Sombrero Beach Road appeared stylish and luxurious. A silver Chrysler sedan nosed out from under the house. We parked on green pea rock—Teresa called it a Cuban lawn—and followed a brick walkway to concrete stairs on the north side.

His voice boomed down from the landing. "Can I help you, asshole? Oh, sorry, ma'am. I didn't see you back around the corner." He waved an open beer at me. "Who's she, your reporter buddy?"

"Teresa Barga," I said. "The city's PIO."

"Ah, Ms. Barga," he said. "I heard about you, too. What do you people want?"

Teresa hissed through her teeth. "Fuck this, Alex. Let's go."

Millican was shirtless, his broad chest covered by hair the same color but longer than his crew cut. "I bet you're here for horse trading," he said. "I heard an hour ago that someone named Timothy's in county custody."

"Maybe I can shorten your time in the barrel," I said.

He wiggled his bottle as if testing for dregs. "And his too, right? I doubt you can do either one. Come on up to the palace."

His kitchen and living room area smelled of socks and eucalyptus, both failing to mask the foul air of closed-up boredom. Two dead goldfish floated in a three-quart bowl on a shelf near the door. The furniture was designer quality, the TV wide as a coffee table. He had muted the Weather Channel. A stack of DVD boxes looked ready to tumble off a footstool. The only good thing about the room was the AC setting—pleasantly cool, not the one step above hard frost so common to indoor Florida.

Millican became the perfect host: "All I can offer is Coors that I forgot to put on ice before daybreak, but it went in an hour ago. It might be cold now."

Teresa shook her head.

"Pass," I said. "I need breakfast first."

Millican dropped his empty in the sink, took a new beer from the fridge, and pointed at the television. "That man is Jim Cantore, and he has redefined the American baseball cap. His brims are perfect semicircles. He could be standing in Galveston or up in Savannah, broadcasting into the teeth of a hurricane, telling the nation and the world about wave height and Safir-Simpson numbers, and that cap brim, his fine roll, would never flutter, never waver. I admire that even more than his perfect tan. I think the 'Cantore Roll' should be the standard against which all cap brims are judged."

Teresa set her eyes on Millican. "How do you feel about perfect justice?"

He stared at Cantore for about fifteen seconds, then said, "Does the city have an interest in this case, young lady?"

"Young lady?" she said.

"Ma'am?"

"Ms. Barga was fine two minutes ago."

"Got it. I acquiesce to the modern woman. Is this a crusade to free up your squeeze?"

"I prefer to call him my gentleman friend."

Millican chuckled with no trace of humor. "I didn't answer you, and you didn't answer me."

"Can I butt in here?" I said.

"Sure," said Millican. "The woman and I were just winding down our match. Now you'll ask me to prevail upon my daughter and her husband to drop charges against your brother. I think they did that after he showed up three days ago and paid them back in cash. Your brother's problem is with the bank that issued the credit card, Rutledge, but you knew that before you arrived."

"It might help if your son-in-law claimed it was a mistake from the start."

Millican smiled like a man getting an award. "What's in it for me?"

"If there's a civil rights case, I back off."

"Which I can't believe you'd be stupid enough to press. What else have you got?"

I shook my head.

He produced a cynical sneer. "Okay, I'll start. Your brother and a woman kidnapped me. A modern woman with exemplary wrist action."

"Tim didn't do it," insisted Teresa. "He was with me."

Millican held up his hand. "At worst that's half true. But let me finish, please. It's only a matter of time before they prove he did it. The FDLE can't wait to find the ski masks the perps wore, because not many people in Florida make frigid-weather fashion statements. Once the feds grab the case, the credit card will get lost in the shuffle. What kind of car does the kid drive?"

"Caprice wagon," I said. He could find out on his own.

Millican nodded. "Those wagons come from the factory with roof racks installed. He had that gold star tied on top of the car, except he had to stop on the highway and tighten his knots because the whole thing started to flutter and shake when we got up to speed. I was blindfolded, but I could hear fine. This is information I gave that morning. It'll also match the vehicle they impounded this morning."

"You said Tim was with a girl," said Teresa.

"I did," said Millican.

"You were blindfolded."

He glanced at Teresa's forearms, then lifted his eyes to hers. "I could tell by the size of her hands and the way she moved them. How do you think she got my dick into that plastic doll?"

Teresa bounced back: "Did she use spray starch?"

Millican paused with that one, then turned to me. "You take chemistry in school?"

"One year. I forgot it after the final exam."

He leaned against a kitchen counter. "Doesn't matter anyway. They hadn't invented cyanoacrylate adhesive when you were in school."

"Superglue?"

"And superglue remover. Gamma butyrolactone, isopropyl alcohol, and acetone. Being roped to a star was nothing but bad theater, and haven't we all wanted to show our ass to morning traffic. After all these years in police work, you get the warm and fuzzies mooning commuters. But the chemicals that the hospital nurse smeared on my dick to get it loose got my attention like she'd rammed a sharp bamboo shoot up the slit. Between you two and me, I feel the pressing need to share this. Some of that chemical stew went up my pipe. I still bleed when I drain the lizard. Is this too graphic for you, ma'am?"

Teresa turned to me. "Alex, did you have bleeding after you got kicked in the balls on Saturday?"

"Still do, Teresa. My attorney asked me the same question."

Millican knocked back a swig, licked loose beer from his lip. "I shiver with fear. You know your good buddy Liska can't be sheriff forever, don't you?"

The wall phone rang. Millican raised his beer to toast the sound of it, and leaned back to grab the receiver. I turned to see Teresa averting her eyes from his full-frontal belly button. Gritting her teeth, she scanned the kitchen, the mess, burns on the countertop.

Millican's side of the conversation was "Yo" and five or six grunts. He hung up and put a smug look on his face. "They found fiber strands on the roof rack of the Caprice. Matches the rope used to tie me to the star. It's fun to connect evidence when it works in your favor."

I wondered why rope samples had made it from the Lower Keys to Tavernier so quickly, and who had worked the microscope. My face betrayed me.

"Gotcha," he said. "You're thinking the rope was used for the nooses?"

"Crossed my mind."

"Negative match, you'll be glad to hear. It disappoints me sure as shit, because I had him for the snuffs and still do. Of course, the star part kills your reason for making a deal. That's all out of my hands."

"Why do you live in Marathon?" I said.

"I love it here. It's clean. I can't imagine how you people live on that funky island at the end of the road. Why do you ask?"

"I'd think a man like you, with your professional background, your accomplishments, wouldn't enjoy anything about this county."

Millican looked out a window. "The great thing about the Florida Keys, you're free to design a lifestyle to your own taste."

"And your ethics?" I said.

He shook his head. "If you didn't bring them with you, you're shit out of luck."

"When we met at the Navarre crime scene you said, 'You don't see hangings that often, unless they're suicides in a locked room.' Was this your first nonsuicidal hanging?"

"We had a bit of everything up north," said Millican. "I got up there in time for some racial unrest. Let's say I might have seen maybe three."

"How about prior to your time up north?"

"There was no prior."

"No other hangings?" I said.

"Never."

"Not in Key West on the Navy base?"

His face froze with his mouth hung open. His thumbnail fiddled with the paper label on the bottle. After he inhaled and exhaled a few times, his eyelids sagged, his gaze went to the floor, his index finger pointed at Teresa. "Did she dig up some dirt?"

"She doesn't know what we're talking about."

"I learned a good lesson back then, in the Nixon years, Rutledge. For my money it still applies. Believe half of what you know and none of what you think."

"Good one," I said. "Especially for a seasoned detective. None of that Jack Webb 'just the facts' bullshit. You want crime solutions, you visit a palm reader, if you can find a parking spot. Fortune-tellers are big in the Keys."

He belched. "You're getting off track. We about through with this chat?"

"I think you pressured Liska to give you a job. I think he compromised by assigning you Marathon. He didn't want you running into anyone in Key West who knew shit from thirty years ago."

"Could be," said Millican. "But I just ran out of time for yakking. You best hustle down the road before I kick your shit again and claim you broke in here without an invitation. You can leave that one with me, if you want to. She's got a butt like a big flower waiting to be plucked, but I guess I don't need to tell you that."

Teresa steeled her face and shook her head.

"When this gets sorted out," I said, "I hope you wind up plucking twangers."

Millican raised his thick index finger. "Hold on a sec." He snatched a pair of delicate-looking reading glasses from the counter—drugstore specials—put them to his eyes, then reached to the wall phone. He pressed an audio monitor and a speed-dial button. His belly muscles tightened. The flab ratio was lower than I'd suspected.

After the dial beep melody, a man's growling voice came from the phone's speaker: "Yo, hot man. Speak."

"Skinny, you still doing big watercolors?" said Millican.

"Every now and then. I got problems with cheap competition this year."

"What kind of prices you get these days?"

"Gold Coast, I quote eight," the man said. "Where you live, I make a delivery, I get a tan, eat shrimp off the boat . . . I'd come down to three. You got a wall you need covered?"

"About to have one," said Millican. "I'll get back."

The connection went silent.

"I'll let you read between the lines," said Millican. "He's never held a paintbrush in his life." He hit the monitor again and another speed number. "Lemme make one more call."

I glanced at Teresa. She was still frowning, staring, shaking her head.

A woman's voice answered: "Department of

Homeland Security. How can I help you . . . Mr. Millican?"

"Is Leslie Dobbs in the office?"

"One moment, please."

Almost immediately a man with a high-pitched voice said, "Chester."

"Les, I heard you took a transfer," said Millican. "I wanted to update my phone list."

"False alarm," said the man. "The wife likes Broward, don't ask me why. You holding back the refugees?"

"We're doing our damn best."

"On Duval Street?"

Millican faked a laugh, "Too crowded. Too many of your people down there hitting on the Czech and Russian shopgirls."

"Gotta go," said Agent Dobbs.

Millican punched an off button and turned to me. "For thirty years I worked where a man isn't a man until he's shoved a pistol barrel into somebody's mouth. I made and kept friends on both sides of the fence." He shook his bottle at me. Beer blew out of the spout and splattered my shirt. "There's not much I fear, take my word for it. And take it the fuck out of my house."

Teresa couldn't get to the door fast enough.

Millican checked her legs and lowered his voice. "Your brother's been in custody less than five hours. Didn't take you long, Rutledge."

"You could've told me that old hanging case was closed and forgotten," I said. "You made a mistake calling up your heavy artillery."

Millican's jaw tightened, his eyes turned cold. "Don't think for an instant I wouldn't commence firing."

21

IN OUR RUSH TO confront Chet Millican, Teresa and I hadn't cracked her car windows. The Grand Am had become an oven bursting with a fresh hatch of allergens. I opened the passenger-side door, rolled down the window, waited for the heat shimmers to dissipate, and kept an eye out for bottles flung from above.

If Teresa's face was a message, I also needed to watch for flung daggers.

I shared her distaste for the man, but I hadn't been the one making suggestive remarks for twenty minutes. If she'd wanted me to punch Millican's nose to defend her honor, tough rats. We hadn't been there to boost our self-images. We wanted information, or at least I did, the cost be damned. By my opinion, she had done enough of her own tarnishing in the past few months to nullify any defense I might have attempted.

We braved the hot upholstery. She started the

engine, flipped the AC to high, put it in reverse, and pressed the gas pedal before the transmission engaged. The gear engaged a half-second later. We snapped backward, scattering green gravel, and just missed colliding with a pickup passing in the street. She almost struck the trash barrels as she repeated her error in drive. A fat raindrop splatted the windshield, followed by several more—preludes to the squall that hit a moment later but did little to drop the car's inside temperature. Teresa's also remained near boiling.

"Did he piss you off so badly that I have to suffer?"

No response.

I rolled up my window. "I flunked my adult mind-reading class, Teresa. How did I upset you?"

"The way you phrase things."

"Things?"

"You said, 'She doesn't know what we're talking about,' and Millican took your word for it. Am I wallpaper?"

"I'll tell you what it was, right now, down to the last detail. That wasn't the time to do it, and it wasn't about Tim."

"It's all about Tim. You think your brother killed two men."

"I want to think that he didn't—"

"That's a bullshit way to put it, Alex. 'I want to think' means you've already devised a scenario and made up your mind to believe in it."

"Look, Millican coughed up a theory on Saturday before he crossed the double-yellow. He connected the credit card to the first two hangings. That's how cops think, and his timeline wasn't outlandish. I didn't know how to disprove it, and I knew it was only a matter of time before I was eliminated as a suspect. Then Tim would drop into the soup."

After a fat pause she said, "Did you think to ask the accused?"

"I was recovering from injuries. I wasn't in touch with him."

"You couldn't reach him through me?"

"I was working through it, trying to be less pissed off."

She kept her gaze ahead. "You want revenge for the way I left you, and he gets to pay the price."

"I don't think like that. I've never seen a future in running backwards."

"Bullshit again," she said. "Your anger with me was stronger than your desire to learn your brother's alibi."

I wondered for a moment if she hadn't called it right.

Teresa took a few seconds to absorb my lack of response. She hit the brakes, turned left sharply, and skidded to a halt in someone's driveway. The rain poured down harder.

"Good driving in the wet," I said. "You've got

every right to be angry, but there's no sense in dying when it's me you want to kill."

"You're right, Alex. Why should I waste energy? I can hire Tim to kill you. That's what you think, isn't it? Someone put him up to all this."

"You're putting words in my mouth without giving me—"

"Get your ass out of my car."

I pulled the handle, cracked the door. Rain blew onto my lap. I pulled the door closer. "I could've been in Georgia," I said.

"What does that have to do with getting your ass—"

"I'm here because you asked for help," I said. "If you hadn't shown up at my house two hours ago, I could have called Connie in Naples and taken a photo job nine hundred miles from here. By two o'clock I'd be leaving baggage claim in Atlanta instead of walking the highway in a downpour. Give me back my damned shirt."

My phone rang. I knew the number. Carmen Sosa, my Dredgers Lane neighbor.

"Can I take this?" I said.

Teresa gave me a sarcastic "be my guest" wave.

"Your tenant is the neighbor from hell," said Carmen. "Is this a bad time?"

"It's a bad week. I'm fighting to have a life. What's up?"

"He's thrown loud parties the last two nights,

almost until dawn. I think he's meeting drunk girls in bars and dragging them back to your place. He had a screamer this morning, or else she was having trouble in the bathroom. She sounded like a jungle cat in high heat. One of those new homeowners on Fleming told my daddy that he was going to turn you in for an illegal rental."

"They'll have to prove he's given me money."

Carmen didn't respond, which meant she hadn't heard what she'd hoped to hear.

"Okay," I said. "Is that all?"

"I don't know how to tell you this."

"Go ahead, Carmen. I'm a big boy."

"There's blood all over the kitchen and bathroom floors," she said. "A couple of stains on the walls."

"No body parts or dead people?"

"No, and no tenant either."

"I'll evict him as soon as I can."

When I clicked off, Teresa said, "Don't get out of the car. I was being an asshole."

A couple of minutes later, driving toward Key West on U.S. 1, Teresa said, "What was the Navy-base hanging?"

"Marnie found **Citizen** articles about a dead sailor from over thirty years ago. It was a suspected suicide that evolved into suspected murder, but never solved."

"Was Liska a city cop by then?" she said.

"He and Millican were the investigating officers. Millican was Liska's boss."

"Is this getting complicated?"

Flashing red and blue lights came on behind
us. I looked around. Deputy Billy Bohner was
waving the Grand Am to the curb.

I said, "More with each passing hour."

Bohner held his cell phone to one ear while he
stared at his computer monitor. Teresa had pulled
alongside a wooden barrier in front of a condo
construction site. He was making us wait, pre-
tending to check out Teresa's car with the DMV.

"Have you got your phone with you?" I said.

Teresa reached toward a canvas cosmetics bag.

"Call your boss," I said. "Tell him where you
are and give him Deputy Bohner's name."

Her hand froze. "I can't," she said. "I called in
sick. I'll get fired."

I dug my phone from my pocket and punched
in Liska's office number. Liska's secretary told me
he'd gone to lunch. She wouldn't give me his cell
number. I rang Bobbi Lewis and got shuffled to
the voice mailbox. I said, "No Jokes rousting
me," and hung up.

When he finally approached the Grand Am,
Bohner remained aft of the driver's-side door as if

dealing with two armed lunatics. He tapped on the roof. "License and—"

"Don't even start, Bohner," I said.

"I want four hands on the dashboard," he bellowed.

The dashboard surface temp was probably 150 degrees. I held my splayed hands just above the surface and said, "You've got a couple of kids to put through college."

"What kind of threat is that?" he said.

"You haven't known Millican for nine weeks."

"He's a better man than you'll ever be," said Bohner.

"In the world of dirty cops, but that's not your world, Billy. I'm not on administrative leave for fucking up, and Millican is. Do you have some great desire to send your eighteen year career down the toilet?"

No answer. I'd made my cast and the fish was circling.

"You want to risk your retirement for a bad apple, it's your choice, Billy."

"I'm a long way from—"

"Two college educations need cash flow."

Another silent pause. I'd set the hook and brought him to the boat.

"Has Millican asked you to account for your whereabouts last Thursday before dawn?"

"Short memory, Rutledge. I was on patrol."

"Between Ramrod and Marathon?" I asked. "Was anyone with you, anyone who can vouch for your minute-by-minute activities?"

No answer.

"Has anyone thought to ask Millican to account for himself during those hours?"

"Now you're in the outfield," said Bohner. "Your license, registration, and proof of insurance, ma'am?"

"No damn way," said Teresa. "I'm not part of your game. I'm going to start my car and drive home."

My opinion of Teresa edged slightly upward.

"Deputy, I've got no choice," I said. "I'm just the passenger. I suggest you go home and think about the stretch between your job and your loyalty to Millican."

The Seven Mile Bridge was like a game of leapfrog. Idiots passing one or two cars, ducking back in line to avoid oncoming traffic, which, up ahead, also looked like another game of leapfrog. I imagined all the postcards that would be mailed back to hometowns: "We cheated death on U.S. 1. We lived it up on Duval."

"Tim's bust this morning in Tavernier," I said. "Who was the arresting officer? Anyone we know?"

"Chris Ericson."

"He should've recognized my name."

"How would that have helped?" said Teresa.

"I guess not at all. He was just doing his job."

"Where in Marathon was that second hanging?" she said.

"Right over there." We were passing the trailer court on the Atlantic side. "Back toward the water. It's a slum that the drive-through tourists never see."

"Sounds like the county commission's vision of affordable housing," said Teresa.

"You just gave me an idea."

Information listed eight CPAs in Marathon. The operator found Downer and Company, so I dialed in but reached a recording. I identified myself and started to ask Gail to call me regarding Milton Navarre.

She picked up before I completed my sentence. "Hey, Alex. How's it going?"

"Sideways, I think. That makes me an optimist this week. When you cleaned out that trailer, did you find Navarre's business records or personal files?"

"Hardly enough to matter," she said. "One expandable file with warranty certificates and coupons. It's in a garbage bag in the trunk of my car."

"How about a property title or purchase agreement?"

"There was a brown envelope with a broker's

address on it, but I didn't open it. I'm with a client right now. You want me to look when I get a chance and call you back?"

"I'd rather pay for the client's time and have you look right away. It's kind of important."

No response.

"Sorry, Gail," I said. "That was a lame way to ask a favor."

"My father's still in jail. Is this call good news for him?"

"It's either no news or good news," I said. "I'm just running a hunch."

"If I had a nickel for every take-out meal I've taken to him the past five days . . . Give me sixty seconds."

Thirty seconds later: "Alex?"

"I'm here, Gail."

"I've got the papers in front of me. He put a thousand down on the trailer and signed a ten-year lot lease. The trailer was only sixty-two hundred, but the lease was forty grand. It was nine years ago, and there's some kind of balloon payment coming up in about five months."

"Did he deal directly with the previous owner?" I said.

"The address on the envelope is Deer Abbey Real Estate, Big Pine Key."

"Does it show a street address?"

"No, but let me . . . Where are my Yellow Pages?" she said. "It's got to be on the highway . . ." She came back on. "Mile Marker 30.4, ocean side."

"Thank you, Gail," I said. "I'll keep you informed."

After I clicked off, Teresa said, "Your mind works in complex patterns. Your brother's the same way. I expect that's no news to you."

In a way it was. For all his tampering with his mind's inner workings, the booze and chemicals and herbs he had ingested over the years, I didn't know what was left. But he'd recalled details of a car chase during our high school days, facts that I had managed, for the most part, to erase.

Teresa spoke softly. "You're quiet. Do you disagree with what I said?"

"Not at all," I said. "For all his crap when we were kids, he redeemed himself most of the time. If something went missing out of our yard, he knew which kid down the street had swiped it and where it was hidden. He could find dogs and missing car keys and knew when books were due at the library. His prime talent—he always knew the perfect person to call each time he needed out of a jam."

"He called me this time," she said. "Maybe he's losing his touch."

"Don't panic just yet." I gave Teresa directions to Deer Abbey Real Estate.

The sign read CLOSED FOR FAMILY EMERGENCY. An attached Post-it note signed by Sharon

Woods, Owner, directed inquiries to a sandwich shop fifty yards west. I hiked over to find a clock-like sign hung inside the shop's glass door. An arrow pointed to four o'clock. Another Post-it note: "GONE FISHIN'." You had to admire their work ethic. These people understood summer in the Keys.

Teresa drove me to Winn-Dixie. I grabbed three real estate tabloids from a freebie rack in-side the door. Back in the car I searched for a Deer Abbey spread, hoping for Sharon Woods's cell or home number. No spread, no luck. Back on the highway we stopped at a broker's office a quarter-mile south. The death-by-tanning recep-tionist said, "We get so many people wondering where that lady is. Her health began to go away last year. I've seen her pick up her mail a few times, but I don't know how she pays rent and taxes. I have four kids, two sets of twins. My whole life's a family emergency."

We tried two other offices with the same luck. The day's heat won the battle with Teresa's air conditioner. I could do better on the phone. We rode the last leg in silence. I kept my nose in the tabloid and made a mental list of brokers to call in search of Sharon Woods.

Teresa pulled into Manning's yard but stopped halfway in. I looked up to question why she hadn't pulled into the parking spot next to my Shelby in the shade under the house.

I thought at first that the Chamber of Commerce had staged an advertisement for doing business in the Keys. Marnie Dunwoody had turned her Jeep's tailgate into a mobile office: a short plastic chair, her laptop on an Igloo cooler, her cell phone hooked to a charger, which she had plugged into an outside outlet.

We got out of the Grand Am and walked under the house.

Teresa said, "It's not what you think."

Marnie kept her face expression-free. "I try not to think, but Alex and I have work to do."

We heard another car coming down Keelhaul Lane. Bobbi Lewis skidded her county car onto the yard's pea rock, angled the sedan so she could talk through her lowered window, then jerked to a halt and levered it into park with a grudge uppercut. After the dust squall blew off with the breeze, I saw my brother in her backseat. I could tell by the set of his shoulders that he was cuffed.

Teresa, to her credit, did not make a scene.

"I hit the jackpot," said Lewis. "Two people I need, both in one place."

"Hi, Bobbi," I said. "How are you doing?"

"Fucking beat, Alex. Save your sweet hellos."

"What do you want?" said Teresa.

Lewis shifted her glare. "Clarification. You had a breakfast meeting with the mayor and his assistant at six-thirty Monday morning?"

Teresa nodded. I heard heavy breathing through her nostrils. "We met at Pepe's."

"A predawn breakfast?"

"The mayor had an eight o'clock flight to Fort Myers. Our meeting dealt with his agenda and two things I had to do later that morning."

Bobbi's radio made a squelch noise. She reached to adjust it, then looked up. "What time did you leave your house on Staples, Teresa?"

"I remember checking the kitchen clock before I walked outside," said Teresa. "It was just before six, maybe 5:57 or 5:58."

"You checked the clock? And Tim was where?"

Teresa grimaced, almost glanced at me, but looked instead to the backseat. "In my bed, Bobbi."

Lewis looked bored. "Fully dressed?"

"No, Bobbi," she said. "Maybe a T-shirt and nothing else. We'd been asleep. Maybe not even the T-shirt."

"It took you thirty-five minutes to drive two miles to Pepe's?"

"I stopped at my office to get my digital recorder, and I went to an ATM on Southard to get cash. Then I went to breakfast."

Lewis lifted an eyebrow. "Is the ATM receipt still in your wallet?"

"It's in a little file box on a bookcase at home," said Teresa. "Two hundred dollars, leaving me a balance of seven hundred and change."

"Make any phone calls from your office?"

"Who would I call at six-fifteen?"

"Right," said Bobbi. "It's a little early for city business."

"No, wait a minute. I called Tim. I couldn't find my watch before I left, which is why I checked the clock. I thought I'd left it at work, but it wasn't in my city desk. I wanted him to look for it."

"At six-fifteen you woke him for that?"

"It's a Gucci watch." She twisted her head toward me then looked back at Lewis. "Alex gave it to me last year. I thought I'd lost it. I panicked, so I called and told Tim to look in my makeup kit in the bathroom. It was in the kit."

"You went without a watch for the rest of the day?"

"I was going to, but he brought it to Pepe's."

"How did he get there?" said Bobbi.

"A Five-Sixes cab. His car wasn't at my house. I forget why."

Bobbi nodded. "Did you introduce him to the mayor?"

"Tim wouldn't come in. He beckoned me out to the sidewalk and fastened the watch to my wrist."

"Nice. Did you see anyone you knew while you were on the sidewalk?"

"What?"

"Someone walking toward Harpoon Harry's?"

"Oh," said Teresa. "Dink Bruce went by while we stood there."

"He was up early, too?"

"He said he was leaving for Montana in an hour. He was going to stop and see a tall girl in Nashville. His sense of humor."

"How did Tim get home?" said Bobbi. "Walk?"

"No, the cab waited for him."

"Good, Teresa. Your story matches and we can check the details. They're good details. You just got your boyfriend off a federal kidnap charge."

"Then let him go."

"Sorry. This all started with credit-card fraud, and we'll follow through on it."

Teresa stared at Lewis, then walked to her car, started it, and drove away.

"Was I the other person you needed to see?" I said.

Bobbi's gaze went frosty. "I bust my brain to script an interrogation that allows me to clear your brother with a clean conscience. Teresa goes away pissed. You stand there like this is old news."

"I'm getting hardened by all the drama."

"You knew about Tim and Teresa, right?"

"Yes," I said.

"You had a good idea where to locate his dark teal Chevy Caprice station wagon."

"Key West is a small island."

"You had all day Sunday to hire someone to retaliate against Millican."

"I just ran this same kind of everyone's-guilty gambit with Billy Bohner. Maybe you ought to arrest everyone and sort out the innocent."

Bobbi nodded. "Then we could claim some progress."

"Did you call it progress when you took that rope from the gold star to Tavernier?"

"I called it my job."

She drove away with Tim in her rear seat. I told myself not to dwell on how at-home he looked as a prisoner.

He refused to look back.

2 2

MARNIE AND I MOVED our op center to Al's kitchen. After I laid out paper towels, a beer, a Coke, and the cold fried chicken that Marnie had brought from Dion's, she handed me a morning newspaper. "Check the personals," she said.

The list was typical. "ATTRACTIVE SENSUOUS WOMAN WANTED," "TANTRA CLASS ALL DAY," "THE RUSSIAN BRIDE SERVICE," "COMPUTER PROBLEM?" and "BACKCOUNTRY TOURS." The last bore the headline TENDER REUNION.

"You think a Russian bride will solve my problems?"

Marnie smirked. "Did you read that bottom one carefully?"

"No."

"Read it out loud to me."

"Tender reunion," I said. "Attention all **Bushnell** and **Gilmore** shipmates. Big reunion scheduled. October in Key West. All hands on deck. Pass the word."

"Sound like an opportunity?" she said.

"If we wait until October, we might learn a few things."

"Is there a number to call?"

"Yes. Two nine four . . . it's your home number."

"It's my ad," she said.

"And?"

"Not a blessed peep so far. The odd thing is, there's a legitimate **Howard W. Gilmore** reunion scheduled eighteen months from now in Seattle. I found the coordinator on the Web. He said I could plant the ad if I sent him contact info for anyone who responds."

"Did he remember the hanging?" I said.

"He didn't come aboard until after the ship left Key West, but he'd heard about it. He said the 'Happy Howie' was five hundred thirty feet long, which gave plenty of room for bad apples who didn't fit the 'military mode,' as he called it. He also said that when the **Bushnell** went out of service in 1970, a lot of men lived in Key West with their families. Their kids were in school and their wives had local jobs. Several hundred were reassigned to the **Gilmore.**"

"Pretty standard," I said. "In those days, at least."

"The man said that the humanitarian transfers resulted in what he called 'an overstock of tropical talent' on the **Gilmore**. He said they were skilled in swapping favors and doing shady deals. Maybe you know the word he used."

"We called it cumshaw when I was on active duty."

Marnie nodded. "That was it."

"It's a barter system," I said. "It supposedly skirts bureaucracy to benefit the military. All I ever witnessed was a mutant version that benefited humans."

"But shady deals would have to come ashore to turn into felony arrests, right? Is that why you wanted to know if any Navy personnel had been nabbed by the city or county?"

"That was my thinking," I said.

"Can we find a better view?"

I carried the chicken to the screened porch. Marnie inspected a rattan chair's salt-crusted cushion, flipped it over, and settled in. "I went to the library this morning," she said. "It doesn't open until ten, but that man in the research room does me favors. He let me in at eight and let me sift through a stack of old newspapers. I started by reading the weeks just before and after the January flagpole hanging. I worked backward, then forward again. In the last four months of '72 and the first two of '73, the hanging was the only crime that wasn't the usual crap. The **Citizen** ran with four major local stories."

"Dirtbags and hippies leading the list," I said.

"Nope. The State of Florida declared the island's sewer system obsolete.' "

"Thereby prompting a thirty-year repair job. What else?"

"Gas prices had driven down tourism, and Duval Street was a wasteland. The Treasure Salvors found the first signs of the **Atocha,** the silver coins and ingots. Finally, the Navy cut out all submarine activity, sent the **Howard W. Gilmore** packing in late January, reassigned to Sardinia, and declared fourteen acres of the naval station surplus."

"Sardinia?"

Marnie nodded. "I noticed two other things during that time period. In October the city manager, acting on a tip, ordered a massive inventory of maintenance equipment. Then, in mid-November, the city was investigating a deficit in its accounts. Three hundred thousand bucks was missing. There was never a follow-up story, no mention of it ever again."

"Nothing related?" I said.

"Not in the **Citizen.** From mid-September to the first week of February, I had to weed through Watergate horseshit, Paris Peace Accords, and gas-station lines. No missing-money follow-up, no crimes involving Navy personnel, no inventory results."

"You're very resourceful, Marnie. You should be a reporter."

She shook her head. "I might have screwed up last night. I called Liska at home. He's a very depressed man."

"What was his side of things?"

"I asked about the hanging," said Marnie. "It was like driving my Jeep into a mountain of Jell-O."

"He stonewalled with fluff?" I said. "Sounds just like our sheriff."

"He talked for five minutes, never said a thing, but the more he jabbered, the more depressed he sounded."

"Did any details sneak out?"

"He tried to investigate the sailor's death without calling it a suicide or a murder. His superiors gave him no support—I assumed that included Millican, but I didn't want to ask outright and tip our hand—and the Navy was no help. A ship's officer told him the higher-ups were afraid an investigation would delay the **Gilmore**'s deployment. Two city commissioners bought him a few drinks and told him he was working too hard. He even talked to a police counselor about it, and the woman told him to let it go."

"Let it go?"

"Those were his words."

"Well, it sure as hell came back to him on Ramrod," I said. "Right about the time he saw Kansas Jack with a stretched neck."

"Can I use that for my story lead?"

"There's no story yet."

Marnie's phone rang. She took it to the kitchen, talked softly.

I used the break in our analysis to call Dave Klein's direct number at the Broward Crime Scene Unit.

"I don't want to be a pest," I said, "but things down here are moving fast."

"I forwarded the results an hour ago," said Klein. "We pulled an image, but nothing too promising. Nothing we'd pursue at this level."

"Thanks for your time."

"I try to do a good job, and like I said, you had a favor coming. Gotta go."

Marnie came back to the porch. "I have to be in the office by four."

"I'll be ten cars behind you," I said. "I might have to evict my tenant."

"That was a quick lease."

"Two months reduced to five days. He moved in on Friday. According to Carmen, the party's been nonstop since then. The neighbors blame me."

"As well they should. You're the slumlord of Dredgers Lane."

"And don't say—"

"Too late," she said. "It's too good a headline to pass up."

"This kid Bixby at the city," I said.

"How did we digress to him?"

"He must have a first name. Any chance you might . . ."

Marnie nodded, punched in a number, and told the city's PIO that the **Citizen** planned a profile of the new photographer. She asked for a few preliminary details, hung up, and said, "E. J. Bixby."

"No name? Just initials?"

"That's it. He's a big bundle of style, that boy."

"Or bullshit," I said. "Or evil."

Marnie checked her watch. "What did we accomplish?"

My turn to shrug.

"We're dead even," she said. "You're hung up on the Navy. My nose for news smells a story in the city's maintenance-gear inventory and the single mention of missing money. If we blend our hunches . . . What if two or three sailors off the **Gilmore** stole a mess of city property just before the ship left port?"

"But why would people be getting killed thirty years later?" I said. "Three hundred grand . . . it's not like they held up a Brink's truck."

"If it all ties together, there's always revenge for some part of it that went haywire."

"Like a murder made to look like a suicide?"

Marnie gathered her things to go. "It's your turn to face down Liska."

"I'll go see him after I deal with my tenant."

Marnie walked to the screen, stared at the canal. "Check it out," she said. "Two girls in a tandem kayak, each wearing a Day-Glo bikini and a lightweight headset. The sweeties are adventuring in the wild Florida Keys."

"Packing iPods and caffeinated spring water?"

"I used to live like that," she said.

"I don't believe you."

"Okay." She laughed. "I never lived like that. Not even for one week."

I walked Marnie down to her Jeep. She pointed out a county cruiser cutting a U-turn at the lane's dead end. The big car rolled back past us, but the deputy kept his eyes on the road. "Think the sheriff's watching you?" she said.

"I can't worry about that. I wonder who's watching the sheriff."

The bastard chirped as I watched Marnie's Jeep disappear onto Pirates Road. Area code 973 meant Monty Aghajanian in his FBI office.

"Alex, that forensic man in Broward County got a bingo on your duct tape. He e-mailed us a palm print."

"No fingerprints?"

"Just a right palm, but it matches a partial print connected to a murder from four years ago. Indirectly, it hooks into two others that same year and one from three months ago."

"Male or female?"

"Victims?" he said. "All male. The perp, too."

"Where were the murders?" I said.

"That's info we can't let slide."

"I'm a security risk? I brought you the tape."

"I can tell you this," said Monty. "They were all over the map, and not in Florida."

"A nutcase?"

"A professional popper, and you need to back your ass off big-time. This boy's on our 'silent' Most-Wanted sheet. It's a list we don't make public. We don't want the cruds to know we're on to their patterns. We also don't think the public can help us without risk."

I said, "A three-year gap between the first three and the fourth?"

"Right."

"Were any hung?"

"Nope," said Monty. "Numbers one, two, and four were electrocutions. We gave him the nickname 'Sparky.' The third was a sicko shot. He used a router on the vic's kneecaps and hooked power winches to his arms and legs. The victim died when his left arm came off."

"Electric davits fit the modus."

"Good deduction, my friend."

"Any of those four related to the Navy?" I said.

"No, Alex, but look," he said. "I've already told you more than you need to know. Our people are southbound right now. Keep your distance from all of this shit, and don't buddy up to anyone with sunglasses and a haircut."

"I'm going to say three names, Monty. You do whatever you want with them. Are you ready to write?"

"Hold on," he said.

Just then my cell phone's second line beeped at me. I recognized the number as one assigned to the City of Key West, but I didn't want to break away from Monty.

"I'm ready to write," he said.

"Chester Millican, E. J. Bixby, and . . . you need spellings on these?"

"Not so far," he said. "That's only two."

"The last one is . . . fuck."

"What's the matter, man?"

"The third name is Timothy Rutledge."

Monty kept silent a few beats, then said, "Sorry you got dragged into this one, my friend."

23

THE CALL I'D MISSED from the city switch-board had been Beth Watkins: "If you get a chance," the message said, "call me back in the next half hour or so."

I scrolled the call log on my phone. Beth must have called me at least once from her cell, but her mobile wasn't in my phone's memory. I called her office line and was shuttled to the KWPD switchboard, a woman with impatience in her voice: "Desk."

"I just missed a call from Detective Watkins."

"She's on an investigation."

"It wasn't three minutes ago, and she asked me to call her back," I said. "Can you patch me through?"

"Hold." The phone fell to a hard surface. I listened to thirty seconds of chatter, code calls, rogers, negatives, and addresses. "Detective Watkins is on an investigation. She can't call back."

"Can you give me her cell-phone number?"
I said.

"I can't give you that."

"All I want is the detective to call me."

"You can leave a message, but I can't guarantee
she'll get it."

"She doesn't have a voice mailbox?"

"Of course she does, but she has to call in to re-
trieve her messages."

"Is that something she usually does?"

"How should I know?"

"Can you get her on the radio and inform her
that I responded?"

"No way, sir. The radio isn't for personal use."

"I hope to fuck this is being recorded."

"It is, and you can go to jail for talking
that way."

"Good. Maybe the detective can find me
there."

The week's miracle took the form of a Wendell-
free exit from Keelhaul Lane, though I still
had the feeling that he was peeking through
the miniblinds, monitoring my moves, readying
himself to pounce into conversation. I supposed
that his free divorce had taken a toll in loneliness. Perhaps his love affair with the ocean
helped to fill the void.

I hooked up with hellbound traffic on Ramrod and escaped the race by thinking through my meeting with Marnie, trying to dislodge details to illuminate the puzzle. Something we discussed wanted to float free of my subconscious fact trap. I wasn't sure what it was, but it had lodged late in our chat. She had placed the Navy-reunion ad in the paper, spoken with Liska, studied four months' worth of old newspapers. What else? Pieces of our conversation faded in and out, but nothing came to me. I only knew that I felt trapped by our dependence on ancient copies of the **Citizen.** We needed a human source.

I needed to test the memory of my Dredgers Lane neighbor, Hector Ayusa.

Crossing Harris Gap Channel my convoy slowed behind an old pickup with a two-story plywood camper teetering on its ass end. A sane person wouldn't drive it in a fifteen-knot cross-wind, much less on a bridge. Perhaps that explained its tortoise speed. My speed run had slowed from full tilt to snail's pace, and my pitted windshield magnified the sunlight's glare. Hurry be damned, I would get to town when traffic wanted me there.

My phone rang as I passed Bay Point.

"Alex, it's Beth Watkins."

I locked on to the mental picture of a trigger finger shot tipless by a police hero.

"I tried to get back to you," I said.

"So I heard. Look, this is a difficult call for me. I'm not a soap-opera fan."

"I wouldn't think so."

"Did you mention to Detective Lewis that I drove up to Little Torch on Saturday?"

"I believe so," I said.

"I called her with some information an hour ago. She was more interested in being rude than hearing me out."

"When she gets focused on a job she . . . well, she gets focused."

"So maybe you'll hear me out," said Watkins. "Tell me if I'm on a wild-goose chase."

"I'm all ears, Beth."

"I'd rather have this be face-to-face," she said. "Any chance you're coming into town this afternoon?"

"I've got to play landlord in the next couple of hours."

"Great," she said. "Call me when you get free, and we can meet in my office."

My memory coughed up an old news item on some cops in Philadelphia who notified by mail dozens of fugitives that they had won Super Bowl tickets. The winners simply had to show photo ID at a storefront office near the stadium to claim their tickets. The police busted each gullible fool who walked through the door and cleared dozens of warrants. With the past week's talk of my being an accomplice, or tampering with evidence, or illegally renting my home, I didn't want to fall for a similar scam.

"Could we meet at the Afterdeck?" I said. "Tell me what time to meet you there."

"I rode my Ducati today. Can you pick me up?"

"I need to run an errand on my way in. I don't know how long—"

"Call me when you pass Home Depot. I'll be waiting outside the police station."

"That sounds okay."

"I get it," she said. "You share the universal fear men have in dealing with women police officers. This is not a setup to detain you, Alex."

"I wasn't suggesting—"

"Quit while you're ahead." She gave me her cell number and hung up.

A few miles later an F-18 landing at Boca Chica flew low enough to scorch my hood paint. The jet's roar unleashed adrenaline, uncorked my brain, and the point I'd tried to recall from Marnie's visit came back to me. When I told her that I'd had to evict my tenant, I had flashed on the timing of Johnny Griffin's Thursday arrival in Key West. If someone wanted to suggest that my brother's appearance coincided with three murders, why not Griffin's, too?

Hell, why not consider everyone I'd ever known?

But I decided to take Watkins with me when I went to Dredgers Lane to evict Johnny.

The new police station on North Roosevelt looked like a corporate headquarters. This was my first time inside, and the first person I saw was Marge Sayre, the receptionist who had migrated from the Angela Street station to finish out her last year before retirement.

"Where do I sign up for the guided tour?" I said.

"There've been a few of those today," she said. "All these state and federal people in here, that all-agency meeting they had earlier in the conference room. Meanwhile, you've been out in the sun, haven't you?"

"Scrubbing a boat on Saturday," I said. "I'm house-sitting on Ramrod."

"We had a canal house up there years ago, before it got crowded. What street are you on?"

"Keelhaul Lane."

Marge got a faraway look in her eye. "I remember when Keelhaul had two houses and three more were built one summer. The old-timers thought the place had gone to hell."

"No vacant lots left now. Is Beth Watkins in?"

"I heard she was looking for you last week," said Marge. "I think the girl's husband-hungry, but you don't need a warning. You've dodged that trap." She called to get Beth's okay, then gave me a clip-on visitor's badge and directed me down a sea-foam green hallway. The place was awash in calming pastels, modular work areas, easy-to-clean surfaces.

Beth's second-floor office with its pale blue walls, three workstations, and a bulletin board fit the uniformity. She was staring at the door, waiting for me to appear. She looked beat and distracted. Mostly beat.

"Marge said there was a big meeting," I said.

She nodded and scowled. "Turned out I'm too junior for a front-row seat. I got a chair by the wall."

"Any breakthrough news?" I said.

"Typical all-agency crap. Everybody lays out their hand, then the FBI shuts up and no one complains. I saw it coming five minutes into the sit-down. I didn't really mind when I got pulled out of the meeting."

"Pulled out?"

"It was almost over anyway," she said. "We had a situation here in town. I'll tell you about it after we have our first drink. Why do you look so antsy?"

I told her about Griffin's noise problems. I

didn't mention my paranoiac questioning of his arrival time.

"You want to take care of it and come back and get me?"

"Why waste the time to go and come back?" I said. "It shouldn't take five minutes. I'll talk to him nicely, maybe ask him to vacate."

"If I get out of your car, my badge stays behind."

"It's hard to picture old Johnny Griffin as the violent type."

"Half of the bad ones look violent. The rest look like puppy dogs, but they're just as mean."

I coasted past a new Ford van in front of my house, a plain-vanilla rental. From outside the place looked quiet and normal. I parked at the end of the lane and led Beth around to Carmen Sosa's back door. Carmen stood in the kitchen, drinking iced tea, hovering over her daughter's shoulder.

I introduced Watkins, then said, "What do we know?"

Carmen pointed at a puzzle book. "Maria's acing a crossword and I don't know shit."

"Mom," said Maria.

Carmen shrugged, groped in her shorts pocket, and dropped a dime in the Bacardi 8 cuss bottle. "He's been home about ten minutes," she said. "Thank you for dealing with it."

Watkins and I walked to my house. I could tell by her breathing that she was readying herself for a confrontation.

Johnny Griffin sat on my porch, a can of beer in one hand, his other hand swathed in cotton bandages. He looked ten years older than five days earlier. His hair and face were grayer and thinner, his eyes fatigued. He pointed to a six-pack with four remaining. "Did your friend see the mess? I assume that's why you're here."

I offered to open a beer for Watkins, but she shook her head. I helped myself, popped its top. "The neighbors are getting uppity about the parties."

"They're over." He lifted his bandaged hand. "I'm officially off hard liquor."

"Someone attack you?" I said.

"I couldn't find any scissors in your kitchen drawers. I needed to open one of those new foil packs of tuna fish. I found what I thought was the perfect tool. My new Griffin Kitchen Rule is you don't open tuna with a box cutter."

"You were sober at the time?"

Griffin shrugged. "Maybe still drunk from the night before. Now I'll be off the water for five days, if they can take out my stitches on day four. The one thing I know for sure is my body needs to dry out."

"No more social functions?"

"None at all," he said. "I hooked up with a bunch of gigglers the other night. I got my fill of their company."

"Everything else okay?" I said.

"Peachy. You going to let me stay? Even with the constant heat, I need this vacation."

I thought about it, then nodded.

"Come by any time next week," he said. "I'll slip you another wad of cash."

As we walked across the street to speak with Hector Ayusa, Watkins said, "Known this Griffin a long time?"

"Since college. We kept in touch, Christmas cards, occasional visits. He and his ex-wife put me up for three or four days when they lived in Knoxville. Why do you ask?"

"How did he make his money?"

"Insurance," I said.

"That's a cash business?"

"All these years in the Keys," I said, "I've learned not to question certain things."

I knocked on Hector's door and waited. A waft of Spanish brandy preceded Hector to his screen door. He waved his hand at the rocking chairs on his porch, then dropped into his favorite seat like a potato into an Easter basket. "You come to tell me you kick out that noisy boy?"

"I had a talk with him, Hector. He said he was sorry about the racket. It won't happen again."

"So why you come by, you miss my face?"

"I need to pick your mind about Weedy Fields."

Hector peered across the lane, tried to send my house back through the years. "Weedy come here from Michigan, so he talk funny like a Swedish, and he probably say that my Conch tongue is funny, but he was a smart old man. One day in 1957 he flies me to Cuba for lunch. I been married maybe not five years, Alex, and he flies me there, we skim close to fishing boats and land near Havana. We have lunch in some old whorehouse, excuse me, miss, but I got six whores mad at me because I tell them my wife is in Cayo Hueso, I got to go back to her. I think those whores might kill me with a knife. Mr. Weedy Fields, he pay the whores to sing us a song, and they happy again. They earn more American dollars to sing than . . . you know what. We leave that whorehouse, everyone smiling. How that man know to pay a whore to sing, I don't know, but he smart as hell."

"You recall his children?"

Hector pushed himself from his chair, stuck his hand between two square flowerpots, and pulled out a pint of brandy. He unscrewed the cap, offered it to Beth. She smiled and waved her hand to decline. He handed it to me. "That boy go off to college, that young girl—they call her Pokey—she went to hell when his wife died."

I tilted it back, took a short swig. "She start hanging out on Duval?"

"Not so much, but she live with that man, he wasn't from here." Hector took a more substantial slug, replaced the cap, put the bottle back in its hiding spot. "Maybe they had a wedding, I don't know, maybe not."

"You recall his name?"

"Alex. My head don't work, all these years. I think I only saw him one time. You better off, you ask Carmen."

"What kind of man was he?" I said.

"He was Navy, I know that. Weedy Fields, he hated that man. One day I watched that one black lieutenant the city had back then, he put the handcuffs on the Navy man in Carlos Market. I believe they caught that man for his work at the city."

"Hector, you've confused me. Pokey's sailor left the Navy and found a job in town?"

"Never left the Navy, Alex. Now, all your questions, you reminding me. That boy and three or four or five other sailors come out and get jobs."

"At the city?"

"They forgot to tell anyone downtown they in the Navy," said Hector. "They forgot to tell the Navy they got all these jobs on the island."

"What kind of jobs?"

"Work crews, just like me at City Electric.

Matter of fact, one Navy man started at City Electric, messed around, I almost lose my job over it. Only time I ever come close to losing my job. They caught him with a box full of new tools, they thought I should have suspected before it happen. A month later, I see him in a city truck. He getting less pay, but he back to having two jobs."

"So someone finally caught on to these boys?"

"I guess, Alex. They were ripping off stuff, I forget what all. Then that big Navy ship went away and took almost the whole Navy with it. That one man they took to jail, I don't know about him."

"After that?"

Hector looked back at my house. "You buy that house, Carmen still at high school, and Weedy Fields goes to Michigan, and we hear he died." He shook his head. "Never saw that girl again. Or the boy again, never."

I sat quietly for a minute or so, juggling facts and half-facts.

Hector spoke first. "You been gone a week, Alex, seems like two years. What you miss about Dredgers Lane beside my face?"

"I miss Carmen's scolding and going out for my morning coffee."

"Over to 5 Brothers?"

"Or to Eden House, if I'm in a hurry. Mike lets me slide in and pretend I'm a paying guest."

"I went crazy, they put that hotel there. I thought, the block was ruined by traffic and racket. Hell, all these years, not problem one. After Hurricane Georges . . . when was that?"

"In '98."

"After that storm, that hotel man, Michael, give us ice and food. Before I die, I win the Lotto, I'll spend a night in that hotel, maybe two, pay him back."

We stood to leave. Perhaps made brave by the brandy, Hector gave Watkins a fatherly pat on her shoulder. "Young lady, you take care on that hot-rod motorbike, you hear me? You don't see it coming, that machine can hurt you bad."

24

BETH WATKINS AND I found Carmen in her backyard, steadying Maria on a pogo stick.

"Johnny Griffin promises total reform," I said, "and your father dislodged a few facts from his memory."

Carmen gave me a forlorn grin. "He pulls details from the past, then forgets to tighten the cap when he hides his brandy."

"His watered-down brandy?" said Maria.

Carmen raised her hand. "Hush, missy. We do it for Grandpop's own good."

"The Fields boy who grew up in my cottage," I said, "you recall his name?"

"Something simple," said Carmen, "like Robert. He was the straight-arrow and Pokey was the wild one . . . Robert, for sure, because he hated the name Bob, and one year—maybe in fifth or sixth grade—we all called him Bob because he was such a goody-boy."

"Was Pokey older than you?"

"Two years by the clock, but a good five in her social life, even with her skinny little girl's body. She was a junior when one of my friends saw her back then, smoking dope with longhairs behind Howie's Lounge. But I guess we all made our mistakes. I made mine so Maria could be perfect."

Maria flashed us a broad smile and hopped away, showing off.

Carmen pushed her finger into my chest. "You owe me a case of wine, minimum price, twenty a bottle."

"I had a premonition that your fee would go up."

"I hope the cost of wine does, too."

"What ever happened to Pokey?" I said.

"No idea."

"How about the Navy man she lived with? Did he ship out with the **Gilmore?**"

Carmen dropped her voice. "I'd forgotten all about him. He died."

"Did he hang himself on the Navy base?"

She nodded. "That's what people said. A few said that he might've had help."

Late-day traffic clogged White Street. I could tell that Watkins hadn't expected to ride in a car without air-conditioning. Waiting for the light at Truman Avenue, she dipped three fingers into

her cleavage, scooped out droplets of sweat, and
flung them out the window.

"Cocktail hour," I declared. "Time to meditate
on all we've learned."

"How about sushi with our drinks?" said
Beth. "In a cool restaurant."

"Ambrosia's one minute away and Louie's
Backyard is a good five minutes."

"I'll buy the fish," she said.

I parked a half-block from Ambrosia near the
fire station on Grinnell and toggled the Shelby's
fuel shutoff switch. With my mind on Pokey's
dead lover, I walked across the street and tripped
over a blue plastic recycling bin on the far curb.
Beth caught me to stop my fall. She saw me
flinch as my ribs took stress.

Instead of checking my scraped shin, I stared
at the bin.

"You've got revenge in your eye," said Beth. "It
wasn't the container's fault."

"I'm not blaming. I just got an idea."

A waiter with a tenor-profundo voice met us
at the restaurant door, seated us at a small table
near the front window, and took our drink order.
I was curious about the "situation" that Watkins
had mentioned, the one that had pulled her from
the all-agency meeting, but I didn't want to push
too hard. After our beers arrived, I asked about
her first weeks on the job, her impression of the
Key West Police Department.

"The veterans' universal goal is to fly under the radar," she said. "The young ones are a mixed bag. Some are too strict and some are slackers. I'd like to toss them all in a blender and pour out a few normals."

Our server reappeared. "Are we ordering?"

"May I?" Beth wanted to pick for both of us.

I shrugged a slacker-like okay.

She ordered dancing shrimp, flounder sashimi, a spicy California roll, four white-tuna sushi, four yellowtail sushi, and four smoked-salmon sushi.

When the server left, I said, "Do you see yourself as a strict cop or normal?"

"I lean toward the strict side," she said. "One thing I've learned is that successful cops form teams and find allies. I'm having a tough time with that."

"Maybe after a few more weeks have passed . . ."

"You think we'd make a good pair of detectives?"

"Why would you want that?" I said. "I'm a loose cannon with no desire to be a cop."

"You have a reputation for taking cases to their core."

"I'm about as official as a plaid shirt."

"But look what you did with that Cuban man," she said. "You got him talking, he went on a tangent about Cuban hookers, and he spilled out ancient details of a work scam."

"I wish, over the last few years, I'd tape-recorded the man's stories."

"You think his information fits with that photo Lewis found in Kansas Jack's home?"

"She told you about that?"

"Yes, she did," said Watkins. "And you're trying to connect dots."

"I suppose you could say that."

"You looked shocked to learn that that Navy man killed himself. Did you know him?"

"No, just the girl, Pokey Fields. I guess I didn't know her very well."

"Do the old hanging plus the new ones add up to a situation?" she said.

"They add up to a goddam mud bath, but things are starting to link up."

"It sounds like you're doing better than the all-agency group."

"I'm juggling theories," I said. "Did they say why the FBI is in an uproar?"

"That summit meeting was like a bridge game. Or maybe not, now that I think about it. They weren't so much holding their cards close as not wanting to reveal that they hadn't a single idea why the murders went down. One man—I think a fed—said their goal was to make connections. I took that to mean they wanted to tie the first two to Lucky Haskins."

Typical Feebs, I thought. They hadn't mentioned the out-of-state hit man.

"That's it?" I said.

"Pretty much. Who's your favorite suspect?"

I held out my hands, palms down, to ask for calm. "It's a thin case, but my first choice is Bixby. I think he's trying to forge his career on a road of bones."

She showed the calm I had hoped for. "Are there second- and third-place picks?"

"Not really. You probably don't know Deputy Billy Bohner. He and Detective Millican are possibles, but I can't see a motive unless someone hired them to kill those poor men."

"Motives don't always jump out at us," said Beth.

"Pathetic list of choices, isn't it? Maybe a solution won't be found. It's been almost a week since three men died, and Bixby is the only person with a plausible motive. No one else raised that point?"

"Nope," she said. "But at least you have the balls to speak your mind. What prompted you to bring up the concept of a hit man?"

I didn't want to betray Monty's confidence, especially if she hadn't heard about the pro in her afternoon meeting. "It's one of a hundred possibilities."

"Maybe the victims were in Witness Protection," she said.

"See?" I said. "Progress. We raised it to a hundred and one. You were going to tell me about your situation in the city this afternoon."

Our dancing shrimp arrived. Beth promised to tell her story after we'd given the shrimp proper attention. I made a remark about dead crustaceans doing the mambo in limbo.

Beth smiled. "Lewis told me about your iguana analogy. If Kansas Jack was an iguana and Haskins a manatee, what was Navarre?"

"An air dance wino."

Beth lifted her glass to her lips, smiled over its rim.

We attacked the shrimp with a flurry of soy sauce, ginger slices, and wasabi and didn't say a word for four or five minutes. When I came up for air, I said, "Tell your tale."

"Your number-one suspect stepped in a bucket of shit. We may need your services at the city for a few weeks."

"I'm someone you call when you can't get another date?"

"Bixby tried to rig a drug buy on Whitehead Street. He overextended himself. He tried to get it on film and he tried to make a citizen's arrest. The other two players took attitudes, with each other and with him. It was knives, not guns. They all survived."

"Jesus."

"The slashees have been sent for repairs. We have a damaged storefront, a parked car with a busted window and dented door, a moped on its side, and a picket fence with splintered slats. And one fewer city employees."

"Trying to create his own headline," I said.

"You won't believe the irony and humor," said Watkins. "Two days ago I considered hiring you as a consultant to bring Bixby up to speed."

"What could I tell a kid with a master's degree?"

"We're in the tropics. He learned under different lighting conditions. Better than that, you could have given him pointers on dealing with locals, from a pro's point of view."

"It might have saved him some blood loss."

"And camera loss, too," said Watkins. "While he was being transported to the hospital, an EMT called the switchboard to check on his gear. No one had noticed the camera bag, so the city will mend his wounds and fire his ass, but he'll have to file the insurance claim."

"Someone needs to go back and look into those crimes he solved in college."

She took a moment to show her empty glass to the server and point to my beer. "Did you ever read any books on JFK's assassination?"

"A few, maybe five or six, half my life ago," I said. "The Warren Commission report read like bad fiction. The others were okay in parts, farfetched in others."

"I lived in California with a guy who collected

anything related to the subject. He got me
hooked on the books that dealt with conspiracy
theory. The most bizarre one of all was **American
Tabloid** by a man named Ellroy. His style was
jerky, his characters were over-the-top, and the
connections he made were off the chart. But in
the end, it was so believable. I finished the last
page, closed the book, and said to myself, 'That
was exactly how it went down.' Since then, every
time I hear or see bizarre, I sift for truth."

"So my being over-the-top and off the chart
makes me a good teammate?"

She went back to eye contact. "Doesn't hurt."

We had finished two thirds of the sushi when
Beth held still and looked puzzled.

"Something wrong?" I said.

She laughed to herself. "I suppose not. I always
think coincidence is funny."

"Which coincidence?"

"Your friend Carmen talked about that man
who hung himself years ago on the Navy base. A
case file came across my desk this morning at
the city. I was supposed to review it and file it
away. This is what I wanted to tell Bobbi Lewis
today when she got short with me. Did you hear
about a suicide on Olivia Street maybe three
months ago?"

"I don't think so," I said.

"I guess we can be grateful it wasn't a murder,
too. There was a suicide note, and his neighbors

weren't surprised he killed himself. He'd always been the mopey sort, down on himself, always negative. The guy dressed up in his old Navy uniform and tied a nylon rope around a ceiling beam, then jumped off his television. He almost screwed up because the nylon stretched. When they found him, his feet were only four inches off the carpet."

"Tell me again, how long ago?"

"The first week of April. Maybe it will juggle itself into one of your theories. Anyway, I'm full and the bill is on me and I don't need to ride my motorcycle home tonight. Can you drop me off on your way back to Little Torch?"

On Big Coppitt I coasted from U.S. 1 to Beth's driveway and shut down the Shelby. Next door, Bobbi Lewis's personal and work cars sat under her house.

"I can't exactly ask you to come in for a drink," said Beth. "You've got a relationship going with my cranky neighbor."

I hesitated out of surprise more than indecision.

Watkins caught my delay. "I could come up to Little Torch and you can bring me home in the morning. She goes to work at six forty-five."

"Then you and I would be the item and Bobbi would take a hike?"

She looked pouty. "All I offered was another beer."

"Can I ask you a question?" I said.

"Sure."

"Why did you look up my property at the county records office?"

She looked into my eyes, slowly nodded. "There went that mood."

"I don't know why I thought of it, but I guess it needs an answer."

"I did it to see if you had a mortgage, or if you had paid cash for your home."

"And if I had paid cash?"

"You probably earned it behind the scenes."

"You mean illegally?"

"I'm the new cop in town. No one offered to fill me in on details that I consider important. I wanted to know what kind of freelancer the city had employed."

"Gotcha," I said. "Thank you for dinner."

She opened the door, eased out slowly, and walked away, leaving the door open. I had to reach to close it before the Shelby filled with mosquitoes.

I found my share of bugs at the outdoor phone a block away, next to the Circle K on U.S. 1. I had promised Marnie I would have a go at Liska. I needed to catch him at home, away from his job, his point of power. I dropped coins, punched numbers, and decided that calling was a bad plan an instant before he answered.

"Mmyello," said Liska.

"What the fuck is mmyello?"

"Oh, it's you. That's how cops in the movies say hi."

"What's your house number on Eagle?" I said.

"I'm not receiving visitors."

"Navy personnel working full-time for the city, early seventies."

"Unless he has a large pizza in hand."

"You order it, and I'll pay when it gets there."

I hung up fast, before he could respond.

25

THE HOUSE ON EAGLE looked neat but dark. King Hangdog answered the door, pushed it wide, and stood back to let me in. The place was stuffy. His center of action was a reclining chair, a gooseneck lamp, and a large flat-screen TV.

"Maybe you could open a window and turn on a second lamp," I said. "What the hell have you been doing in here?"

"Absolut vodka and the evening news." His voice sounded like a rusty hinge on a hatch cover.

Many moods traveled on Chicken Neck Liska's glum face. If you thought he looked sad or displeased, you could be dead wrong. He might be basking in tranquility, ready to write you a million-dollar check. If you chose to ignore his sour expression and let his words tell the story, you saved time and brain cells.

I opened the fridge. "Two left in this six-pack. Can you spare one?"

"I'll take a few bites of that blueberry pie."

I handed over the whole pie. "You didn't call for a pizza?"

"It's coming. I'll save room." He dug a forkful from pie center, stuffed it in his mouth.

I twisted the cap from some kind of light beer. After the Kirin, it tasted like fizz water.

Liska quit chewing with his mouth half full. "Your reason for this house call?"

"This is Wednesday," I said. "We haven't seen each other since last Friday. As county sheriff, you would like to formally apologize for the brutal actions of your detective."

"Right, your run-in with Millican. How are your nuts?" He put down the pie, tore off a paper towel, swiped it across his face. He sopped up more sweat than blueberry dribble. "Never mind my intrusive query. I presume your equipment worked fine three nights ago with the other detective."

"I was convalescing, but my attorney will love your concern," I said. "Let's call those Millican episodes his run-ins with me, not the other way around."

"Whatever you say."

"What's your opinion on why he risked his job to rough me up?"

Liska shook his head. "Maybe he was upset by the unique murder scene."

"An old pro like Millican, upset?"

The doorbell rang. I walked across the room and opened up.

"Anchovies and mushrooms?" said the delivery man.

"That's all the toppings we get?" I said.

"Double-extra cheese."

Liska ate three pizza slabs while I sipped watery beer. He finally quit and said, "Why did you come here?"

"I had a chat with my secret weapon," I said.

Liska pondered that a moment. "The old Cuban who lives on your lane?"

"You're still a fine detective."

"He worked for City Electric, didn't he?"

"He remembered the sailors who took jobs at the city. Marnie found archived news on the suicide—investigated by you and Millican. By your titles, Millican was senior, probably your boss. She also found mentions of the city's missing money and its sudden ordering of maintenance inventories. I think it all ties together."

Liska looked me in the eye. "So I bungled my first case as a city lieutenant. Now my fears of being exposed have shafted this current investigation?"

"I couldn't have said it better, Sheriff."

"What do I do," he said, "erase everything and start over?"

"Might be the best approach, all the bullshit of the past few days."

"And these are days which you spent snooping around, piecing together the puzzle so you can astound the establishment with your deductive abilities?"

"I asked a few questions," I said.

"Rutledge, have you ever walked past a house with a dog in its yard? That dog barks at your approach, keeps yipping as you pass, then barks you good-bye. He stops when you're out of sight. You ever wonder what that dog's thinking?"

"That question fits our discussion?"

"That dog defended his turf and your departure proved that he succeeded. It doesn't matter that you weren't attacking, or that you were going down the street anyway. In that dog's mind, he drove you away."

"So everything I think I do," I said, "you're a step ahead of me."

"You deciphered the mutt analogy."

Liska tried again to offer me pizza, closed the box, and dropped it to the floor. He stared at me without speaking, looked away, then brought his eyes back to mine.

"Did you recognize Kansas Jack the minute you saw him?" I said.

"It took me a minute or two. When I asked you to e-mail me photos, it was to compare them to the old file. Once I got the five-by-sevens from your man Duffy Lee Hall, I knew for sure."

"Did Millican call and tell you that he'd recognized Navarre?"

"No," said Liska, "but he didn't spend years studying the cold case. He didn't say shit, so neither did I."

"You think his memory's gone soft after all this time?"

"His brain's like that orange juice I like."

"Not from concentrate?"

"Close," said Liska. "I was thinking 'Lots of pulp.'"

"How did the whole mess get stovepiped into a cold-case file?"

"Got time for a long lead-in?" he said.

I shrugged in the affirmative.

He reached behind his reclining chair, extracted the bottle of Absolut, poured a triple into a juice glass. "I got an education in hearing lies," he said. "I took a job where all day, all year long, people tell you lies. Every criminal's mission as a lawbreaker is to confuse the issue and bullshit the man. But never did I hear lies like from our government officials. I've never been a revolutionary or an anarchist, and I'm not going to tell you that our system doesn't work and that any toad on government pay is full of crapola. But the batch I ran into, in 1973, would rather climb trees to tell lies than sit on their butts and tell the truth."

"Do tell," I said.

"You turning the tables here, Rutledge? Doing a one-man good cop, bad cop on the old master?"

"I have no desire to be a policeman, or to mimic their acting techniques."

Liska took a sip of vodka. "Get yourself that last fucking beer, Rutledge. I'm not going to sit here and drink alone."

I returned to his sofa, raised the bottle a notch before tilting it back.

"Brick walls were a dime a dozen," said Liska. "The city, the county, the Navy. I went to an FBI agent. He freaked out. In those days they didn't like to tread on the military, or on any other agency for that matter."

"That's changed?" I said.

He shook his head. "I got one good sniff on that case. I forget the wee details, but I wanted to interview a few more sailors and the Navy didn't want to pull men off the ship. By then the **Gilmore** was in the Mediterranean. Something was going on. A multinational submarine and amphibious exercise, whatever. They insinuated that we had a lame case and they couldn't spare the manpower. I thought someone like the local commander had gotten to the mayor, but he denied it. The sheriff, Bobby Brown, denied it, too. I asked the state representative and got no answer, so that's when I knew it came from Washington. Come to find out, the Navy wanted so bad for us to back off, they threatened to renege on an offer to give the city their surplus land."

"Truman Annex?" I said.

"You got it," said Liska. "The biggest land fiasco in county history. Anyway, after all the horseshit, the prosecutors couldn't have budgeted a drawn-out trial. It would have cost a fortune to fly men in for grand juries and trials. The city pulled everyone off the case."

"Just like that, it was closed down?"

"Yep."

"Did the Navy conduct its own investigation?" I said. "Or make arrests?"

"Hell, back then the Navy was lax on haircuts and beards. You think they kept decent files?"

"There's something missing."

"Justice?"

"No," I said. "You're leaving something out."

"What might that be?"

"Your determination."

"You mean my months of work and years of concern? You're right. To me, down deep, it always was a cold case, always unsolved."

"That was then and this is now. This is a new century, for Christ's sake. It wasn't the embarrassment of a blown case that kept you quiet this week."

He took a deep breath. "Not entirely, no."

"Did you make yourself as dirty as the rest of them?"

"The Navy was good for and good to Key West. I was a green recruit, and I didn't want to single-handedly screw up the relationship. I was cautioned not to make waves."

"Waves, Navy. Good imagery. Did someone slip you a thick envelope?"

He tilted the glass of vodka, then let it rest against his lower lip. "A new roof on my mother's house."

"For that you would never go to jail all these years later."

"Might lose my job."

"Who has the horsepower to fire you?" I said. "At worst, you retire early."

"What would I do if I retired? I mean, what would fill my days? I'm packing too much bull-roar in my head to relax. I'm better off working to the day I die. Otherwise I'll go nuts."

"Is anyone alive who even remembers that roof?"

"I don't fucking know," he said. "I mean, my mother died a year later, but I sure as hell couldn't tell you who hauled shingles and pounded nails."

"Don't you think you would've heard from them by now, if they wanted to harm your reputation? When you testified against their cousin in court or when you ran for office?"

He tried to sip from the empty glass, then reached for the bottle. "You looking for me to unburden my soul, Rutledge?"

"I have a feeling that Millican's name is coming back to our conversation."

"He caught on to a scam run by some Navy guys who called themselves the Oblivion Division. He started taking little envelopes. I should have turned him in, but you know how that works. It got bigger and bigger. The envelopes turned into little brown bags like they wrap around beer bottles. There was plenty of cash going around, but I wouldn't take any. Millican advised me to let them do my mother's roof, so they wouldn't see me as a risk. They almost got caught once or twice, for petty crap, but we smoothed it over. From then on, my silence as good as implicated me."

"When did it fall apart?" I said.

"After the city and the Navy washed their hands of that flagpole hanging, I was plain disgusted. I didn't care about being a cop, so I had nothing to lose when I told Millican he was history in the Keys. I told him, 'You leave town, go away and leave my life, and this never happened.'"

"So he went up north and got a job?"

"One of those thieves was dead and Millican was scared shitless. He didn't need much of a push."

"Except he came back earlier this year and you hired him," I said. "How did he pressure you into giving him a job?"

"The place he worked, he was right at mandatory retirement age. That wouldn't have been a problem in my department. He had family down here, and I needed a good man. It was time to forgive and forget. Or let's say I thought it was. I hadn't done either one, and now I'm stuck with my decision."

"Stuck with that dead sailor years ago and deaths by hanging of Kansas Jack, Milton Navarre, and Lucky Haskins. The chance of bad press from your mother's free roof is the least of your worries."

"End of history lesson," he said. "Go the fuck away, Rutledge."

"Something else went down. You either overlooked it, covered it up, or took part in it."

Liska reached for the vodka and said nothing.

"Were you informed of a suicide in the city about ninety days ago?"

He nodded, took a slug. "Help me out of this chair."

Liska spent about five minutes in the john. I heard the retching sounds, the flushes and sounds of a cleanup. Then a battery-operated toothbrush.

He came back to the living room, screwed the cap on the vodka, and sat.

I said, "Did you follow up, look into it yourself?"

"The old-style Navy uniform got my curiosity," said Liska.

"How did you see it?"

"Like the city's best detectives, I saw a typical sloppy, sad suicide. Unlike the others, I saw a well-orchestrated murder. When the fingerprints came back I confirmed that the dead man had been stationed on both the **Bushnell** and the **Gilmore.** I didn't remember him from the old files, but . . ."

"Is that when you called Millican and told him to get his ass down here?"

Liska nodded again. "I told him his messy past might be coming back around to haunt him. I covered it up once, I wasn't going to clean the decks again. You're going to have to excuse me. I'm going to kick you out and go to bed."

"One last thing," I said. "Do you remember when the Full Moon Saloon moved from United Street to Simonton?"

Liska looked at the floor, didn't move, didn't even twitch a facial muscle. Right about the time I thought he'd gone to sleep he said, "If I had to guess, 1983. Don't bother telling me why you wanted to know."

There was another piece of history I wanted to dredge from his memory, but I forgot what it was.

"One last favor," I said. "Can I bum a couple Ziploc bags?"

26

THE SHELBY HAS A distinct exhaust sound, even more audible at night, so I parked on George and walked two blocks to Tanker Branigan's house on Johnson. I didn't see a soul or—local miracle—prompt dogs to bark. On a crapshoot I was going to harvest a recycling container for potential evidence, assuming that Tanker was a friend of both my brother and the environment. My thinking rode the concept that, if I could deliver Tim's empties to the FBI, via Bobbi Lewis, his palm prints would condemn him or clear him. As Liska had said, it would all come out in the end. Forever the optimist, I saw no choice but to try.

I found the bin and cursed the darkness. I didn't want to rattle bottles or cut my hand on a can lid. Master of stealth, I positioned myself to catch street-lamp reflections off the Michelob labels. Then I felt metal press against my neck.

"Move a muscle, motherfucker, and your mouth's an exit wound."

I froze, heard only the wind rustling the plastic bag in my hand. My penchant for quick comebacks died. I pictured my teeth in an outward spray of enamel and fillings.

"Jesus Christ, Alex," said the gruff, sleepy voice. "You need deposit nickels that bad?"

My knees went soft but I felt the cold pistol barrel lift away. I turned to find Branigan looking sheepish, his weapon now pointed downward.

"Do you need to guard your trash with a gun?"

"My tow-truck days, I had to show this monster once a week, but I only flashed it. I never fucking aimed at a human before. What the hell are you doing?"

I explained why I was there. I knew the police had Tim's fingerprints, but the key to the nightmare was a palm print. Tim's palm print, even if obtained by unofficial means, might lift all suspicion before the legal machine put unstoppable gears in motion.

"You could've rung the bell," he said. "I got two weeks' worth of trash you can have for free. Just take it outside the door."

"You might have been asleep. I'm sure this bin will give me plenty."

"But that plastic bag will smear the shit out of prints. You want to pick them up, you need to run a stick inside their spouts. I'll get you an empty six-pack carton to carry them. And take an empty Ice House. They'll need my palm print so they can differentiate."

After we'd lifted six bottles and placed the carton in a paper sack, Tanker said, "We okay on every little thing?"

"I've been thinking about your plan," I said. "You were going to challenge Tim to raise his self-esteem. It lifted my hopes for another shot at the friendship we had as kids. Now he's sitting in jail, most likely in retribution for your trick with Millican on the star."

"Fear not, big brother," said Tanker. "He's building character as we speak. It ain't over 'til it's over. He'll surprise all of us one day real soon."

I pissed off Bobbi Lewis by calling late.

"Why six bottles now?" she said. "I can't do squat until morning, anyway."

"We wouldn't have to connect in the morning. I could go home now and sleep late."

"Were you creeping around my house an hour and half ago? I heard your dual mufflers."

"I gave your neighbor a ride home," I said.

"From which restaurant?"

"She was drinking and didn't want to ride her crotch rocket."

"She want to ride yours?" said Bobbi.

"It didn't come up."

"I'll leave that line alone, thanks. If those bottles are so damned important, bring them to my office at eight-fifteen. You can personally hand them to a black suit with a Quantico accent."

I began to say something, but I was talking to dead air.

My drinking plus the blood-pressure spike from Branigan's weapon had me toasted. I didn't feel like driving twenty-five miles to Little Torch, and I kept thinking of Teresa's line about people hiring people to kill people. After all the info I'd pulled together, I felt closer to solving the puzzle. But that made me superstitious. What was to stop a pro from waiting in the shadows at Manning's house, hoisting me up for a midnight ride, making me an air dance Dumbo?

I needed a spiritual lift, but not by the neck.

I drove fifteen blocks, parked in front of Sam and Marnie's house, and dialed the inside number.

"Yes, Alex," said Marnie. "I'm on the porch listening to tree frogs and eating Healthy Choice ice cream and looking at your car behind the hedge. You may think of our couch as your home away from home."

Marnie was stretched out in a long T-shirt and surfer jams.

"This peaceful pose," I said. "May I assume you heard from the man we knew as Sam Wheeler?"

"It's rained for three straight days in Baldwin County, Alabama. He got fed up and he'll drive as far as Gainesville tomorrow. We have an actual, real dinner date the next night."

"Any response to your classified ad?" I said.

"One call, from one Mayra Culmer, a widow with the emphasis on lonely. Her late husband, Elmer Culmer, was a first-class boilerman on the **Bushnell.** Elmer went down to cancer in 1988."

"Elmer's going to miss the party."

"Mayra said that the crew and their wives, especially those who lived in town, were a tight-knit group in the early days. She wants to help organize the festivities. She talked to me like her new best friend. I gather it's been a long slog since '88."

The Conch Train woke me. Marnie was in her office on the phone. I hadn't meant to sleep so late. When I came out from brushing my teeth, Marnie had coffee for me. "You didn't hear the phone?"

I shook my head. "I heard the train driver on South Street yakking about sea-grape trees. Is that your reality gong every morning?"

"That was the third train today. You were out cold. Meanwhile, I got another call from Mayra, the lonely Navy widow. She's going through some old boxes because she thought she still had a cruise book. She thought it might help me find **Bushnell** and **Gilmore** crew members."

"We want that," I said. "They were skinny, hardbound versions of your high school yearbook. Big on squadron logos and phony-ass pictures of the captain schmoozing with snipes and deck apes."

Marnie's phone rang again. She ducked away and I spread the morning's newspaper across a table, sipped my coffee. The real estate ads inspired my next move, an idea that promised fewer speed bumps than pilfering bottles. The white pages had no listing for Sharon Woods. The Yellow Pages listed a title-insurance company on Big Pine. A bubbly-voiced woman answered my call. I told her I needed to find the owner of Deer Abbey Real Estate.

"Sharon?" she said. "We've been trying to reach her since last Friday."

"I'm an old friend, not a client, but I can't find her anywhere."

"I've heard that she's trying to cut back on work. Do you live on Big Pine?"

"Little Torch," I said.

"Heck, honey, try the house."

"I hate to barge in on her," I said, "and I misplaced her number."

"Well, that's a problem. She's unlisted, you know, which has always been odd for a real estate broker. You might have to drive by."

"That's another problem. We never socialized at her house. We met at restaurants, so I don't know where she lives."

"The lady I work with knows where it is, but she's gambling in Nassau. I'd tell you to call the utility companies, but they're sworn to secrecy anymore. All these new rules. If Edith calls in, you want me to get directions and call you back?"

"Love it." I gave her my name and number.

"I'm Honey Groves," she said. "I know it sounds fake, but it's not."

"That's refreshing," I said. "Our world is awash in fake names."

I stopped on Stock Island to give the six-pack of empties to Bobbi Lewis. I had blown the eight-fifteen appointment, and Bobbi wasn't in her office. The duty guard recognized me. He checked the paper sack and probably pegged it as a joke. He wasn't anxious to believe that rattling bottles were possible evidence. I asked him to let Lewis decide.

I made good time up the Keys. The sky was so blue it looked plugged in, and I rode the easy chair between an Immigration and Naturalization bus and a box-shaped delivery truck. The INS bus had BORDER PATROL across its stern. Another boatload had hit the beach, the bumpy bus ride the best thing desperate Cubans had experienced for years.

No surprise, Deer Abbey Real Estate was closed up tight. The same FAMILY EMERGENCY sign hung in the window. I drove to the sandwich shop, parked out front. The smells and the sight of the cook stacking bacon, lettuce, and tomato made me instantly hungry. I was the only customer. I sat and offered the young counter server twenty bucks for the BLT. She laughed and said, "Fine. I was going to save it for after work, anyway."

"Deal's a deal," I said, and opened my wallet.

She put the sandwich in front of me, along with a minibag of chips and a glass of iced tea. "We'll settle for five dollars and fifty cents."

"I might have to leave a fourteen-dollar tip."

She smiled. "That's up to you."

I took time to enjoy the food. The young woman went about her job, set up her work station for the lunch rush. When I was down to my last few bites I said, "Sharon Woods come in for breakfast?"

The girl shook her head but tapped a photo tacked among a dozen others on the wall. A woman in a Halloween witch's costume stood in front of a cute cottage. The print quality sucked. I couldn't make out the face.

"You want to rent that house?" she said. "My

daddy owns it. If you know Sharon, you probably know she's going to a bigger place."

"I'd be interested in renting, but I have to say, I didn't know she was moving. Actually, for all these years I've known her, I've never been to her home."

"My daddy's cottage is too small for her wheelchair. I'm not supposed to show it until the day after tomorrow. Sharon doesn't want to be bothered while she's packing to leave."

"I'm easy," I said. "If I like the neighborhood, that's eighty percent of my decision. Write down the address, and I'll drive by and check it out. If I see her outside, I won't let her know why I'm around. For certain, I won't mention your name."

She smiled. "You don't know my name."

"So your secret is safe with me."

"Okay." She wrote the address on her order pad. "It's a mile and four tenths from here. Can I really keep the change?"

A white picket fence, a screened porch, board-and-batten siding, and a plastic trellis hid the double-wide aspects of Sharon Woods's small "manufactured" house. A metal roof and green shutters made it look like a Conch cottage, or at least attempted. My knowledge of Big Pine put the closest canal four blocks distant. I'd expected to find a real estate broker in better circumstances.

I parked on the street and walked toward the house.

A graveled woman's voice barked, "Stand out there in the sun and tell me why you're here."

She was behind a screen door and looked to be sitting. I couldn't make out her face. "I'm looking for Sharon Woods. My name is Alex Rutledge."

She coughed. "You're a policeman?"

I shook my head. "No. I wanted to ask you about three of your real estate deals. Milton Navarre, Kansas Jack Mason, and—"

"Haskins," she said. "Lucky and Tinkerbell Haskins. Can you imagine going through life with those names?"

I shook my head and kept quiet, tried to adjust my eyes to the darkness behind the door.

The rough voice: "I know about those killings and I hate the thought."

"I know you sold—"

"Yes, I did, and I've been waiting five days for detectives to knock on my door. A woman called about Jack Mason but she never followed up. If you're not a policeman, what's your interest in those people?"

"I'm a part-time photographer for the county. I had to take the crime-scene pictures of the first two deaths. That got me involved. Then a detective showed me a photo she found in one of the men's effects. It was a young girl standing in front of my home in Key West before I bought the house. I got to know the girl, a long time ago, then lost touch with her. Knowing that a murdered man had her photograph, I was worried about that girl I hadn't seen in years. She'd be a grown woman by now."

"And that"—the woman coughed again—"that brings you all the way to Big Pine?"

"Not that far." I reached down to slap a mosquito on my leg. "I'm watching a friend's house over on Little Torch, on Keelhaul Lane."

She hesitated, then said, "I don't mean the distance you traveled. I just wonder about your curiosity. Was that girl in the picture your only motivation for coming here?"

"It's a long story, but there's a real chance my brother will be accused of the first two murders. He's had what they call a rough go all his life. What's the old cliché, 'bad choices'? The detectives might find him an easy target for suspicion, guilty or not."

I saw her hand wave behind the dark screening. She pushed open the screen door and rolled forward a foot or two in a wheelchair. "Get out of the sun and bugs. There's a bench up here."

On the porch, in the shade, I had a better view of the coughing woman in her flower-pattern robe. She lit a cigarette, shifted her position, and rubbed her tongue on the front of her teeth. She took a drag, then said, "I take it you're trying to be a private eye. You solve the case of the hanging bums and your brother's off the hook, so to say."

In the still-dim light Sharon Woods's mannerisms gave me a spooky feeling. "That's part of it, too," I said. "Anything that might help find the real killer, any connection, I'd appreciate."

"Right, plus the little girl you're worried about."

"Yes," I said.

"Well, like I said, Alex Rutledge, I've been waiting for days for the detectives to show up or else"—she shifted her cigarette to her right hand and raised a pistol from next to her thigh, lifted its barrel, then dropped it back to its hiding spot—"or else, because of my connection to the victims, I wondered if a murderer might show up. I wasn't sure, but I never thought it would be Alex Rutledge."

The speech patterns matched the mannerisms, but it took me almost ten seconds to make the connection. When my mind zeroed in on the fact, it struck me like something physical.

"You're Pokey Fields."

She clenched her jaw, reached to fluff her hair. It looked unwashed and needed more than fluffing. "You're the man who wouldn't throw me a quick roll in the hay. I'm surprised you'd even talk to me all these years later."

27

"WHICH ONE OF THEM had my picture?"

"Kansas Jack Mason."

Pokey coughed to clear her throat. "You told me to stay away from put-down artists, men who would keep me under thumb so they could be more important and powerful."

"Was I wrong?" I said.

"I have no earthly idea. I didn't follow your advice."

I kept my trap shut. I didn't want to pass judgment half a lifetime later.

"Before I met you," she continued, "I fell in love with a man who died. I never fell in love again. For a few years I tried more men than I could count. My deceased mother used to warn me, it's a long way from the mattress to matrimony. I finally got married and stayed that way for a hell of a lot longer than most marriages last these days. That deal went down the crapper, too."

"Did I make a difference in your life?" I said. "Any difference at all?"

"Those books did."

"How so?"

"I learned there was a world north of the Seven Mile Bridge," she said. "I didn't soak up everything the world has to offer, but the books sure as hell clued me in. I also learned you can't be a whore where everyone gives it away for free. I'm not talking about sex, you understand?"

"What do you mean?"

"Friendship. I was going after it on the barter system."

"Tell me about the Oblivion Division."

"My word, Alex, you've done your homework. Before I start, I'll warn you. This isn't going to help stop or solve a single damned crime."

"That's fine," I said. "I'll take it as a history lesson. Local color."

"There'll be a mess of that. God, I've been waiting a long time to spew this out. You're going to hear more than any job-whipped cop, that's for sure."

"I'm in no hurry to be anywhere else," I said.

She coughed a few more times, picked up a pack of cigarettes, looked at it, then put it aside. "Lucky Haskins's daddy was a chief in the **Bushnell** disbursing office and later on the USS **Gilmore.** He died, I don't know, around 1980.

But back in 1970 Chief Haskins was a card player. He got himself into a game upstairs at Captain Tony's. That bar's still there, I believe, but I haven't been on Greene Street since a Fantasy Fest twenty years ago. Anyway, there were some charter-boat captains, the Monroe County sheriff, a few bartenders, the city manager, Captain Tony, and a dentist they called Dr. Bill. Those are the ones I remember, because I used to pick up fancy cash making their drinks and letting them pinch my fanny. They played once a week, hot and heavy, from ten at night until whenever.

"Anyway, one of those games, the city manager complained about a major problem with the accounting in his maintenance department. The chief told him, 'Let me come in and take over, and your grief is ended.' The city manager asked if he would get in trouble with the Navy, and Chief Haskins assured him that he could take care of that. The ship was a tender; it was there to service submarines and never left the dock. All the chief needed was forty minutes' notice of meetings ashore so he could get himself off the ship and over to city hall.

"Well, that started it all, and this was back in the **Bushnell** days. I guess the chief got the city manager out of a bind and put the books in fine shape. But he found a loophole in the system, and real quick four or five boys from the ship were employed off-base. And wasn't my new boyfriend one of them?"

"Your first lover?" I said.

"Paul was the only boy I ever loved," she said.

"Was he the one who died?"

"Don't get ahead of my story, okay?"

I sucked in my lips to show her my mouth was sealed.

"There were five sailors moonlighting in broad daylight," she said. "People in town never suspected, and aboard ship Chief Haskins covered for their absences. It began with each man earning two incomes. Paul told me that the chief figured how to skim each man's Navy paycheck—that was his profit on the deal. But the chief didn't stop there. He came up with a larger scheme that took a brilliant mind to dream up, even though sooner or later it would fail. He and those boys weren't thinking too far ahead, and it started to crumble in 1972 when word came down that the submarine base was closing. The **Gilmore** received deployment orders for the Mediterranean, and Chief Haskins was first to go. The war was ending, and they needed disbursing personnel to process Vietnam discharges on the West Coast. The chief hadn't been gone three weeks when a clerk at the city found a pattern of overpayments."

That must have been the city's $300,000 shortfall in autumn of 1972.

"Real quick, it all went to hell," she said. "The city commission ordered an investigation and an inventory, and it took them about six weeks to find a major hitch. Chief Haskins had decentralized storage to save transportation costs and time. The city procurement people had been ordering for three maintenance sheds around the island. For two full years the city had ordered three of each tool, pipe, spare part, and piece of gear. The inventory of the first two sheds came out almost on the money. But the last one, they found an empty building on Whitehead Street."

"A bogus shed?"

"Only the BlivDivs knew about it—the Oblivion Division."

"How did they sell the stolen equipment?" I said.

"Construction crews out of Miami. Like clockwork. I don't think a delivery truck left the island empty for almost two years."

"Did you know about it all?" I said.

"Let me finish. A city personnel-records check showed that five people in maintenance hadn't shown up for work after January 1, 1973. No one knew where they lived or where they had gone."

"So they went back aboard to wait for the ship to sail to the Mediterranean?"

"For the most part. In mid-January, they all took leaves and went to Reno, Nevada, to celebrate their great wealth. What could it have been, maybe ten or twelve grand apiece? Anyway, yes, they confined themselves to the ship, with one exception."

"And none of the city's discoveries made the news?"

"Oh, major embarrassment," said Pokey. "The politicos didn't want to know about it. There was so much other crap going down—commissioners smuggling pot, cops on the take, you name it— a few missing lawn mowers was small-time. No one in town ever linked it to the Navy. Of course, the city manager who hired Chief Haskins in the first place kept his mouth shut. I assume that cost somebody some cash."

"What was the exception?" I said.

"When they came back from Reno, everything was different."

"How so?" I said.

"They made a pact to stick together and never rat on each other. Even if one of them was caught, he would never tell on the others. They wanted my boyfriend to promise not to sneak off the ship so he could visit me, and of course he was sneaking off to see me. One night at dinner-time Paul went to Carlos Market on Caroline to buy us some burger meat. A city maintenance supervisor recognized him and called the police dispatcher and Paul was arrested. He bonded out the next day, but BlivDivs heard that the city was going to send a bunch of people onto the **Gilmore** to look at faces, to see if they could find the missing maintenance workers."

"Was Chief Haskins's son named Lucky?"

Pokey nodded. "He was a teenager who became the Oblivion Division's mascot. He may have made some pocket change, but no more than that. He stayed in town to finish high school when his father shipped out for San Diego."

"Did the city send people on board?"

"I think the ship left port before they had a chance."

"You mind if I ask your boyfriend's full name?"

"His first name was Harvey," she said. "He went by his middle name, Paul. His last name was Evans."

I pressed on. "And you, after he died?"

"I cried for ten hours and I married him the next day. He couldn't make the ceremony, but I had friends in town who fixed the paperwork. You could get stuff like that done in Key West back then. If it hadn't been for that Navy widow's pension, I might have starved those first couple of years."

"You were still in high school?"

"My senior year," she said. "And my father wouldn't allow me in his home. Even when my mother died, I couldn't go inside. That's why I came around after you bought it."

"Must have been tough."

Tears streamed down the woman's face. "It still is, Alex. You have to go now."

28

AFTER THREE TRIES I connected with Bobbi.

"Where are you?" she said. "Talk fast, I'm in a hurry."

"On the bridge between Big Pine and Little Torch. Did you get the bottles?"

"They're being analyzed as we speak. What else?"

"The Michelobs were Tim's. The Ice House, for reference, was his roommate's."

"What else?" she said.

"I found and spoke with your little girl in the photo. I'm out on a limb here, but there's a chance she hired the hit man who killed Kansas Jack, Navarre, and Haskins."

"Meddling again, Rutledge?"

"And here I am, fool that I am, trying to pass credit to you."

"Her name and address?"

"Sharon Woods." I told her the street address on Big Pine. "Get her phone records and you'll find the FBI's secret Most Wanted man."

"You know too much for your own good," said Bobbi. "But thank you."

I found Tanker's roommate, Francie, in a chair under Al Manning's house on Little Torch. Her jaw was set tough, but she curled one side of her mouth to a sly grin. She wore a forehead sweatband, running shorts, and a cut-off tank top that said, IT AIN'T GONNA LICK ITSELF. Perspiration sparkled on her upper lip.

I shut down the car and stared at her.

"The horny toad I picked up in the Hog's Breath last night had a dentist's appointment on Big Pine," she said. "I'm looking for new accommodations."

"Tanker jealous of your new chauffeur?"

"Tanker and me were mostly just roommates," she said, "but he watched sometimes."

"Watched."

"Me and other guys," said Francie. "That's why he let me stay there. This morning he said he was closing down the hotel. I was riding a cock-horse to Banbury Cross. Next thing I know I'm on the sidewalk with my hair dryer and four grocery bags full of laundry." She pointed. The kayak held her makeshift luggage. "Can I use your outside shower? I smell like a gym locker."

"It was on my list, too," I said. "This time of year, you go two days without a bath, you don't even get solicitation calls." I gestured toward the yard.

"I already looked inside. It's big enough for two."

She walked toward the rear of the house, checked over her shoulder to make sure I was following, and peeled off her top. She gave me a dirty smile and swung open the shower door. Off came the sandals and shorts. She had an all-over tan, not a wisp of hair from the neck down.

"I'll let you go first," I said.

"You don't like my looks, Alex, I'm not gonna get my imaginary panties in a wad over it." She tapped her finger on a bar of soap. "Can I borrow shampoo?"

I came back down with a washcloth, a towel, and Pantene. She was lathered up, looking slippery. "I like the philodendron in here," she said. "All we need is a tiger peeking through the leaves, we could be a tropical painting. Come in and I'll scrub your back."

"You ever wear a bathing suit?"

"The two things I need least in my life are boring people and tan lines."

"And I get categorized if I don't strip down?"

"You're already categorized. You're bashful."

"Let's work slowly on our relationship," I said. "It'll mean more to us down the road."

"I'm almost done here."

"Take your time."

Twenty minutes later, after our separate showers, we sat on the porch, beers in hand. Francie stared at the canal view as if it were a big movie screen. "We're a long way from Kansas," she said. "Four months ago me and my girlfriend were evicted from a trailer east of Lawrence. We thought we'd wind up sleeping on benches with newspaper quilts. We had a yard sale that lasted only an hour. Some creep gave us three hundred bucks for all our old underwear. That night we caught a Greyhound to Miami, and the next day a pimp from the bus station brought us down here. He got creepier than the thong-sniffer, so we ditched him on Duval."

"What happened to your friend?" I said.

"Found herself a boyfriend who mates on a charter boat. When he first met us, he called us the wild sport fuck and the pink frustration."

"You being . . ."

"I'm not the chicken-head, if that's what you mean. I like to project the image of being almost a virgin. Does that mentally show on my face, from your way of seeing it? Or does that make sense?"

"I almost couldn't have said it better," I said. "How did you meet Tanker?"

"I met him in Rick's Bar. He gave me the ultimate pickup line. He was impressed because I could walk and chew gum at the same time. My dirty mind went to work, and I asked what he could do at the same time. He said, 'Floss and piss,' so I said, 'You either floss one-handed, or piss hands-free. Who cleans your toilet after you clean your teeth?' "

"How did he react to that one?"

She raised her eyebrows. "That's when he said he loved me."

"Other than sex games, how was he as a room-mate?"

"In this town, you have to be careful when you complain about cheap rent."

"So you admit to an issue or two?" I said.

"When Tanker cleaned the bathroom, he called it 'the Annual.' He got pissed a couple times when I left the toilet seat down. And he cared more for that policewoman blow-up doll than he did about me. The doll and his precious stack of little blue books."

"He was a reader?"

"Skinnier books than ones you'd read. I got the impression they were bankbooks. The top one was a passport, and the rest I never saw. He waved that stack at me once and said, 'Don't ever forget that money buys freedom.' He counts his pennies and cries poverty all the time, but I think he's rich."

"Does my brother know he doesn't have a place to live anymore?"

"What do you mean?" said Francie. "After the

second night, he never came back. That Teresa works for the city and she was his sugar mama, best we could guess."

"Were you the Michelob drinker?" I said.

She grinned again. "Tim left a case and a half and the price was right . . . Wait, was that you last night in the garbage? Tanker said some ass-hole was looking for deposit bottles."

I nodded. "It's a long story. You came here looking for a place to crash? Why me?"

"I need short-term stability."

"What about mine?"

"Is that your cell phone?"

I caught Marnie's call before my message service did its thing. "If you're in town, you might want to drive over," she said. "Mayra Culmer found that cruise book, and it's full of photographs."

"I'm on Little Torch," I said. "I can be there in a half hour. What was the date of that Navy flag-pole hanging in '73?"

"Hold on . . . January twenty-third."

I couldn't remember the date engraved on the silver Zippo from Reno. But I knew it was before the twenty-third.

"You might want to start looking for a Harvey Paul Evans."

"I found his name in an old police report on the flagpole hanging," she said. "He was a ma-chinist's mate."

———

Francie proposed that she take a nap while I went into town.

"It's not my house," I said. "I can't invite houseguests."

"I make a mean cheese-and-sausage omelette and a beef stew that will turn you into a sex fiend."

I shook my head. "I'm afraid you'll turn me into a thong-sniffer."

"So much for stability," she said. "Take me back to the crazy island."

I helped Francie load her bags into the car and made sure Wendell Glavin wasn't in my rearview. Inbound was a piece of cake. Outbound rush hour was a long train of bumper jumpers, Lower Keys commuters heading home to Cudjoe and Summerland.

I made four calls from the four-lane around Boca Chica Naval Air Station. A woman I knew at a downtown bail-bond outfit assured me that, for anything short of felony weapon use or manslaughter, Tim would see daylight by sundown. Good trick, I thought. Tim might show his appreciation by throwing us a moon at high noon.

The second call was to Carmen. With her job at the post office, she knew how to find little-known apartments and decent landlords. She told me to drop off Francie on my way into town and promised to find her the cheapest efficiency on the island. She also said that Johnny Griffin had kept his promise. Dredgers Lane had enjoyed a silent night.

My call log gave me Gail Downer's office number. It was late but I gave it a try. Maybe it would forward to her home phone. It rang twice and jumped to a recording. I was trying to click off when she picked up.

"I'm sorry to bother you at this hour," I said. "I need a favor. If you have that Zippo lighter handy, I need to know those engraved initials."

"Easy," she said. "It's with those papers in the trunk of my car. Hold a sec."

I dug a ballpoint and a paper scrap out of my glove compartment and handed them to Francie.

Gail returned to the line. "The date is 1/12/73."

"Okay," I said. "But go slowly. I have to re-peat all this to my secretary."

"The next line reads 'Nevada,' and under that is "R.I."

"R.I., as in Rhode Island." I said. "Then?"

"M.J.W."

I told Francie and said, "Next?"

"Umm, E.J.B."

Coincidence? Only Bixby knew for sure. "E.J.B.," I said. "Got it. Keep going."

"J.P. Mc-W., with a small 'C,' not 'M-A-C.' "

I repeated it for Francie.

"Then H.P.E."

I said, "H.P.E." Harvey Paul Evans.

"Is this information good for my father?" said Gail. "Or your brother?"

"I'm still not sure of a damned thing, but I think it's good news and I'll let you know as soon as anything makes sense."

Finally, I called Liska's home number.

"There's no more beer, there's no more vodka."

"Don't need either, Sheriff," I said. "Who was the ex–Navy man who died on Olivia Street in April?"

"He used a fake name for fifteen years. His real name, which I assume you want, was Morris J. Wells. Can I ask why you need to know this?"

"His initials were on that Zippo lighter that Lewis found."

"Oh, Jesus."

I kept telling myself that the weeklong puzzle had come full circle. But a few stations on the circumference remained in fog. Twenty-four hours earlier I was banging my shin on a blue recycling bin. Now I felt close to banging my nose on a solution to three murder cases and, from a personal standpoint, to getting out of the police-photo business. Perhaps Johnny Griffin's rent cash would kick off my easy future, my world travels, my precious collection of little blue bankbooks topped by a passport.

How many bankbooks does one man need?

I took Francie to Dredgers Lane and helped her move her makeshift luggage from my car to Carmen's kitchen. As soon as I was clear of the lane, I pulled out the cell phone and punched in Bobbi's number.

"What now, Alex? I sent deputies, but whatever you said to Sharon Woods scared her away. She closed up her house and bolted."

"Those bottles?" I said. "Check the Ice House for a match to the FBI's wanted man. Tim's buddy called himself Tanker Branigan. A girl who shared his house at 1878 Johnson just told me he had a collection of little blue books. She thought they were bankbooks. What makes more sense is that they're passports with phony names. I think he's your hit man, and he knows we're on the edge of finding him. You need to act fast."

"If Sharon Woods hired this hit man and she's gone, it stands to reason that Branigan will be gone, too. You're so good at figuring things out, tell me exactly what I need to do."

"I'll call you back in an hour," I said.

"So I sit here on my ass and wait for you to solve the crimes?"

"Maybe you could order a roadblock at Jewfish Creek."

"I'm going to order lunch instead."

On my way to Marnie and Sam's I drove past the house on Johnson.

Closed up and dark.

Tanker wasn't home.

29

ELIZABETH STREET SMELLED OF frangipani and recent rain. I hadn't seen puddles on South Street. In Key West, that's a 10 percent chance of precipitation. It's going to rain for sure, but only on 10 percent of the island.

Marnie met me on her wide front porch and handed me a skinny nine-by-twelve book without a dust jacket. Its front cover was elaborately embossed with the title **USS Bushnell, AS-15, Springboard '68** and a simplistic rendition of a large ship surrounded by destroyers, helicopters, and submarines. I took it inside to a table. Marnie had set up a desk lamp.

"It commemorates a training cruise to the Caribbean." She handed me a magnifying glass. "Mayra said there's a bunch of these men who wound up on the **Gilmore.** You feel ready to look at five hundred faces?"

I pulled out my note with the Zippo initials and the packet of Duffy Lee Hall's photo prints.

I told Marnie about "M.J.W."—Morris J. Wells—the questionable suicide from early April, then shuffled photos to find the least gruesome head shots of Kansas Jack Mason and Milton Navarre. "Here are our current-day murder victims," I said. "Harvey Paul Evans and Morris J. Wells and three other sailors were running a scam to rip off the city, hence the city's missing money and need for inventories. Evans was the sailor having an affair with Pokey Fields, aka Sharon Woods, now a real estate broker on Big Pine."

"Did her father hang Evans?" she said.

"According to Pokey, Evans was the only one arrested. She didn't say they killed him, but it stands to reason that his scam partners didn't trust him to stay clammed up."

I perused the book. Informal shots on every third page or so bore captions with weak attempts at humor. A young boatswain's mate in a light denim shirt, dark blue jeans, and a sailor cap stood over a spilled bucket of paint. The caption read, "Gee, Chief, you said you wanted a thick coating."

Studying tiny faces in old photos could take me all night. I began to scan name rosters of the posed groups of shipboard divisions and teams. I found the first set of initials only ten minutes into my search. "Bingo," I said, but E.J.B. wasn't named Bixby. I didn't need the magnifying glass to see that Milton Navarre had once been petty officer third-class Edwin J. Bacon, assigned to the **Bushnell** Supply Division.

With 'E.J.B.,' 'H.P.E.,' and 'M.J.W.' identi-fied, I suspected—hell, I knew—that the last group of initials—"J.P.McW."—would match a much younger Kansas Jack Mason. I still wanted to confirm it in black and white, but something didn't add up. If there were five sailors in the scam, I needed to find two more faces but had only one set of initials. I scanned for a last name that began with "McW."

Marnie brought me coffee. "Can you talk to me while you search the book? This could be my big story, but all the facts are in your brain."

I spat out my take on Tanker Branigan, and Bobbi's nonreaction to my news. Then, ten or twelve pages in, I studied a picture of a dozen sailors from the ship's print shop. The stern, al-ready weathered face of Kansas Jack jumped out at me. I read the caption but found no "McW." name. I counted heads from the left, then names from the left. Kansas Jack had been Petty Officer Robert Ingersoll.

The "R.I." on the silver lighter had not stood for Rhode Island.

"Talk to me," said Marnie.

I tapped the evidence photos I'd shot a week earlier. "I've accounted for four men," I said. "That leaves one more group of initials."

"Don't forget Lucky Haskins," she said.

"But that was his real name. We still need a
J.P.McW."

"Is there a body we haven't connected to all
this?"

"He could've died years ago," I said. "Or he
still could be on Tanker's list, if he's the killer, except he's probably north of Orlando by now. Either way, you've got your story."

"You're not leaving the house until I finish
writing it," she said.

"I'll keep reading this book while I fill you in."

I turned a page and found a photo of the
eight-man ship's underwater repair team. My finger stopped on J. P. McWerter. Again I counted
names then faces. It was Wendell Glavin whose
broad, much younger smile spooked me. Wendell, the avid diver.

"Marnie, the phone book. Look up Glavin on
Little Torch. Call him on your phone."

I grabbed my cell and punched in Bobbi's
number. For once she answered.

"Branigan's house is dark," I said, "so you were
right. He's on the move. His next victim is my
neighbor across the street on Little Torch, Wendell Glavin."

"You've got to tell me why you think that,
Alex," said Bobbi. "I can't dispatch units based
on a hunch."

"I'm looking at an old cruise book that Marnie
Dunwoody located. Glavin was on the **Bushnell**

and **Gilmore** with Kansas Jack and Milton Navarre. The three were hooked up in an old scam to fleece the city. The sheriff knows the background on it."

"I'm already dialing Liska." Bobbi hung up.

"Glavin doesn't answer on Little Torch," said Marnie. "It just keeps ringing."

Marnie insisted on riding with me. She wanted me to talk her through the story while I hurried up the highway. I kept it under forty out Flagler, but once I rolled into county jurisdiction and crossed Stock Island, I hit the pedal hard. By the time I passed Key Haven, I was clocking sixty-five. Clear of Shark Key, when there were no on-comings, I took it over eighty. Anything more on that washboard surface, we'd go airborne.

For six days Wendell had been eagle-eyed, always aware of comings and goings at Al Manning's house, especially after he learned of my quasi-official connection to the cases. One of the first things he'd talked about was the murder on Ramrod Key, though he'd tried to pass it off as the work of Cuban refugees. If I had wanted to engage him in conversation, I could've pointed out that the last thing a refugee would do, after risking his life to reach the beach, is commit a crime. But Wendell had been alerted when he found out who was killed on Ramrod. He must have gone to full panic when he learned that Milton Navarre died the same day. He knew that he fit the potential-victim category. He might even have thought that I was his executioner.

I gave Marnie the gist of my Liska interview, leaving out the free roof on his mother's home. I ran what I remembered of my conversation with Sharon Woods. The mile markers flew by. I passed only five or six cars and watched my temp needle creep toward the H.

Crossing the tall bridge from Summerland to Ramrod, I saw a mass of flashing blue and red lights in the near distance. I lifted my foot from the accelerator.

"A roadblock for us?" said Marnie.

"I must have passed a deputy in a radar cruiser."

I didn't want to confront a highway-patrol roadblock in an overheating car. They might not be impressed by a civilian hurrying to stop a crime. I pulled into the Boondocks lot and shut off my lights. We were two miles from Keelhaul Lane. Walking could take a half hour, and by that time anything could happen.

Two civilian cars and a pickup truck rolled past us heading south.

"Shit," I said. "A roadblock would stop all traffic, not just the northbound flow. The flashing lights are on Keelhaul."

Ninety seconds later I turned down Pirates Road. My headlights caught two people next to a car on the shoulder. They waved for help, but tough shit. I couldn't fix their problem. I floored it, swerved to pass wide, then recognized them. I stopped long enough to get Tim and Teresa into the backseat.

"My car ran out of gas," said Teresa.

I checked my own gauge. The needle was solid on E. "Why are you here?"

"Marge Sayre called from the city. She heard a crime report come across the county's radio circuit and got worried. You must've told her you were staying on Keelhaul Lane."

I couldn't pull my car under Al Manning's place. Cop cars blocked his driveway. But the action was across the street at Wendell's house. I parked forty yards away.

"Do you know what the fuck is going down?" said Tim.

"Yes," I said. "You two need to slide up the side stairs and hang in my kitchen."

"No argument there," said Tim. "I'm allergic to this lighting scheme."

Marnie and I approached Wendell's driveway. I spotted Bohner and Millican, then Bobbi Lewis.

"I won't press you to work," said Lewis. "One of the deputies had a camera with him."

The silhouette of Wendell's wet suit was right where he'd always hung it. A rope ran upward from the body inside the suit to an under-house beam.

"We were too late to save Wendell," I said.

"Our sicko killer hung up two wet suits," said Bobbi. "That's the city's uniformed doll, Matilda, still in the air."

Tanker Branigan had offered a farewell practical joke. "Where's Wendell?"

Bobbi flipped her hand toward the ambulance. "We asked a neighbor to look. She'd never seen the victim before. The body in there is not Wendell Glavin."

I walked past the hard stares of Millican and Bohner. The rear doors of the ambulance stood open. The victim stretched out in the lighted interior was an ashen version of the man I had met and come to know during the past week.

I turned around, found Bobbi right behind me. "Your murderer's the dead man."

"Come again?" she said.

"That's Tanker Branigan."

"Need help here?" Millican appeared large by Lewis's side. Bohner stood next to him, his hand positioned close to his weapon.

"You've been returned to duty, Millican?" I said. "They didn't tell your victim that all was forgiven."

"Nothing's forgiven," he said.

"There's your abductor, laid out in the wagon. Does that make you happy?"

"That's good, asshole," he said. "Blame your shit on a corpse."

"You fucking crook," I said. "If you had shut down that scam in '73 instead of taking brown bags stuffed with cash, this whole week wouldn't have happened. Who was sliding you money, Chief Haskins or the man they hung? Was that why you hurried up north and took another job, Millican?"

"You are fucked beyond belief."

A new voice said, "No you're not, Rutledge. You're exactly right."

Sheriff Liska and a black-suited crew-cut stranger had joined us. Behind him stood the woman with the short brown hair whom I had offended on the airplane. A new Crown Victoria stopped in the street. Two Florida Department of Law Enforcement agents in matching polo shirts and khaki trousers stepped out. The FDLE's crime-scene van stopped behind the Crown Vic. The new scene command team had arrived.

The FBI agent with Liska requested palm prints from Branigan's corpse and insisted that the body be taken to Miami for autopsy. The prosecutor— my plane companion—confronted a distraught

Chester Millican. So as not to be snagged in the net, Deputy Bohner hurried to his cruiser and drove away.

I started walking toward my car so I could move it under the house. I felt limp as an eel, like I hadn't slept in a month. Then Bobbi caught up and we stood next to someone's mailbox, briefly speculated on Millican's future.

"Wendell Glavin was waiting for Branigan?" she said.

"If three of my former associates had been murdered, I'd be in the driveway with an AK-47."

"Three?"

"Lucky Haskins," I said. "He was just a kid who idolized the scamming sailors. Except all these years he knew that his heroes had killed a man."

"Can I have all the details tomorrow?"

"You're not going to look for my murdering neighbor?"

"The FDLE is all over it. I told them that Wendell probably stole Tanker's collection of fake passports. They notified every airport from Atlanta south, but they're afraid he flew out of Miami ahead of their alert."

"You want to spend the night across the street?"

She shook her head. "Three different agencies need my written report by seven A.M."

"You know the weird thing about Branigan?" I said.

"His sense of humor?"

"He came to me last Sunday at the Lodge with a plan to boost Tim's self-image. He wanted my okay."

"And you gave him permission?"

"I told him my brother's life was not my responsibility."

"You posted bond for Tim's release this evening," she said. "How long will you be his enabler?"

"Millican and a few others had declared him guilty before trial. I wanted him out of the system, out of custody."

"Even if he was a murderer?"

"Didn't I give you beer bottles with his palm prints?"

Bobbi nodded, looked pensive. "We arrested Bixby in his hospital bed on a warrant from the Missouri State Police. One of the murders he solved was solid, but the second one didn't add up."

"He'll finally get the fame he wanted so badly."

"I owe you a list of apologies." She put her arms around me and remembered not to squeeze too tightly.

"I recommend debt consolidation, Bobbi. Roll them all into one boat ride."

"Clothing optional?"

30

JUST BEFORE DAWN I heard a short downpour, could taste the rain, feel its presence like a cooling blanket. The birds woke me for good. I'd given Tim and Teresa the bedroom and Marnie the couch, so I drew the porch hammock. The arrangement was fine with me.

Between ten and midnight, after I'd pulled my Shelby under the house, the four of us had polished off my beer supply while I dictated details for Marnie's morning article. Tim listened while Teresa curled herself into a rattan loveseat and buried her nose in a Lorian Hemingway book on fishing. Marnie decided to leave Liska and Millican out of the story's background, at least for the initial report, and we timelined the rest of her piece. She kept herself awake long enough to e-mail it to the **Citizen**'s night desk. I opened a tin of cashews, ate the equivalent of a high-calorie, three-course meal, brushed my teeth, and took a snifter of Mount Gay to the hammock.

The cop radios and flashing lights across the street hadn't kept me from falling into deep sleep. I had no idea what time they closed down their crime scene.

The morning begged for the kayak ride I'd postponed so often. I wanted to give it a try before the day's heat set in, so I hoped I had sufficiently healed in the six days since the car wreck. Prowling quietly so I wouldn't wake the others, I found a ball cap, a white T-shirt, khaki shorts, and some bug repellent. I started humming an old Sheryl Crow lyric about a beer buzz in the morning. That inspired me to stop in the kitchen and twist the cap off an Amstel Light. Descending the outside stairs, I caught a déjà vu of Millican's ambush the previous Saturday, then comforted myself with the knowledge that he wouldn't be power-tripping any citizens in the months ahead.

In a lapse of come-awake drowsiness, I wondered why Wendell's wet suits weren't in their usual spot across the street. I was thankful that I hadn't been the one to find Tanker Branigan hung from the rafter, and I thought back to our little drama at the recycling bin. I had been a trigger's pull from death with a professional hit man holding the weapon, and I'd thought at the time I was fortunate not to have peed my pants. Hell, I was lucky not to have joined his strung-out roster of victims.

Distinctive sounds don't have to compete with

other noises at daybreak. As I lifted one end of the kayak from its cradle, a neighbor's air conditioner switched on with a loud thud. Even with the added noise, I heard feet shuffling behind me.

"Why did you have to stick your damn nose in all this?" said Pokey Fields.

I turned to find her aiming a pistol at me. She stood in a near-perfect ready stance, her feet apart, knees bent slightly. No wheelchair in sight.

"I wasn't sticking a thing," I said. "I was a bystander, if anything. I wasn't more than curious until I saw that picture of you."

"What was I, unfinished charity?"

"That's a pretty cold way to describe it," I said.

"Say it in your words, Alex. I was naked in your living room. You were counting my pubic hairs, watching my nipples like little weights on metronomes while I walked toward you. What was your plan, exactly?"

The pistol was in her left hand. When she had flashed her gun yesterday, it was next to her left thigh. She was the left-handed noose maker, and I'd missed the cue.

"I thought I could shake loose the bitterness in your life," I said. "You'd reached the point of hating every man who stuck himself inside you, and I didn't want to join the club."

"You didn't want the poontang?"

"I wanted to show you there was more to this existence than living with losers."

"Which brings us around to this time around," she said.

"I told you yesterday. A murdered man had your picture. You could've been in danger."

"Put the bottle down, Alex. I don't like it in your hand."

My back muscles danced with energy and I calculated the odds of survival if I leaped forward, grabbed for the gun. Would I be wounded instead of shot dead? Would I postpone the inevitable or give myself a chance? Would she go upstairs and start shooting the others after she'd taken me down? I forced my face muscles to droop as if a predeath stupor had taken over my mood. Without losing eye contact I reached sideways to put my beer and the bug repellent on the kayak.

She said, "You made me your personal crusade, right?"

The bottle fell to the concrete, broke, and sprayed glass against my ankles.

It didn't faze Pokey. "Or was it a different kind of crusade," she said, "like one of those dead men was your relative or something? Why did you have to fucking meddle?"

"The brother factor. I told you that, too. Tim was all set to be designated fall guy."

"Tanker told me he'd met you. I told him to go easy because you were okay. It saved your skull when he caught you taking beer bottles the other night."

"If Wendell was a target," I said, "why didn't Tanker kill him last Thursday morning?"

"Tanker wasn't even supposed to kill Eddie Bacon that day—the man you called Milton Navarre. He was supposed to take them out on different days as different forms of suicide, just like they disguised Paul Evans's murder in 1973. But Tanker was so proud of his davit deal that he did two the same day and brought police attention. We made an adjustment on his fee after that crap. To answer your question, Wendell wasn't home. When Tanker drove away, he saw him kissing that lady in the muumuu down the street. Wendell must've been screwing my old neighbor, and it saved his life."

"Your old neighbor?"

"You don't get it, do you? I was married to Wendell all this time. I left him last year after Lucky, when he was drunk one night in the Sugarloaf Lodge, let it slip that they'd hung Paul Evans from the flagpole. I always wondered if they'd done that, but I never knew for sure."

"Why did you marry Wendell?"

"Meal ticket, Alex. You wouldn't understand. You've never been that desperate. I just wish to hell Tanker had killed Wendell first. Lucky Haskins would still be alive."

It registered. "Wendell killed Lucky?"

"He figured out who told me that Paul wasn't a suicide."

"So it's everyone's week for revenge. Why are you pointing that thing at me?"

"Survival tactic."

"There's no connection to you," I said. "Who's going to prove that you hired Tanker?"

"You."

"I might know you did it, Pokey, but I can't prove that you did. The FBI was overjoyed to find Branigan, but if you kill me, they'll have a new murder suspect to hunt down. Where will you hide?"

"Easy, Alex. Everybody who disappears from the Keys goes to a Third World country and drives a taxi. You want to find me, look for a lady cabbie who lives near the ocean."

"I won't want to find you."

"Well, I guess the point's pointless, anyway." She waved her pistol toward the canal. "I made you a going-away present."

From where I stood I could see only one davit. A fresh noose hung from its hook.

"No fucking way," I said. "I saw how those men died."

"You get to join the club."

"I want you to shoot me."

"Maybe I won't kill you," said Pokey. "Maybe

I just want to see how you look with that rope around your neck, see how you look with no future, no fucking hope. Maybe I'll look at you like that and take pity and go away and let you live."

A voice from the backyard said, "Maybe you got the wrong man, Pokey Fields."

I turned to see Tim walking toward the noose. He wore khaki shorts, a ball cap, and a loose white T-shirt to mask his bulk. Except for his size, he was my mirror image.

Tim stopped under the davit, lifted the noose, and positioned it on his shoulders. He reached upward to snug it tighter against his chin. "Maybe you got my little brother at the end of that gun. How many people you want to kill today?"

Pokey was a cold soul, but not that cold. She aimed her gun at Tim, then back at me. Her eyes lost just enough focus to tell me she hadn't anticipated complications. She hadn't thought that anyone else was in the house. She hadn't thought that I'd refuse to move. She sure as hell hadn't guessed that an unarmed man would walk onstage when she held the only bullets.

Her focus returned with the chill and hate inside her. "You boys think you're too clever for an old hippie girl," she said. "You put a problem in front of me—which isn't a problem because what you and me have said the past two minutes, only the real Alex could know about—but I'm going to let you resolve this shit. That way one of you might not die."

"Come on, Pokey," said Tim. "You can flip this switch and solve your problem."

"No," she said. "I think you're Tim Rutledge and your brother's going to flip that switch. I could shoot you both, but if he turns on that davit, he gets to live."

"Bring it on," said Tim. "I'm about hungry as hell. Turn it on or I'm going to walk away and get breakfast."

Pokey aimed the pistol at my head. "Go out there," she said, "or I'll shoot you both."

"Aren't you worried that Wendell's going to come back and get his own revenge?"

"He's history and you know it. I could see from the highway all that activity last night. Tanker gave him the farewell party that I paid for."

"Then you didn't read the paper this morning," I said.

She checked to make sure Tim was standing still. "What I know couldn't be in the paper, Alex Rutledge."

"Wendell surprised Tanker and hung him and went away."

"What do you want to gain with that bullshit?" She glanced toward Wendell's house, the direction I wanted her to look. "You think if you confuse me, I'll crumble and cry and hand you this gun?"

"Wendell was on high alert after the other two deaths," I said. "It was Tanker Branigan they took away in the ambulance. Either way, I guess, it doesn't change my predicament."

"Right." She canted the pistol toward Tim. "Walk."

I shrugged, took one or two steps toward the backyard, and Marnie made her move. The karate kick from behind caught Pokey at the base of her skull. She and the pistol flew from under the house and landed in the yard. I couldn't tell if she was out cold or dead.

A moment later Billy Bohner's cruiser wheeled onto the pea rock. Teresa must have called 911. Thank goodness he'd taken his time.

We took Al Manning's motorboat to Picnic Island that afternoon. The statements and legal hubbub were behind us, and Bobbi took the afternoon off. Sam wasn't due back in the Keys until sundown, so Marnie had run to Murray's on Summerland for a satchel of sandwiches and wonderfully unhealthy chips and a refill of my beer supply.

A few other boats were anchored near us, one playing an Alan Jackson CD, people in lawn chairs in eighteen inches of water. It reminded me of the seventies when the gang I hung with would go to Ballast Key to skinny-dip and play volleyball and not give a damn about the rest of the world.

The authorities had dominated our morning, so we hadn't had time to talk among ourselves. Teresa was particularly quiet, still in shock over the risk Tim had taken. I couldn't figure out how to thank him without causing her more alarm.

Bobbi rescued me from my struggle by bringing up the subject. "I still can't believe Tim put himself into a hostage situation," she said. "Every guideline I've ever seen says it never works."

Tim responded with a no-big-deal wave, as if swatting a pesky bug. "You hear breaking glass and look outside and see a noose on the boat lift, you gotta do one thing or another."

"He did more than walk into the yard," I said. "He put his head in a damned noose. If she'd turned on the davit . . ."

"The fuse box was on the kitchen wall," said Tim. "I flipped the breaker before I came downstairs."

I smiled with pride and relief. "You've always been smarter than you looked."

"Thank God for that," he said. "I look like you. People might judge me by my sibling."

"Hear, hear," said Marnie.

"I forgot to call Gail Downer in Marathon," I

said. "I wanted to tell her she can have her father back."

Bobbi raised her Mountain Dew for a toast. "That's been done, Alex, and you're welcome. Now I'd like to salute two men. Each, in his own way, got his brother back."

"Hear, hear," said Marnie.

DATE DUE